Revenge Café

LISA SHIOFF

Tasfil Publishing LLC

New Jersey, USA

This book is a work of fiction. Names, characters, and incidents are products of the author's imagination and are used fictitiously. Any resemblance to actual events or persons, living or dead, is entirely coincidental.

Front cover image credits:
Palm Trees on Deserted island from Dreamstime.com

ISBN: 0692232311

ISBN-13: 978-0692232316

DEDICATION

To my husband and family who don't seem to mind my obsession with the islands.

Contents

Preface

Most who visit the U.S. Virgin Islands can easily attest to the natural beauty of the landscape and the easy friendliness of the people who live there. Those who are more sensitive can feel the almost palpable vibrations left by the myriad souls who had made the islands their home, either intentionally or unintentionally, since pre-Columbian times.

A unique characteristic that is plainly evident, though, is the way the Islanders have transformed the English language to fit them and their unique style. To honor their distinct use of the language, I sought input from Islanders on pronunciation and even spelling to do my best to reflect it in this work.

I also tried hard to stick to the real geographic layout of St. Thomas, but I did use a little poetic license for this book. The Revenge Café is a fictional restaurant. The Villa Olga estate, however, is a real place that also happens to have a real restaurant on premises, one with amazing food, views and (rumor has it) there might just be a ghost there, too. But the similarities stop there. All people, events, and even menu items are figments of my imagination. And Villa Olga in the book sits in a slightly different place than it does on the real island so that it can be seen from a (fictional) sundry shop.

Enjoy!

Chapter 1: In Search of a Key Ingredient

A Rastafarian man I'd never met held a cardboard sign with my name scrawled across it in black marker. Wearing dark sunglasses, wrinkled green khakis and a bright yellow T-shirt, he leaned against a trashcan in the arrivals pickup area of the St. Thomas airport in the U.S. Virgin Islands.

"That would be me," I said, pointing to the sign. "I'm Mandy Breen."

"Welcome!" He smiled like a Cheshire cat and lifted his sunglasses to look at me below their rims. "I am Charlie."

He took my carryon and led me past the taxis and courtesy car shuttles. We crossed a throughway, entered a rental car lot, meandered our way to a set of stone steps in the back, climbed up and then proceeded down a road. Eventually we stopped in front of an illegally parked, once white but now mostly rusted pick-up truck.

"I'm sorry," I said. "But I think there's been a mistake. A man named Chance Abbott was supposed to arrange a car for me."

"No mistake." Charlie threw my carryon into the truck bed. "I's taking you to Chancey."

"You?" I rubbed a spot of powdery rust on the hood. My finger poked through. "In this?"

"Yeah. I drive you to him." Charlie jumped over the tailgate and into what appeared to be leftovers from a garage sale piled in the truck bed. His waist-length dreadlocks swung behind him like wind-whipped tree branches. Or maybe like tentacles reaching out to capture prey.

"That's a good one." I forced a laugh. "I don't know what Chance put you up to, but the joke's over. Where's my real ride?"

"No joke." Charlie stood straight. "I take you to Chancey."

"Chance hired you to drive me?"

"Chancey needed a favor." He shrugged. "I owed him one."

"Oh God." I leaned against the truck and rummaged through my purse for my cell.

"You sick?" Charlie asked.

"Not in the way you mean it." I rammed my hand through every nook and cranny of the bag until I unearthed my phone. Chance's end rang only to be answered by voice mail. I hung up without leaving a message and threw the phone back in my purse.

"So did Chance mention anything to you about my condition?" I asked.

"Condition?" Charlie stopped rearranging his loot and looked at me. A shadeless lamp was tucked under one arm.

"I suffer from something called amaxophobia. Ever hear of it?"

He straightened and shook his head.

I cleared my throat and swallowed my pride.

"It's the fear of riding in cars."

Charlie's mouth twisted into a shape that suggested there might be bad fish nearby. "What you mean?"

"I mean I get scared, really scared, and for what most people think is no reason, when I'm a passenger in a car. Sometimes I get so scared I kind of freak out."

"Ah." He nodded. "I get it. I don't like snakes. I's afraid of dem and freak out when I see one." He set the lamp on top of my carryon, which was on top of an old tool chest. "No worries. I be careful." He bound everything together with a fraying bungee cord and gave me a thumb's up before jumping out of the truck bed.

"Don't supposed I could drive, could I?" I asked. "I usually don't have a problem when I'm the driver."

"She got a touchy clutch. You good w' a stick?"

I shook my head.

"Like I say. I be careful." Charlie's smile was wide enough and bright enough for me to believe he meant what he said. He fumbled in his cargo pockets, presumably looking for his keys. I watched him and took long, deep, calming breaths. Sometimes they were aptly named. Sometimes. Sometimes they made me hyperventilate.

With keys in hand, Charlie manually unlocked the passenger door and opened it for me.

"H'yeh," he grunted. I wasn't sure if he'd said "hey you," or "here," or if he had simply hiccupped. Every time I'd been to the

Virgin Islands in the past, I'd picked up a little of the dialect, but I had a long way to go before I could say I was fluent. "Fo' true. I be careful," he added.

I channeled my inner-red engine and took a step toward the truck. After another long inhale, I ducked inside and sat down on the bench-style seat, which happened to be held together with peeling silver duct tape. Charlie closed the door and I exhaled. On the next in breath, I reached for the seatbelt over my shoulder. There was none. Fear bubbled up from my bowels. My fingers scrambled along the floor, near the door. No belt. I slammed myself upright and opened my mouth to speak. But I couldn't make any noise with all that breath whooshing in and out.

Next thing I knew, Charlie was in the driver's seat. The truck's engine was gunning and we were pulling out into traffic.

Within seconds, I was in a full-blown panic attack. Yet, Charlie drove like he had not a care in the world. With one hand on the steering wheel and the other waving in the air, he crooned to a Reggae beat and bewailed the dangers of island politics as if *that* were all we had to fear in this world.

"Use both hands!" I screamed, batting at his free arm.

Thunk! The truck slammed into a pot hole. I bounced hard in my seat. My head bumped against the dashboard.

"Jesus! You're going to kill us!" I yelled. "Slow down!"

But Charlie was deaf to my screams, unaware of my pleas to be careful, oblivious even to my fingernails digging into his arm and thigh. My ears tingled, my cheeks burned: tell-tale signs I was on the verge of fainting. Frantic to stay conscious, I threw my head between my knees and clutched the bars on the underside of the seat.

I rode in that almost fetal position for the rest of the ride. My tears splashed the filthy floor boards and I swore I would kill Chance. I would tackle the British bastard, wrap my hands around his neck, and squeeze until he turned purple and died, or until my arms gave out.

A lifetime later, the truck slowed to a stop. I heard the gears shift and the engine shut down. With the caution of a snake handler, I lifted my head and dared to look out the window. Much to my relief and surprise, we were not dangling over a cliff. We were in a parking lot edging a harbor and all four of the truck's wheels were touching the pavement.

Relief washed through me as I recognized the area. In front of me, the port city of Charlotte Amalie spread in a half-circle around Long Bay. Just beyond the sea wall was a busy strait separating St. Thomas from Hassell Island. Off to its right was Water Island. The tiny, emerald green, palm-tree dotted isles created a postcard backdrop for the cruise ships and luxury yachts sailing in the dark blue water around them.

The boats glowed ethereal white in the early evening sun, like transporters from heaven anchored in the harbor for a Caribbean holiday. The smoothness of their languid dance as they glided past each other soothed me. My breath slowed. The pounding heartbeat in my ears faded. The adrenaline oozed out of my system.

"We here," Charlie announced after a few minutes of me not moving. I heard his door squeak when he opened it to step out of the truck.

I exited my side. Grateful to be in contact with the earth again, I stretched, arching my back until it cracked. The Rasta's eyes zeroed in on my chest. "So, uh, where's Chance?" I shrugged into a slump.

"Probly up dere, in de restaurant." Charlie tilted his head toward a set of stone steps climbing a hill. "Yeah, Chancey be here. Dere's his Jeep." He pointed to the end of the lot where a newer, dark green, Jeep Grand Cherokee was parked.

It was the closest to love at first sight I'd ever experienced. As part of the deal for me to move to the island, Chance had promised I could drive his car until I bought one of my own or found a place to live within walking distance to the restaurant. I'd been dreading his old Jeep, an abused, ancient, rag-top Wrangler. But this beauty had potential. It looked capable, rugged, reliable, tough, almost safe.

Charlie pulled my carryon from the truck. "Eh, why you no go w' me to Duffy's?" he asked. "I go dere now, you know. Maybe you could ha' a drink an' relax some 'fore you meet up w'Chancey." His eyes returned to hover below my neck.

"No, thank you." I took my bag, amazed yet again, by the power of boobs. Nothing rivals their ability to make a man overlook truly pathetic qualities, even bizarre phobias, in a woman. "I need to meet up with Chance. I'm sure you're right and he's just inside."

"OK. But I be dere if you change yo mind." Charlie returned to his truck.

I headed over to the stairs and glanced back at the Grand Cherokee. Now that the initial rosy glow of my crush had passed, the Jeep bothered me. It looked lonely there in the lot. And I found it odd that Chance hadn't mentioned buying it. Its shiny and obvious newness suggested he'd only had it a short while. It would have been smarter of him to buy it after I was done using it. Cars don't stay shiny and new very long for me. I wondered how long I'd be able to keep it pretty and whether or not Chance would renege his offer after the first scratch.

With a sigh, I climbed the stairs, letting my carryon bang against each step behind me.

At the top I found a walkway flanked by a series of small potted palm trees and covered by a crimson awning. It led to a pristine, white stucco building whose roof matched the awning, as if both were equally burned by the tropical sun. Pink bougainvillea climbed the walls on blue trellises and carved into the hill on one side of the walkway was a limestone patio area, complete with an empty fire pit and unlit Tiki torches.

I headed down the walkway and stopped before a set of closed, oversized, frosted-glass doors. Etched palm trees ran the full height, providing swaths of clear glass that were not quite wide enough to see anything recognizable within. Above the doors hung a lacquered wooden sign: *Welcome to the Revenge Café.*

"Wow." I paused for a couple of heartbeats, my hand resting on a door handle. Adrenaline re-emerged and sparked throughout my body. This time from anticipation, not from fear. Here it was, framed in a tropical island setting, our, my, dream-come-true.

I was on the cusp of an exotic new beginning. One I'd been fantasizing about for far too long. No longer would I be a TV investigative reporter wearing straight skirts and high heels working in a tough city. Instead, I'd be a restaurateur, working my dream job in breezy tops and flip flops, living in paradise.

I could feel the smile spreading across my face. I was almost tingling with excitement, almost giddy. Only almost, because my reporter's hackles were raised. The place was stunning and ideally located. I'd been expecting a tiny hole-in-the-wall that was more bar than restaurant. One where Chance and I would probably be the only two people working, maybe the only two dining as well. I wasn't aware Chance had the means to buy a property of this caliber.

Ignoring the doubt trying to settle on my shoulders, I pulled open a door. No one greeted me.

"Chance?" I hollered. No answer. I walked toward the host's pedestal. "Yo! Chance!"

Still, no reply.

"Yeah. You should be scared," I said as I entered the dining room. "After that ride you just put me through."

I rounded the host's pedestal on tiptoes, expecting him to yell "Surprise!" at any second. But no one greeted me. The place was empty. Perhaps he was giving me the opportunity to savor the sight. He did, after all, manage to create our ideal restaurant, just as we'd always envisioned. Dark rattan furniture was balanced out with crisp white linens. Brass accents shone as if freshly polished. Ceiling fans rotated in languid circles and live palm trees framed the doors and windows. There was even a gleaming white piano on a tiny stage in one corner. The restaurant was the perfect dining tableau.

Except near the back. Something was wrong. It looked like someone had ripped the cloth off a table, not caring that a candle had toppled over and a crystal vase went flying. Letting go of my carryon, I walked toward it. Broken glass crunched beneath my sandals.

"Chance?" I stopped. "Is everything OK?" I kicked the shards from my shoe and gingerly made my way to the other side of the table.

"Chance?" I tried one more time. I was at the rear of the room and not sure what to do. To my right was what looked like a dark office area; to my left appeared to be the kitchen, where the lights were on. I chose the lighted route and pushed open a swinging door.

Again, perfection greeted me. Red tiled backsplashes gleamed along the walls. Obviously new pots and pans were lined up according to size and hung from hooks extended from the ceiling. Shiny stainless steel sinks and appliances stood next to each other at the ready for service like soldiers at boot camp graduation.

Something smelled delicious–a lobster or crab something. My nose led to me to a slow cooker pot, the kind you'd find in a home kitchen, not in a restaurant. I thought I knew what was inside and unlocked the lid to discover I was right: lobster stew, one of

Chance's favorite recipes. Inhaling deeply, I completely forgave Chance for Charlie and the rickety truck. The stew was good enough to be his penance for just about anything.

On the counter opposite the slow cooker was a large wooden salad bowl surrounded by an assortment of greens and vegetables. Next to that counter was an open door to a refrigerated pantry. By the looks of things, Chance had been frantic to find something and had tossed about fresh produce in a desperate search. Had he realized he was missing something important for our meal and gone out on foot to get it?

"Chance?" I slammed the pantry shut. "C'mon! Where are you?"

I spun around. My sandal slid on something squishy and I lost balance. Reaching out to grab hold of anything to keep from falling, I unintentionally pushed down on a different door handle. That door opened and I discovered Chance hadn't gone in search of a key ingredient. He was still in the restaurant, in the walk-in freezer to be precise.

And he was dead.

Chapter 2: Breathe Deep

Chance's body was seated in a giant, white cake. His arms pulled behind him. His head pressed into the top tier.

"No, no, no." I heard someone saying. It had to have been me since there was no one else around. I backed from the freezer, unable to look away from him. His lifeless lips and one eye were swollen, almost distorted out of shape. The other eye bugged out at me as if surprised by my arrival. Icing covered most of his face, but for one clean cheek. I found myself reaching out, wanting to touch that cheek.

I slammed the freezer shut instead.

My breath gasped, my vision tunneled.

"Oh my God!" I fell to my knees, pressing my fists hard into my eyes as if that could erase the vision. My ears filled with static that was so loud I could barely hear the tiny voice inside my head telling me I should do something useful.

With the side of a counter for leverage, I managed to make myself stand and, after a nanosecond too confused to move, I ran out of the kitchen. A phone was near the end of the bar. I picked up the receiver and punched in nine-one-one.

Sometime later, I wasn't sure how long—an hour? Two? Three? I found myself being fingerprinted and then told to wait by a desk in a tiny, orange, windowless room at the Alexander Farrelly Criminal Justice Center. The police station was in the island's Superior Court building, a large stucco facility across the street from the harbor—the same harbor that housed the Revenge Café. Like the harbor, I was very familiar with that building. I had spent a considerable amount of time there a few years earlier while I'd investigated a story. But I'd never been in that room before.

I wasn't sure how I'd gotten there. I was in such a traumatized state after seeing Chance in the freezer, I couldn't quite recall everything that had happened immediately afterward. I remembered a rush of energy, flashing lights, and uniformed people running and shouting. Then everything slowed down when I heard someone say "the body," which meant "the dead body," which meant Chance's dead body.

The words swirled around my head unwilling to settle down and make a meaning I could accept. *How could Chance be dead? Was he killed? Could it have been some kind of accident?*

I ran my hands through my hair. The movement pulled the fuzziness from my brain and I realized that, not only did the police think Chance had been murdered, but since they fingerprinted me, they must consider me a suspect.

I reached for my purse to get my cell. It was late on a Sunday evening so I wasn't sure whom I could call for help, but it didn't matter. I had no purse.

As if suddenly exposed to the elements, I covered my chest and stomach with my arms. They had my bag! My phone! Judging by the behavior of the Virgin Islands PD from back in my reporter days, it was too easy for me to imagine the police planting evidence on me, in my purse. It would be very bad press for an island whose main industry is tourism if the murderer of a white, British citizen was never to be found. But powerful and good press if they could quickly find a handy, white mainlander to pin it on.

I stormed over to the door, yanked it open and nearly ploughed into a tall, solidly built, Islander man. I met his dark brown eyes and had to grip tighter to the doorknob to keep from falling over. They were the kind of eyes that, if I met them in a bar, tended to get me in trouble. And at first, they seemed equally surprised and intrigued by my baby blues. But then I caught the glimmer of a VIPD badge clipped to his collar around the same time it appeared to register in him why I was in that room. We both regained composure and his eyes went into attack mode, reminding me I was the one who most recently had ink on her fingers.

"Can I help you?" he asked. He looked to be a few years older than I was, maybe in his early or mid-thirties, and had an air of authority about him that gave me the impression he took for granted he was always in command.

"I'd like my purse." I glared at him, forcing him to recognize me as the alpha female.

"It will be returned to you shortly." He stepped past me and walked to the desk. "Please have a seat. I have a few questions for you."

Not wanting to be chased through the building, I did as instructed and returned to my chair. He sat on the other side of the desk and flipped the pages back on a yellow notepad. I couldn't help but notice how his biceps flexed, just a little, beneath the sleeves of his navy blue, Polo-style shirt.

"Ms. Breen, I'm Detective Matthew Piper." He spoke slowly, sounding like a mainlander. "Before you say anything, I'd like you to know this was my weekend with my sons. They were supposed to be with me through dinner tonight after which I was to put them on the water taxi to go back to their mamma on St. Croix. I had to send them to her early because of this incident today. I'm not happy about that and I'm hungry. Let's not waste time."

"Sounds like you should have grabbed the stew." Similar to Pavlov's dog drooling at the sound of a bell, I turn into a sassy reporter at the sound of a jaded cop.

"What stew?" Piper asked.

"The lobster stew cooking at the Revenge Café."

He walked over to the door and leaned out.

"Ho, McFadden!" he yelled down the hall. "Make sure someone at that restaurant checks the stoves and ovens. We can't let that place burn down again."

"What do you mean, 'again'?" I asked when Piper returned to his seat.

"You're not the one who gets to ask questions right now."

"Oh, right." I leaned back in my chair. "That would be you."

"Correct." He took position with his hands together over the legal pad, eyes leveled with mine, back straight, biceps slightly exposed. "You were unintelligible when you arrived. I just need to clarify some information and then you can go. When was the last time you saw Mr. Abbott?"

In my head flew the myriad phone calls and emails, but nothing face-to-face seemed to be a recent memory. "Maybe a year ago?"

"You don't sound certain."

"I am. I think. Maybe." I blinked a few times. "I mean, the last time I saw Chance alive, *in person*, was about a year ago."

"In person, huh?" He dropped his pencil and rubbed his forehead as if he had a headache. "Does that mean you've seen him, *alive*, in some other way? If so, when and how?"

"We web-cammed recently." I watched him make a note and noticed it was half-way down the page. "So when do you think I could get my purse back?"

He looked at me from under his eyebrows. "Let me check," he said and stood up.

After he exited the room, I stretched over the desk as far as I could without completely coming off my chair to read what was on the notepad. Unfortunately, there weren't as many lines as I'd thought and apparently the buff detective never got an "A" in penmanship.

"How recently did you webcam with Mr. Abbott?" Piper startled me when he returned. I sat back in the chair and accepted my purse from him. He took his former seat and tapped the notepad closer to his side.

"I think maybe two days ago." I combed through the mess in my bag unable to determine whether they'd taken anything.

"And then you decided to visit him?"

"I'm not really visiting. I was to move here."

"Was to? Are you still?"

"I don't know. I was also to become his business partner, co-owner of the restaurant and—"

"Again, what do you mean by 'was to become?' Who owns it now?"

An awareness of just how screwed up my life had become slammed into me. I closed my eyes and held my head in my hand, taking my time to answer. Apparently, I took too long.

"Ms. Breen," his voice raised a decibel. "I can easily find who the owner of the property is tomorrow morning, when the—"

"I'm sorry, jeez." I threw up my hand in exasperation. "You know, this isn't the easiest thing in the world for me. It's a little hard to think straight right now."

"I apologize if it seems we're being impatient."

"I would call it harsh and insensitive."

"It appears your business partner was murdered and the sooner I get all the facts regarding his situation the better," he said.

"Of course. I—"

"Who owns the restaurant now?"

"Chance owned the restaurant."

"By himself?"

"I believe so."

"Does he own any others?"

"No."

"Where did he work before?"

"For himself. He was a special event photographer."

"He went from photographer to restaurant owner?" Piper tilted his head to one side. "That's quite a career change. Was there a sudden incentive for him to do it?"

"Not really. It was a long-awaited dream come true."

"How long?"

"I don't know. Maybe ten years?"

"That must mean he wanted you to be his partner because you have the experience?"

"No. I just shared the dream."

He stared at me instead of writing that answer down.

"How long have you owned that property?" he asked.

"Chance bought it a couple of months ago."

"And aside from yourself, are there any other investors?"

"N- no." I verbally stumbled.

Piper's eyes pierced mine like specialized x-ray machines programmed to detect lies and sins. "Are you sure?"

I nodded even though I wasn't.

"So, about your arrival today, he knew you were coming?"

"Yes."

"He knew the exact date and time of your arrival?"

"Yes. He made the flight reservations." I shook my hair out of my face, feeling the need to appear stronger. "In fact, when you get around to looking over his credit card transactions you'll learn he also paid for my trip."

Piper raised his eyebrows at me in such a way I understood he didn't appreciate my tone.

"I'm sorry," I conceded. "I'm an investigative reporter, well formerly, for a TV station in south Florida. Before that I'd written numerous articles, some of them award winning, about criminal activity in the Caribbean. I understand how police agencies are supposed to work."

"I see." He pounced the eraser end of his pencil on the pad, obviously hiding how impressed he was by my credentials. "You told us someone drove you to the restaurant. Did Mr. Abbott arrange that for you as well?"

"Yes, at the last minute. He originally said he would meet me, but then something came up."

"What came up?"

"I don't know."

He pulled up a few sheets on the legal pad and glanced over the notes. I couldn't help but notice those biceps flex again. "You said the driver's name is Charlie but I don't see where you gave us his last name, or the company he worked for."

"I don't know either."

"What about the make and model of the truck?"

I shook my head, regretting I'd told him I was a reporter. That was a rookie mistake.

"Can you remember anything about him that might help you find him again?"

"He looked Rastafarian."

"A Rasta named Charlie?" He sucked on his lips as if he was trying to repress a smile or hide a private joke. His eyes remained fixed on the legal pad, though he had stopped writing.

"Yes, a Rasta named Charlie," I echoed.

"Any other detail?"

"He was going to someplace called Duff's or maybe Duffy's afterward."

"How do you know?"

"He invited me to go with him for a drink."

"Did you?" He tilted his head up. A hint of a grin on his face.

"No. That Charlie guy met me at the airport and drove me straight to Ch— . . . to the restaurant."

The grin faded. "How did you know Mr. Abbott sent the driver?"

"He'd left a voice mail for me right after my plane took off today. I heard it when we landed."

"What did he say?"

I fished through my cluttered purse and pulled out my cell. The phone felt unusually heavy. Or maybe it was just that my hand felt unusually weak. I had to summon a hidden reserve of strength to force a finger to touch the voicemail icon. Then with the phone on *speaker,* I placed it on the desk and hit the *play* arrow before quickly hugging my purse so tight I was able to wrap my arms around my stomach. I hoped it was enough to keep my insides on the inside while my dead friend spoke to me, sounding as though he was still alive.

Hey babe. Good news: I'm making one of your favorite meals. Not-so-good-news: I won't be picking you up at the airport. Don't worry, though. I made solid arrangements for you. So just breathe deep."

"What does that mean? Breathe deep?" Piper asked.

I stared hard at the phone hoping the visual exertion would somehow close my tear ducts.

"Ms. Breen? What does that mean?"

I sniffed and looked at the detective. "Oh, I uh, I get nervous when I ride in cars. I have an issue."

"That explains your arrival here," he muttered and leaned back in his chair. "So the driver takes you to the restaurant and leaves," he said a little louder. "Then what did you do?"

"I went in and . . . I found—" My voice caught.

He made another note then sat quietly, as if mentally chewing on my answer. His eyes were still trained on mine, but they were no longer fierce, super-powered optic machines. They were very human and hinted at sympathy.

"I think we are done here for now. Thank you, Ms. Breen." He flipped all the pages over on the legal pad. "I must tell you it will be in your best interest not to leave the island until this case is solved. We have your cell phone number. Where will you be staying?"

"I was to stay at Chance's house."

He stood up. "Please alert this office if you have a change of plans." He walked toward the door and opened it.

I remained seated, feeling drained and weak while Piper stood in the doorway, seemingly fortified with a steel spine.

"You may leave now, Ms. Breen," he said and walked away.

I did as suggested and followed him out. In fact, I tailed him through the building until he stopped and sat at another desk. He seemed surprised to find me standing beside him.

"Is there something I can help you with?" he asked.

I opened my mouth, but nothing came out. I had no idea what I should do or say next and I think part of me hoped he would give me a clue because there was no one else around for me to ask.

He only waited, patiently.

I looked down at my hands and realized I didn't have my other bag.

"Can I get my carryon? I think I left it at the restaurant."

"No. It's part of a crime scene now and will need to be searched thoroughly before it can be returned to you."

"You've got to be kidding," I huffed. I wasn't sure if I wanted to grab him by the shoulders and shake some sense into him or kiss him in gratitude for riling me back into sassy reporter mode. "Do you really believe that after I killed him, I carefully tucked the murder weapon back in my suitcase? Cleaning it first, of course. Wouldn't want to risk any of his bodily fluids staining my favorite blouse, right? How can my bag be part—"

"It was on the premises where a murder was committed. That makes it part of a crime scene." I thought I saw the corners of his mouth twitch.

I sighed and put my hands on my hips. "So do you have any idea when your officers will be done rifling through my underwear?"

Piper grinned and opened a drawer in his desk. "There's a possibility you could have it back tomorrow morning." He retrieved a business card and scrawled something on the reverse. "Here's my information. My cell phone number is on the back. You can call me in the morning and I'll let you know whether or not you can have your bag then."

Chapter 3: Face the Traffic

I stopped outside the criminal justice building, entered Piper's information into my cell and looked at the time. It was just after nine o'clock that Sunday evening. I needed to find shelter and come up with a plan. A big plan. For the second time in my life, I was jobless and homeless with Chance being the root cause of both problems. The difference being the first time it happened, he was also the one who helped me get back on my feet and figure out what to do with my life. With no Chance this time, I wasn't sure how or even where to start.

I was okay with making that a secondary problem, though. Jobs and homes come and go. Losing a friend, particularly to a murderer, was a primary one.

I wasn't willing to leave it up to police work to solve Chance's murder and it wasn't because I had a tough time trusting Caribbean men in blue. Chance was my best friend and closest ally. I owed it to him to make sure the right person was found, held accountable, and possibly castrated.

It seemed to me, the smartest thing to do would be to head to Chance's house for the night. I wasn't sure how well I could stomach staying there knowing he'd never return to it, but I had to think like an investigator. If his death wasn't a random act of violence, and instead was something personal, maybe I'd find a lead there and get a head start on the police.

The challenge was: Chance's house was on the north side of the island, about ten miles away as the crow flies. Actually, it was about ten miles of mountainous terrain, which meant I needed to get a taxi. Even if it wasn't mountainous, I'd still need a cab. Charlotte Amalie could be a pretty dangerous, gang-infested place at night. Walking through it would put me at risk of becoming yet another person shot in one of those wrong-place-wrong-time kind of events. And which would be worse? Getting caught in the crossfire of rivaling gangs or having a panic attack in a cab?

I figured getting shot would be worse. If I survived that, I'd probably end up having a panic attack while I bled to death in the back of an ambulance.

However, I'd also need to get another taxi the next morning to come back for my carryon. I promised myself that would be the only two times I'd be driven around by someone else on the island. I would just have to force myself to handle it, somehow. And then, since I was still blacklisted from all the car rental agencies on St. Thomas, I'd find a hotel in Charlotte Amalie between the restaurant and the police station. That way I could walk wherever I needed to go

There! I had the beginnings of a plan.

But I was instantly sickened by a memory of the day I was fired from the TV station. I'd refused one too many assignments based on the fact that the crime did not happen within walking distance to the jail and courthouse. The old adage *be careful what you wish for* ran through my head.

"I'm so sorry, Chance," I said as I started walking toward the edge of Veteran's Drive. "I didn't mean it. I really didn't."

Out on the roadside, I turned to face the traffic. Within a few minutes, a silver SUV with a lighted yellow *taxi* sign on the roof came into view. I waved to get the driver's attention. The SUV was big and rugged with no signs of recent damage. But as soon as the driver rolled down his window, I noticed a street lamp glint off his glasses and had second thoughts.

"So, do you *have* to wear those glasses to drive?" I asked. Standing by his door, I leaned my belly toward him, in a semi-flirtatious gesture. Maybe he'd take them off to get a better look.

"Yeah. Me no see wit'out 'em." He flashed me a charming smile. "Where you going beautiful?"

"Estate Mandahl." I got down to business and leaned my hands on his window seal. "OK, really, have you ever had any problems with those glasses?"

"You try to sell me new specs? You gotta deal?"

"No. Nothing like that. Listen. Has an on-coming car's headlights ever created a glare on your lenses?"

"What?"

"Have you ever been blinded by another car's headlights? Have you ever wrecked because you couldn't see?"

"Pretty gyul, you wanna ride or no?" He tilted his head and again, the lamp light glanced off his lenses.

"HO!" someone shouted. I looked down the road and saw a couple of young men had met up several yards away. They slapped hands in greeting and shouted good-natured barbs at each other before disappearing into the shadows of an alley.

"Yes, I guess so," I half-groaned and half-said to the driver.

I gave him the address and went as far as I could in the rear of the SUV. Sitting backwards, crunched in a ball, I pressed my face hard against the seat so I couldn't see out any of the windows and started the deep breathing techniques.

The driver must have been late to a party. He sped the entire way across the island, bouncing over the twisty-turny, mountainous roads as if the shocks were made from industrial strength Slinkies. Keeping my hands in a death grip around the headrest, I continued breathing deep and attempted to visualize lounging on a beautiful, sunny and safe beach. My ears rang and there was a buzzing sensation in my forehead, but I was able to keep the panic attack at bay.

Eventually the driver slammed on the breaks. I swayed back with too much force and banged my nose on the seat on the rebound.

"We h'eh," he said. "Heh. You alright?"

Without answering, without even making eye contact, I shoved some cash over the Plexiglas divider and slinked out of the cab.

Stepping onto Chance's front porch, I triggered a motion sensor that turned on an outside light. I stood in its beam, pretending to search through my purse for keys. When the cab began to back out the driveway, I took for granted the driver had the good sense to look behind him and bent down to pick up the conch shell beside the front door. A key was always in it. Chance had gotten the idea from a Kenny Chesney song.

Once inside the house, I punched the last four digits of Chance's cell number into the alarm system to silence its warning. I flipped on a light and waited, for what I wasn't sure. It just seemed like the appropriate thing to do. Besides, I needed a moment to gather myself. Because suddenly I knew how Alice felt when she landed at the bottom of that rabbit hole.

If I hadn't needed *that* key to get in and *that* code to shut the alarm, I would have thought I'd stepped through a warp machine and ended up in a final grand prize showcase on *The Price is Right.*

Chance's house was missing some interior walls. Always in the past, whenever I had entered his house, I walked into a tiny living room, at the rear of which was a door to the dining area that abutted a galley style kitchen hidden from view. And the entire house had been outfitted with cheap, necessary furniture.

Now there was an open floor plan. I could see all the way through to the back sliding glass doors. Directly in front of me was a new red leather sofa and two chairs surrounding a new glass-topped stone coffee table. Beyond them was a new teak dining table and new black Parsons chairs. To the right was an ultra-modern and sleek new kitchen with a new bar separating it from the living room. All the newness took my breath away. Or maybe it was the evident expense of all that newness.

Like a wary cat, I stepped lightly across the floor. I turned on every light I could find and tried to pretend my stomach wasn't tying itself into a tighter and tighter knot.

I'd always thought Chance told me about everything going on in his life. But, like the new Jeep, he had never mentioned the home makeover. His apparent secretiveness was out of character for him. As was the idea that he'd paid for everything himself, with well-earned money. Chance seldom had more than enough cash on hand to pay his bar tab. And lines of credit were never very friendly to him.

I made my way to the kitchen, which could have served as a backdrop for a TV celebrity chef show. Sand-colored quartz counter tops were streaked with the same terra cotta hue as the tiled floor and backsplash. The dark wooden cabinets had a satin finish, brushed aluminum knobs, and clouded glass doors. The appliances were all large, commercial-grade, and stainless steel top-of-the line products. Inside the cabinet doors and drawers I saw he'd even purchased new china, flatware and cookware.

I ran my hand down the quartz countertop, awed by its smooth coolness, worried by its obvious price tag. Confused by the whole situation.

Roaming through the house, I turned over books and magazines, glanced through a stack of mail, and rifled drawers. I wasn't sure what I was looking for other than something that didn't seem to belong where it was, or something that wasn't right somehow, or maybe even a note that read: *If I'm found dead then . . .*

But the house had recently been cleaned. Nothing was out of place and it smelled like synthetic lemons. Inside Chance's bedroom was a perfectly made bed, suggesting the housecleaner had come in after he'd left that morning. All clothes were put away. There wasn't even a dirty towel in the hamper. The guest room was equally clean. And the one bathroom was spotless, nothing even in the trash bin.

"But wait." I stopped in the bathroom doorway as I spoke to myself. "It's Sunday. What kind of housekeeper cleans on Sunday?"

I made another loop through, this time making sure the window curtains were shut, the front door and back sliders were locked, and that the alarm system was armed. Secured, I was now just starving and suddenly lonely and sad.

I opened the refrigerator. One of the things that had forged a bond between Chance and me was that we both believed food was our cure-all, our savior, our true and constant addiction. But not the ingestion of it. We weren't problem eaters. We were problem cookers. And Chance had created the ideal setting for us to feed our habit. I knew I could sufficiently chop, grind, pound, fry, batter and bang around in his beautiful new kitchen and successfully drown out those sad and lonely feelings—as long as there was something good to work with.

There was. The fridge housed a beautiful New York strip steak and enough lump crab meat to make a stuffing for it. In the pantry were potatoes and heads of garlic. And in a small wine storage unit, a lovely bottle of Cabernet.

"Wine!" My head reeled. I shut my eyes and retraced my steps going into the Revenge Café. I couldn't remember seeing any wine, but I could remember the mess in the dining room.

I looked up Detective Piper's name in my phone.

"I have to be quick," I said when he answered. "My battery is low. But I was wondering, can we arrange a tit-for-tat kind of deal?" I put the phone on *speaker* while I peeled potatoes.

"What do you mean?"

"You know, if I should ever discover some information that could be helpful to you while you look into this case and—"

"Then you should just give it to me so I don't have to arrest you for obstructing justice. Unless, of course, you're withholding evidence. In which case, I will arrest you for that."

"Well, aren't you up to date on judicial semantics?" I flicked potato skin off my hand. "I didn't mean anything like that. I wouldn't step on your department-mandated, shiny toes. I know—I *knew* Chance better than anyone. And I'm going to get to the bottom of his murder with or without your help. It'd just be easier if I did it with. So, when I find out something, I promise to share with you immediately and I was hoping you'd reciprocate."

"I see. Well, as a *former* investigative reporter, you should know I can't divulge information while investigating a case."

"I know that's the official line. And I wouldn't expect you to tell me anything that could hinder the case, but if say, I asked a pointed question, maybe you could answer it?"

"Hm." He paused. "I could possibly. But I would need full disclosure as to why you were asking and it would depend on the question."

"Did you find the tablecloth?" I rinsed the vegetable peeler.

"What tablecloth?"

"The one missing from the Revenge Café."

"This is where full disclosure would come in."

"In full disclosure, I know how Chance cooks." I let the water wash over the potatoes in the colander.

"Back up. Are we talking about cooking, tablecloths, or are you trying to make sure I don't find something?"

"I have nothing to hide."

"And I'm to take your word for that?"

"I'm sure the coroner has already done the math to see how long his body was in the freezer. If you check with that office, you'll discover I was on a plane when he was killed."

"And you know that because?"

I sighed with a loud *ugh.* "You're wasting my battery life."

"You don't have a charger?"

"Y*ou* have my charger. It's in my carryon." I pulled a long chef's knife from its slot.

"You can have it back tomorrow so speak quickly. How do you know you were on a plane when the murder occurred?"

"That lobster stew is one of Chance's trademark foods," I said as I chopped. "It's a slow cooking stew. He starts it early and lets it sit, barely staying warm, to let the flavors intensify while he makes the rest of the meal. After it gets going, he'll cut up the ingredients for a salad and then prepare a main course, last he'll toss the salad and make a dressing. He'd just pulled out the stuff for the salad and I didn't see evidence of the main course anywhere, which suggests he was killed at least an hour, maybe two prior to my arrival. I'm going for two, because he's very slow. In other words, he was killed shortly after he'd called and left the message in my voice mail, which is when I was still in flight."

"You have good math skills. But now tell me, what did they clean up?"

"I don't know. That's what I wanted to ask about."

"Again, why would I answer?"

"Because I just helped you."

"No you didn't."

"Because I have something for you if you'd let me give it to you." The knife banged on the cutting board.

He barked out a laugh. "You going to give me the recipe for that stew?"

"Maybe. Where's the tablecloth?" I dumped the potatoes in a pot, threw in some garlic cloves and filled the pot with water before putting it on the stove. I turned the burner on, opened the pantry door and found breadcrumbs. Piper remained silent. I assumed he was debating over whether or not he could tell me about the tablecloth.

I began mixing the breadcrumbs with the crabmeat and heard a shuffling sound and a door closing on his end.

"We are looking for the tablecloth," he said. "Now, why are you asking about it?"

"There should be an open bottle of wine somewhere." I stirred horseradish and mayonnaise into the crab and breadcrumb mixture. "Chance never cooks without drinking wine. I don't remember seeing glasses or a bottle in the kitchen." I sprinkled jarred parsley in the bowl.

"And how is that supposed to help me?"

"I'm guessing if you find a wine bottle in the trash behind the restaurant, it's probably wrapped in that cloth because whoever killed him must have picked it up." Not wanting to battle the no-see-um bugs outside to grill the steak, I turned on the broiler.

"He wasn't killed by blunt trauma."

"How was he killed?" I slit the New York strip and stuffed it with the crab mixture.

"You still owe me information. That wine bottle doesn't count, though I found it interesting enough to give you the blunt-trauma teaser." He clicked off.

Chapter 4: A Nice Jagged Edge

I drained the potatoes and garlic then returned them to the pot to mash with milk, butter, and salt. Once satisfied with the texture, I sprinkled in grated parmesan cheese and stirred until it melted. I pulled the crab-stuffed steak from the oven, arranged it on my plate with the potatoes and sat down to eat.

The meal was delicious. I almost got lost in it. What kept me too stuck in reality was that I happened to notice a framed picture on a sideboard against a wall. Actually, it wasn't a framed picture. It was a framed magazine from the last story I'd covered while working as a journalist for a print media outlet. I'd spent several months on St. Thomas investigating that story. I stayed at Chance's house, drove his old Jeep, and had even asked him to help me as my photographer. In fact one of his pictures made that front cover.

I walked from the table and picked up the frame. Lines from the article emerged from the depths of my mind: ... *multiple international governments mishandled the same situation and ultimately caused a man to die ... a circuit of corrupt officials and authorities in the Caribbean working diligently to keep a supply of cocaine traveling safely to the mainland states . . .*

It was an inflammatory, accusatory article. Names were named. Covert operations were brought to light. Powerful Caribbean public figures were exposed to be frauds and traffickers of illegal pharmaceuticals. They were stripped from offices and many were incarcerated. But not all. Within a few months of the piece being published, the magazine headquarters were bombed. Thankfully the editor had the foresight to insist it was written by an anonymous source, otherwise I might not have outlived Chance.

Instead, he did not outlive me.

I set the frame back down, trying to ignore the shaking in my hands. Could someone have found out Chance took the pictures for that article and his death was another act of retaliation? If so, did that mean they knew I wrote the piece and were looking for me now?

Hopefully they'd gone to my old home in Florida.

It was one of those rare moments when I lost my appetite. I dumped my half-eaten dinner in the trash, re-filled my wine glass and felt the heft of the bottle in my hand. I poured the remaining wine from the bottle down the sink drain and silently thanked my uncle John.

He was my mom's brother. My dad had disappeared on us shortly after my sister was born and in a sweet attempt to make sure we got some kind of fatherly influence, Uncle John would come by every now and then and try to give my kid sister and me advice.

After my mom died and we were living with my grandmother, he'd moved on to teach us self-defense moves. He didn't know karate or any kind of martial art, but the man had never left a bar as the loser in a fight.

I knew exactly how to hit that empty wine bottle on the quartz counter to make just the end break off, leaving a nice jagged edge. I had a feeling it would come in handy if someone happened to come around Chance's house during the night looking to see if he had any visitors from the mainland.

Early Monday morning I woke up on Chance's red sofa with a stiff neck and determined thoughts. If indeed I was right, and his death was retribution for my magazine article, then I had even more of an incentive to find the murderer. I wouldn't just be righting the wrong of his killing, I would also be making amends for causing the mess to begin with.

Of course, if I succeeded, that just might place me directly into the crosshairs of the killer. But I decided to worry about that later.

I took a tepid three-minute shower to preserve the water in Chance's cistern for whoever purchased his house next and groomed myself to the best of my abilities with his bathroom supplies. I did, however, stop short of using his toothbrush and ran my toothpaste-laden finger around my mouth instead.

Like a typical guy, his hair products were minimal, actually aside from shampoo, they were nonexistent. And I think I must have looked in the cabinet under the bathroom sink at least fifteen times before I was able to accept the fact the man didn't even own a hair dryer. I wasn't sure how my hair would turn out without my anti-humidity gel and spray. It was probably going to be a mess. But I had nothing to work with. Not even a bread tie to pull it back and secure into a pony tail.

It's not that I'm vain. Chance used to tease me and say my bravado was held up by a layer of lipstick that I really didn't need. And he may have been right. I'd always felt a kind of power when I knew I could control how people responded to my looks. I knew the right shade of lipstick or a curl placed just so would enable me to get whatever I needed. Done up right, I could easily flirt information out of an old man or encourage a bartender to break his code of discretion and gossip about a regular. But I could only do it when I knew I looked good. Unfortunately, I was going to end up at the police station asking for my carryon bag looking like a strung out mess in day-old, wrinkled clothes, un-styled hair and only a touch of makeup from the pressed powder and lipstick in my purse. I wasn't sure how well I'd be able to handle it.

I used the house line to call directory assistance and then the Islander Taxi service, who told me it could take as long as a half hour for a cabbie to get to me. Which meant I had around thirty minutes to distract myself from worrying about the upcoming car ride.

Wishing my cell battery wasn't dead, I searched through Chance's kitchen drawers looking for a spare charger—he'd had the same kind of phone I did.

In the third drawer I found the charger. I also found a brand new Jeep key fob. It looked just like the one my most recent therapist had when she insisted we use her car for a desensitizing exercise because mine was in the shop again. I knew it would start a car, not just unlock it. I also knew it was an expensive little item. My therapist had added the replacement cost of it to my last bill. Apparently her original was too damaged to be of use after I'd wrestled it away from her and threw it into traffic, successfully preventing her from turning the car back on after I'd turned it off. But Chance's seemed invaluable to me. If I was right, and it did go to his new Cherokee, I could use his car until whoever held the bank note realized he was no longer in a position to drive—and if it wasn't impounded by the police.

I dropped the fob in my purse, taking it as a sign that the day was getting better. Now I wouldn't have to worry about taxis or be at the mercy of poorly skilled drivers. Nor would I have to walk everywhere in the heat while I tracked down a killer. Granted, driving my own self around wasn't any less scary than being in a cab with a stranger, particularly on an island with some of the worst roads and traffic on the planet. But I knew I was a much more cautious driver than anyone I'd ever met. Also, I was more tolerant and accepting of myself than a stranger would be. Should I panic, I'd let myself pull over to relax and get control of my breath without a meter ticking.

I plugged in my cell for a few precious moments of charging and, once it came back to life, scrolled through to my Aunt Maggie's number. I called her cell from the house line and stood in the window, looking for the taxi.

Aunt Maggie's voice mail picked up after several rings. I didn't leave a message. As a medium in Cassadaga, Florida, the Psychic Capital of the World according to her business card, she claimed to commune with dead people. If she really was all that good at her job, I figured she'd know why I was calling.

Next I found my cousin Babs' number and again used the house phone to call her. Although she is Aunt Maggie's daughter, she doesn't speak with dead people. She does, however, read Tarot cards and is an intuitive, whatever that means.

"Mandy?" she answered.

"Yeah. How did you know?" I went out to the porch to talk with her from there.

"I've been getting the craziest vibes from you since yesterday. Where are you? Did you make it to St. Thomas? How's the restaurant? How's your friend?"

"I made it. I'm on island. The, uh, the restaurant is beautiful. But . . . but . . ."

"But what, hon? What's wrong?"

"Chance is dead." I sat on the steps and closed my eyes against the tears that were ready to drip down my face. I shouldn't have called her before going to the police station. I needed to stay strong, clear headed, on top of my game and all the other clichés that were supposed to mean something other than being overwhelmed with emotion.

"My God! What happened? Are you OK?"

"I don't know what happened. I think he was murdered–"

"Did you talk to Mom?"

"No, I got her voice mail when I called. I just, I don't know. I guess I just felt like I should tell someone." I heard the honk of a taxi and opened my eyes. "Look, Babs, I gotta go right now. I'll call later or something."

I hung up before she could respond.

I put the phone back in the house, reset the alarm and locked the door, keeping the house key in my purse. The taxi driver looked nice so I explained to him how I was a nervous passenger. He promised me he was a good driver.

He lied.

He was rude, too.

When he dropped me off at the police station he actually refused my payment.

"No. You go! Don't you call for us again!" he shouted at me as if I was the one who'd nearly killed the two of us even though he was the one who had driven through a yellow light. "You yell too much. Make *me* nervous." He threw my cash back at me and flew out of the parking lot.

I gathered my money from the ground, straightened up, pretended I still had my dignity and stared at the building before me. Bat wings of fear flapped in my stomach. I was taking a huge risk coming here.

There was a definite chance that someone currently in that building was involved with or connected to the people I'd written about in that last magazine story, and they wouldn't be happy to know I was the author. Key power figures and police personnel in the Virgin Islands, St. Thomas in particular, were arrested due to that piece. Others were still roaming the streets, possibly fired from their positions but still in contact with their old department friends and co-workers. Maybe a few remained on the force because not enough evidence against them could be found, yet. And what better way to make sure that evidence never surfaced other than to kill the people who discovered it to begin with?

Was I was walking into a mousetrap? Could Chance's killer

could be a good officer of the law with the VIPD? Is brawny Detective Piper "in" on Chance's murder and now need to cover that up by getting rid of me, too?

I reminded myself, I'd just risked my life traveling across the island being driven by a taxi driver with a death wish, I could handle this. Besides, it was a Monday morning. All departments would be opened and staffed. No one would be stupid enough to hurt me in front of witnesses, right?

I headed straight toward the doors and went inside, walking with the cocky swagger of a professional basketball player. Just inside, I caught a young uniformed officer checking me out from the rear. It boosted my determination. I almost felt sexy, strong, and I even toyed with the idea of easing my budget by cutting back on hair products. I strutted up to the information desk, asked to see Detective Piper and was led to the same orange room I had sat in the night before.

"Good morning, Ms. Breen," Piper said a few minutes later as he entered the room with his yellow legal pad and a manila folder. He took his former chair and assumed his school-boy position with hands clasped together over his notepad, biceps peeking out below his shirtsleeves. "How are you holding out?"

"As well as possible given the fact my best friend was killed yesterday." I looked into his eyes. They were tired, the skin under them papery, as if he didn't get much rest the night before. It threw me off a little. It almost softened me until I noticed he didn't have my carryon. "Where is my bag?"

"An officer is retrieving it from the locker now. You'll have it in a few minutes." He paused as he opened the file. "I'm curious about something, though. Why do you call Mr. Abbott your 'friend'?"

"What?"

"When you called emergency services, you told the dispatcher something had happened to your 'friend,' and just now you called him your 'best friend.' Why do you call him that?"

"Why wouldn't I?"

"Pure speculation on my part, but I believe it's normal for people who are engaged to call each other 'fiancé.'"

Chapter 5: Interesting Set of Circumstances

Well, that certainly wasn't the way I expected the conversation with Detective Piper to go. In my semi-frizzy, but still apparently presentable head, I had envisioned two scenarios. One, I'd be given my carryon and then sent on my merry way. Or two, I'd find they had planted incriminating evidence in my luggage, in which case I'd have some verbal sparring to do while I figured out how to secure an attorney. Either way I had formulated arguments and had a surplus of verbal ammunition at the ready. But before I could even take aim, the man threw a grenade in my lap. I wasn't prepared for incoming explosions of that nature.

"Though I guess your engagement is a little unusual," Piper continued. "Since you hadn't even seen your fiancé in person for a year. You did say that, did you not? That you hadn't seen Mr. Abbott for one year?"

I nodded.

He waited for me to explain myself, which was a waste of his time. I thought it was better if I sat mute while I conjured a way to explain my bogus wedding plans that wouldn't put either Chance or me in a bad light.

But Piper was a patient and possibly sadistic man. He openly grinned as he held my gaze for an uncomfortably long time.

"You *were* supposed to get married tomorrow, weren't you?" he eventually asked.

"Yes." I fingered a lock of hair.

"You neglected to mention that yesterday."

"Did I?"

A quiet knock on the door saved me.

"Open!" Piper called. A uniformed officer wheeled my bag into the room, nodded at the detective and left.

"Interesting set of circumstances, don't you think?" Piper asked, raising his eyebrows.

"I'm not sure if I know all the circumstances."

He placed his elbows on the desk and pressed his fingertips together. The movement was self-assured, as if he had all the cards, which I figured he had though I still wasn't sure which game we were playing.

"Among Mr. Abbott's personal effects was a business card for a Chester Butterworth. Do you know him?"

I shook my head.

"We spoke to Mr. Butterworth last night and learned he gave your fiancé legal advice." He raised his eyebrows again. I began to think it was a signature habit for him. "In fact, Mr. Butterworth went on at length about how he'd just helped your man open his restaurant."

"I see."

"Mr. Butterworth did more than that for Mr. Abbott. It seems," Piper slowed his speech, "that on the same day, just last week, your intended applied for a marriage license and created a will leaving everything to one Amanda Breen. His house, his car, even his newly purchased restaurant, the Revenge Café, now belong to you." He paused, I guessed for dramatic effect. "Don't you think that's a rather interesting set of circumstances?"

"Interesting but false." The tension in my body lifted as I called his bluff. He had nothing, nor had he planted anything, on me. He was fishing. "There's no way in hell Chance made a will."

Piper's eyebrows lifted even higher. "Why would you say that?"

"Chance doesn't create wills. He doesn't do those kinds of things. He's a perpetual Peter Pan, never growing up, always living in the moment. Making a will means planning for the future. That is completely out of character for him."

"Was."

"What?"

He didn't answer, but I got what he meant. Tears blurred my vision. I bit my upper lip and made myself look into his eyes, hoping for the lie-detecting x-rays or something else that would encourage me to fight. Instead, I got tired shadows filled with sympathy. I didn't want his sympathy. It wouldn't be good for me. I wanted, I needed something else to keep from breaking down. I ripped open my purse for a tissue.

"Besides, even if he did make a will, isn't that normal?" I slammed my wallet on his desk, topped it with the car key fob and a powder brush that I always forget to put in the zippered compartment and so everything in my purse has a dusting of *ceramic bisque* powder. "Don't most people make their *intendeds* their heirs?" I plopped my phone, a notepad, pen and a handful of change on his desk. "I mean, I would think that should be expected, right?"

"I suppose." He gave me a lopsided grin. "Only most people don't make a will then get murdered shortly before they are to marry their *friend*."

"Right . . . well," From a side pocket, I extracted Chance's spare house key, a pack of gum, my lipstick, and a small mirror. "OK, so yeah, maybe that's a good point, a very good point." Another side pocket held a couple of mints, and a flash drive that I'd swore up and down at a relatively high decibel to my former boss that I'd already given to him. "But still, it's normal for people to make wills when they're on the verge of a major life change."

"Like getting married." His grin broadened into a full-on smile.

"Yes. Like that." I wrinkled my brow at him with as much ferocity as I could muster and threw a pack of matches onto his desk.

"Or starting a new business." He leaned back in his chair, still smiling.

"Or starting a new business," I echoed and dug out my Florida house keys, a stamped envelope that I thought I had mailed to the Broward County Clerk of Court's office, and a small eraser that looked like salmon sushi. Finally finding what appeared to be a barely used tissue, I blew my nose and shook my hair away from my face.

"It might have been easier if you'd just asked if we had any tissues." He nodded at the mess on the desk.

I looked at the pile of debris. At first I didn't understand what I was seeing, but then I realized my purse felt unusually light. What the hell was I doing?

I slumped against the back of the chair and stared at the rotating ceiling fan. Sassy Reporter girl deserted me. Maybe she needed better hair. All that was left was Mandy. Confused, unshielded

Mandy. I decided to wave a white flag, which in my case meant a crumpled tissue.

"The thing is," I said and began re-loading my purse. "I don't know why Chance would have made a will. He doesn't, didn't really, own anything."

"He at least owned a house, car, and restaurant."

"I mean," I stared at the pack of matches in my hand. Why was that ever in my purse? Smoking was one of the few vices I'd never indulged. "I just find it odd that he made a will right after–"

I caught myself.

"Right after what?" His smile gone, he leaned forward over the desk.

I resumed replacing the contents of my purse, slowly, deliberately, taking great care where I tucked it all.

"So, um." I coughed. "Chance got the funding for the restaurant, bought a new car, and had recently renovated his house. I uh, well, I was a little surprised he could afford all those things."

"I see. You don't know where the money came from."

"I'm guessing he got a loan." I peeked at him, hoping he'd tell me that Butterworth person had said something about a huge credit line to a local bank.

"Guessing or believing?" he disappointed me.

I shrugged.

Piper resumed his school-boy posture but with eyebrows in their natural place. "Are you sure there were no other investors?"

"He never mentioned any."

"Do you know if there was anyone in the past, an old partner perhaps who would benefit by having Mr. Abbott pass away before getting married and giving half his net worth to you?"

"Not that I'm aware."

"I don't suppose you'd know of anyone who would have liked to cause Mr. Abbott harm, do you?"

"You know, if Chance was alive right now, that would be a funny question."

"Why?"

"Ha! There are probably a couple dozen men whose American wives found Chance's accent and flattery too sexy to ignore. There're a number of third-world bar owners who, I'm sure, believe he owes them large amounts of cash. And . . ." I was about to tell him that Malcolm, my ex-boyfriend, hated his guts more than anything in the world but the look on his face suggested I'd said more than enough.

"And yet you were going to marry him?"

"Oh, well, you know . . ." I flapped a hand. "Water under the bridge, right?"

"Right." Piper's head bobbed a couple of times before he continued. "Thank you." He ripped a page from his yellow pad. "I will be in touch with you if I have further questions. In the interim, I suggest you contact Mr. Butterworth. Here is his information." He reached across the desk and handed me the paper. "Since you are responsible for Abbott's estate, you will need to contact the morgue. Once the death certificate is filed you will also be responsible for arranging burial and whatever necessary memorial services."

A battalion of medieval Crusaders on horseback stampeding through the room would have made less of an impact on me.

"What? I have to . . . I'm what?" *Why me? It wasn't going to be a real marriage!*

"Mr. Butterworth probably has all the details regarding Mr. Abbott's final wishes—that is if you don't already know them."

Once again, I left the police station on foot. This time I dragged my carryon behind me as I headed toward the Revenge Café just down the harbor. Midway along I approached Bumpa's Ice Cream and Sandwich shop and popped in for lunch.

I ate, sitting upstairs at Bumpa's, at the edge of the covered outdoor area where I had a nice view of the bay. The land arced out to a point where St. Thomas jutted toward Water Island. In front of it, I could see Hassell Island across the straight from the Revenge Café. The walls of my restaurant, if what Piper had said was true, blazed white in the sun up on its hill.

In between bites of my BLT with extra mayo, I pulled out the paper Piper had given me and entered Chester Butterworth's information into my phone. I dialed and his line went to voice mail immediately.

"This is Mandy Breen," I said, and found myself without words. *I need to talk to you about my dead fiancé* seemed like something you should never leave in a message. Instead, I asked him to please call me and left my number.

Bumpa's didn't have a line of people waiting for a table so I got a refill for my coffee and pulled out my laptop. With an AirData wireless access card plugged in, I went online and learned from Intellius that Piper had transferred from the police department over on St. Croix to St. Thomas about a year and a half earlier. The timing of his transfer suggested he came as part of the replacement team for the personnel who'd been fired or incarcerated due to my investigation. On the surface it appeared that he was safe for me to confide my suspicions about my story, but only on the surface. I still didn't know if he had been specifically chosen for his current job because he had similar loyalties as his predecessor, who was still in jail. That kind of stuff I'd get from his co-workers, neighbors and friends, not from the Internet.

I also looked up all the names I could remember of the people I exposed in that article who were involved in the illegal drug trade. It seemed most of the major players were still incarcerated, except for one: Reggie Callwood, a former police lieutenant on St. Thomas. I couldn't find any information on what he was now doing for a living and when I plugged into Google Earth the St. Thomas street address that was listed for him on Intellius, I was told it was invalid.

I wondered if Piper knew him.

I left and headed toward the Revenge Café, walking on the opposite side of the street from the harbor. The early-afternoon sun was intense. My skin burned, sweat dripped down my back and my hair stuck to my neck. After only a few blocks, I had to stop in at a sundry shop.

I was willing to pay the ridiculously high price for the sunscreen. It was a necessity and I was the foolish one for not bringing any from the mainland. But I couldn't accept the cost of a package of three hair clips.

"Do you have anything similar that doesn't cost a month's rent?" I asked the clerk.

"You no live on island do you?" she laughed.

"Actually, I think I do now." I placed my basket on the counter.

"You jus' tink?" She squinted one eye at me.

"I just inherited a place."

"Nice. You inherit a job, too?" The register beeped when she scanned the sunscreen with a hand-held device.

"No, but I inherited a restaurant. It's that place up on the hill over there." I pointed through the front window along the bay to the Revenge Café. "It's that white building across from that little island."

The woman twisted around and stared, for what I thought was too long, out the window. When she turned back around her eyes were open wide.

"H'yeh." She ripped open the hair clips and pulled one out. "You have dis one and go. Be careful of de jumbies."

I thanked her and left the building, stopping outside to slather on the sunscreen and pull my hair up to clamp it at the top of my head. Jumbies? I stared down the curve of the island to my new restaurant wondering what she meant. Jumbies are supposed to be bad spirits. The Revenge Café glistened too white and bright to be associated with any kind of bad spirits.

Then again, good spirits probably wouldn't have killed Chance.

The dark green Grand Cherokee looked as if it was waiting for me at the end of the parking lot when I arrived about ten minutes later. Not another car was in sight, not even a police car.

I neared the Jeep and stopped to fumble in my purse for the fob I'd found. Holding my breath, I held it up and pressed the button with the opened lock symbol. The Jeep's doors clicked in response.

"Yes!" I reached out to the driver's door and noticed dark powder residue. The police had checked it for fingerprints. There wasn't any yellow tape around it though so the Jeep was now mine for the taking. Perhaps permanently, if I could afford the payments that I assumed I inherited along with the actual vehicle.

I tucked the carryon on the passenger side floor and sat in the driver's seat. The stifling, stale air engulfed my face in a suffocating embrace. I pressed the ignition button and waited for the air conditioner to have its way with me while I tried to figure out what my next step would be.

I was ready to do something. Go somewhere. Solve Chance's murder somehow. My fingers drummed the steering wheel, the sound almost echoed in my blank brain. Where the hell was I to begin? I guessed I needed to finish researching Piper. If I could clear him of any connection with my article, then I'd tell him about it and ask about Reggie Callwood and any of the others who may be out wondering the streets.

I decided to go back to Chance's house, which apparently was mine, where I could charge my phone and do more research on the Internet.

I pressed the brake pedal, grabbed the gear handle and looked into the rear-view mirror. Of course no other cars were in the parking lot, but suddenly there were a couple college-aged, white girls visible. I turned my head and watched them moving away from the steps that led up to the restaurant, walking toward the road. In skimpy, strappy tops, very short shorts and flip flops, they seemed out of place, as if they got lost walking to a beach.

The only reason I could think of for two, white, twenty-something females to be in an empty parking lot in the Caribbean was for them to meet their contact to buy drugs. It was an intriguing concept with far-reaching implications. Was Chance's restaurant a popular illegal stop-and-go pharmacy? Was his death because he'd witnessed a deal gone awry outside the kitchen window and therefore *not* because of my article?

Chapter 6: Despite the Odds

I thought about getting out of the Jeep to talk to the women, but answered my cell phone instead. Chester Butterworth was returning my call.

He had a British accent that was different from Chance's; he sounded more like he was from one of the islands formerly or currently under British control. I explained who I was and said I needed to speak to him about Chance.

"I'm available now, love, if you'd like to pop by," he said.

"Sure, um, I could do that." I fished for the pen and notepad in my purse and gave a micro-prayer that he was within walking distance. "I'm at the Revenge Café now. How do I get to you from here?"

"It's simple."

"Good." My prayer was answered. "I'm ready." Unable to find the pad, I held the pen poised above an empty, torn envelope.

"OK then, leave the restaurant driving away from the harbor. Take the first left branch of the road. Cross over Veteran's Drive, and veer off to the left again. You'll want to make a right when you see a mahogany tree beside a pink building, and then a left at a white wall. Got it?"

"Well–"

"And then travel 'bout a half kilometer and you'll see an old peachy-colored, two-story, stucco house looking over a rock outcropping. I'll be in that house. *Easy*!"

"Sure, but–"

"I'll see you soon, love." He clicked off.

Easy, he'd said. Right, easy.

I was sure it would have been easy if I were a driver trained to race in the Grand Prix of Monaco. However, I was a very bad and nervous driver, who comes from a family of very bad and nervous drivers, who learned how to drive (being taught by a very bad and nervous driver grandmother) on the straight, wide, flat back roads of central Florida.

I was also a very bad and nervous driver who happened to be the driver and sole survivor of a car wreck that killed my little sister and that same grandmother.

No driving was ever easy for me.

Regardless, with hands gripping the two and ten o'clock positions on the steering wheel, I pulled out of the parking spot and stopped. I congratulated myself for the good job of going backwards without hitting anything and put the Jeep into *drive*.

"So far so good, Chance."

The girls had disappeared. I glanced around for them as I left the lot and nearly slammed into an open-top tour bus loaded with passengers. I swerved, remembering almost too late that despite the fact I was in a U.S. territory, and I was in a car with the steering wheel on the left, I'm supposed to drive on the left side of the road, not on the right as is normal in the mainland states.

I'd just crossed over Veteran's Drive when the truck driver in front of me stopped, with no warning, to have a conversation with a pedestrian friend. I stomped on the breaks so hard I bumped my chin on the steering wheel. The second time it happened, because that is a normal and acceptable reason to hold up traffic in St. Thomas, I lost control and veered up along the side of the truck. If it weren't for that pedestrian's quick reflexes making him jump onto a wall to escape me, I might have hit him. Instead, I hit the wall.

"I'm so sorry!" I yelled as I rolled down my window. "You all right?"

"You drunk?" he asked.

"No, I just . . . your friend . . ." I covered my eyes with my hand. "I'm sorry. I'm a nervous driver."

"You not drunk? Fo' true?"

"I'm sober, honest." I put the car in reverse, pressed the accelerator apparently with too much force and bumped into a light pole behind me. The man, still sitting on the wall stared at me, as did his friend, whose head was sticking out of his truck window.

I put the Jeep in drive, lurched forward and stopped to wait for the other driver to go.

"EH!" he yelled. "Scatta!"

"Excuse me?" I called back to him.

"Scatta yo baxide!"

I waved *thank you,* in case he was politely telling me to get in front of him, and pulled back into the street.

After stopping to have my own roadside conversation with a stranger about what a mahogany tree looked like, I wound up at what I thought was Butterworth's office: a large, pink West Indian style house, with a red barreled roof and white verandah across the street from a loose pile of rocks.

I guessed the house had been built over a century earlier when the Danish ruled the island. It probably once was the home of an important government official or a wealthy colonial businessman but had since been converted into modern offices, predominantly unoccupied offices because it appeared to be vacant. The verandah was empty of furniture, the upstairs windows were shuttered, and the downstairs ones had the blinds pulled. I saw no signs on the front door and no mailboxes lined up on the porch.

Knowing it was very possible I had turned at the wrong tree, I knocked on the door. After a minute of silence, I knocked again then shuffled in my purse for my cell phone to call Butterworth.

The blind in the window beside the door flipped up and the window opened with a rumble. The face of a white, chubby male poked out and smiled at me.

"Miss Breen?" he asked.

"Yes. I'm here to see—"

"Oh, do come in!" The head disappeared inside.

I opened the door and before I had a chance to let my eyes adjust to the dim interior, I saw the man pouncing down a hall toward me.

"Chester Butterworth," he said tugging on my arm. "At your service." He pulled me inside the house and slammed the door behind us.

I got the feeling Chester Butterworth's childhood dream was to be a Tommy Bahama model living a Jimmy Buffett lifestyle. Tragically, there was evidence he had yet to achieve a level of income, or a trim enough physique, to do it with panache. His khaki shorts, which hung below his well-endowed tummy, were more wrinkled than my day-old ones and I could recognize the flowers only on the sides of his Hawaiian-style shirt where the sun couldn't reach to bleach out the colors. A barely lit cigar stub was crammed in the corner of his mouth and dark sunglasses perched atop his tousled head. I was torn between deciding if his two-day old beard and gold hoop in his left ear made him resemble a pirate or a has-been rock star.

But his appearance made sense to me. Chance would never have used an attorney who owned a suit.

"I hope I was easy to find," he said as he escorted me to a back room. He walked so quickly his worn down flip flops clicked like cards in bicycle spokes. "I'm sure it's been a trying day for you, love."

"It has, thank–"

"Please, do sit down." He nearly shoved me into an old, scratchy plaid chair before flopping on the mismatched one next to it. He rubbed out the cigar in an ashtray in need of emptying and clutched my hand. "You must be devastated. Simply devastated, darling."

"It's tough." I pulled out of his grip and tugged on the hem of my shorts to protect my legs from the chair's upholstery. "I think I'm still in shock."

"Shock!" His body bounced with the exclamation. "Yes, well I guess that would be expected." He leaped out of his chair and headed toward a side door. "Maybe you would like some water?"

"No, thank you. I just–"

"Coffee then?" He spun back around and gripped my chair.

"Really, no. I only came–"

"Something a little stronger?" He raced to his side of the desk, ripped open a drawer and produced a bottle of Cruzan rum.

"Maybe just a sip."

I have a thing for Mount Gay rum from the Barbados, but Butterworth's bottle of Cruzan, which is made in the U.S. Virgin Islands over on St. Croix, was top shelf. He held an impressive single-barrel variety I saw no reason to reject. Besides, although it wasn't even close to five o'clock yet, I was on an island where drinking is not a vice or a habit; it's how everyone lived, twenty-four-seven, and now that I lived there . . . when in Rome . . .

"So yes," Butterworth said as he handed me an on-the-rocks glass with no rocks and a half-inch of rum. "I guess you would be in a state of shock. How can I help you, love?"

“This morning,” I started and stared at my glass. I tried to convince myself the splotches near the rim were water spots, clean water spots. “I met with a Detective Matthew Piper and—”

“I know Detective Piper well.” Butterworth nodded over his drink.

“Right, well, he said you handled Chance’s estate and—”

“Yes, I knew Chance well, too.” He beamed. “I know everyone on island.”

“Well, Piper suggested I contact you. He said—”

“Aha! I spoke to Terry in the coroner’s office. I know what happened. No worries there.” He reached over and clinked our glasses. "A crime of passion is very easy to persuade a judge and jury to be lenient on."

“What are you talking—”

“A crime of passion is often seen with a kind and empathetic eye.”

“I don’t think you understand—”

“Aw, it’s OK, love!” He popped out of his chair and came around to sit on top of the chipped Formica desk in front of me. A little rum sloshed out of his glass. He licked it off the back of his fingers before continuing. “It’s so easy to understand. You come to the island excited and happy to see the man you agreed to marry. But where is he?” He slugged down his drink, thumped the empty glass on his desk and leaned toward me to whisper. “Anyone could understand. Anyone can relate to a woman breaking down in an hysterical fit when she finds her beloved in an intimate, and apparently kinky, embrace. I’m sure his bound hands only incited the hurt burning inside—”

“What are you talking about? I wasn’t hurting. I—”

“You were angry. I get it.” He gripped my arm. “He was probably drunk. She was probably just a stripper hired for his stag party. But all you saw was betrayal and—”

“No! That’s *not* what happened!” Suddenly sure the alcohol would kill whatever germs were on the rim, I gulped my rum.

“Oh. I’m so sorry.” As if on springs, he popped off the desk. “But I still understand, love. Not everyone is into the whole bondage scene, but I think most would agree that accidents can happen anywhere, especially when ropes and spicy foods are combined. I promise you, it will still be easy to justify.” He paced in circles. His words came out quickly, growing louder and louder as I became more and more perplexed. "Why, I've even seen research where if you get a woman's feet warm, she'll have an easier and stronger orgasm. We can convince the jury that's what *you* were trying to do to help *him*. Yes! You were heating him up so to speak and . . . I got it!" He was close to yelling, forefinger pointing to the ceiling. "You were trying to save his life by putting him in the freezer, yes?"

"What the hell are you talking about?" I stood and shoved my glass in his hand.

His face froze in a frown as if he were the confused one. "So you didn't kill him?"

"No!"

"Oh." He ambled back behind his desk, sat and pulled out the rum bottle again. "So you don't need help coming up with a defense?"

"No!"

"Well, that's probably a good thing." He gave us both a liberal pour and handed me his former glass. "You would have been the first murder suspect I'd ever worked with." He leaned back to put up his feet and clutched my glass over his stomach. "So what is it that I can help you with, love?"

I switched our drinks, in the off chance the glasses had been clean to begin with and returned to my chair. He grinned and did a *cheers* in the air before sipping. I *cheered* him back and drank.

"I came here . . . wait, first, what were you talking about?" I perched on the edge of the scratchy chair.

"Chance's murder of course."

"But ropes? Spicy food? What was that about?"

"Oh, the police believe he was killed with hot peppers."

A little voice in the back of my head said I should get up and leave. It suggested I was talking to a crazy man, possibly even the person who had killed Chance, and that maybe I should get my ass to a hospital before the poison in the rum got all the way through my system and made me as nutty as he was. But as I sat there contemplating his words, I took in his eager face.

Despite the frat boy appearance, he looked older than I was. There were well-set creases at the corners of his eyes, deep smile lines making parentheses in the stubble around his mouth, and streaks of gray naturally highlighted his hair. And overall, there was a Boy-Scout earnestness about him that made me think that, despite the odds, he looked sane.

"I think I misunderstood," I said. "Did you say—"

"They believe he was killed with hot peppers," Butterworth repeated.

"What? How do you know?"

"Like I said, I know everyone, love. As soon as the police left me last night, I called Terrence King, the coroner. He told me everything."

"And everything is?"

"This is confidential, now," Butterworth lowered his voice. He brought his feet down to lean over the desk toward me. "Terry told me Chance's shirt had been ripped open. His hands were bound behind his back with cloth napkins and his mouth was stuffed with hot peppers. Terry hasn't filed a complete report yet, but as of this morning he was waiting on toxicology test results to confirm it was the peppers."

He tilted back to take a drink and a button popped off his shirt. I watched him as he set his glass on the desk and look at the floor between his spread legs for the rogue button.

"How long do you think that will take?" I asked.

"Shouldn't be long, really." He gave up on the button and opened a desk drawer. "Since they know what they're looking for."

"What kind of peppers were they?"

"Oh, a couple varieties. The chef, Harold, said he had some intense ones in the kitchen. Terry thinks the kind used on Chance were habanero and something called rocoto."

"Rocoto? Are you sure?"

"As sure as Harold is."

"Who spoke to him?"

"I think Matt Piper." He looked up from trying to secure his shirt shut with a paperclip. "Now then, why did he send you to me?"

"Oh, right! That. Um, Piper told me that you did the will. Did Chance—"

"He left everything to you."

"Okay, but did he say—"

"You'll need to contact his bank and all that."

"Yeah, but wait." I held up my hand. "Did Chance say why he

was making a will?"

"Oh just crossing his T's, dotting his eyes. You know, the usual."

I frowned and sipped my drink. "But that doesn't really make sense."

"How so?"

"Did he happen to tell you why we were marrying?"

"Actually," Butterworth hunched forward, his eyes shifting left and right as if looking to see who else could hear. "I was the one who told him it'd be easier to become an American citizen if he married an American woman."

"Well, that's my point." I leaned over the desk toward him. "Don't you find it odd that he left everything to me when it was supposed to be a marriage of convenience?"

"Oh! I thought he'd found someone he fell in love with."

"No. We're just old friends."

"Ah, I think I see what you're getting at. And why yes, that does sound rather odd. Do you think maybe Chance felt his life was in danger?"

"That's what I was trying to ask you."

"I haven't the faintest idea, love. Sorry." He leaned back in his chair and smiled at me.

Chapter 7: Iguanas, Goats and Ponies

"So, uh, anyway, you know what I need to do, right?" I asked Butterworth.

"I do?" he asked.

"I hope so because I don't." I paused and waited. He said nothing. "I need to contact the morgue and, you know, make arrangements of some kind." I thought he looked as if he was on the verge of saying something. He wasn't. We sat quietly for a full minute. "I thought maybe you could tell me what to do. You did make the will, right?"

"Yes!" he shouted. I jumped. "Of course! The will!" He spun his chair around to face an open laptop and typed like a professional. "Yes, yes, here it is. Just a minute." He punched a key, lurched from his chair and nearly ran out of the room. I drank.

"Yes, yes, yes," I heard him saying as he re-entered with a thin stack of paper in his hands. "Here is the will and the details of everything he owned, which now you own." He thumbed through the pages while still standing. "The good news is there is no debt. He owned everything free and clear, as you probably already knew. Regardless, that's a good thing as debt of the deceased can be difficult to clear up."

"I don't understand." I reached out and took the papers from him.

"When someone dies and they owe a lot of money, often creditors—"

"No, that's not what I mean." I looked at him across the desk. He was back in his seat, fingers drumming the Formica, leaning forward as if eager to hear my next words so he could interrupt. "How could he not have any debt? He just bought a restra—"

"Everything was paid for in cash." Butterworth blinked several times before he continued. "The house, the car, even the restaurant."

"Where did he get the money?"

He shrugged. "I didn't ask."

"Wow." Forgetting about the semi-sticky scratchy nature of my chair, I leaned back. "Hmm. So if he . . . then I . . ."

"Yes?"

I shook my head. "First thing's first." I waved the will in front of me. "Are there directions in here discussing his final wishes?"

"Final wishes?"

"What to do with his . . . uh, his . . ."

"Oh that." Butterworth plucked the papers from my hands. "I used a program where we just had to fill in the blanks." He shuffled through the pages. "He did most of the typing so I'm not sure, but it sounds rather like standard normal practice, yes?"

I looked at my unfinished second drink instead of responding and shoved the glass out of my reach before it tempted me.

"Yes. Hmmmm, here it is." Again the fingers of his free hand drummed the desk and I could hear his foot pumping on the floor as he read. "He wanted to be cremated. His ashes spread in the harbor before the Villa Olga, which is quite coincidental."

"Where? And why coincidental?"

"Villa Olga is the name of the estate he bought where the restaurant is. Parts of it have burned down several times in the history of St. Thomas. Chance was apparently killed with hot peppers. And he wants his body to be burned. Don't you think all that fire is a bit coincidental?" He handed me the will.

I took the pile and put it in page number order again.

"Yes, I suppose you're right."

Our eyes held. For a nanosecond, Butterworth stopped moving but then he burst out of his chair as if to tackle something on my side of the desk.

"Of course, Ms. Breen, if you need any help with the arrangements, please feel free to call me. You have my number, yes?"

"Yes." I stood to go; he didn't hesitate to lead me toward the door.

"And if you need recommendations for where to house off-island guests, I can probably help with that, too."

"I don't think that will be nec—"

"Well, sometimes in-laws can turn into guests who stayed too long very quickly. Not that I have ever had that kind of problem, but that's what I've heard."

"What do you mean?"

"His family. I know he wasn't close, but I assumed you'd let them know about, well, about his passing."

"Oh, that," I said realizing what lay ahead of me. My stomach churned. "I just haven't had a chance to think everything through, yet."

"Yes, right." We were at the door. "Well, again, if you need—"

"I'll give you a call," I interrupted.

I returned to the Jeep, got in and turned it on so the air conditioner could cool me while I processed what Butterworth had just said. I wasn't so sure the killer was connected to that magazine article anymore. It remained a possibility, but now I had a feeling the money trail was more apt to lead me to the murderer. But I couldn't ignore the fact that the hot peppers were the murder weapon.

In the two months since I'd agreed to the crazy deal of marrying Chance in exchange for half of the restaurant, he'd inundated me with food and menu ideas. He took full advantage not only of my love of food, but of my resources. My journalism career had started with me being a food writer for a magazine my old boyfriend, Malcolm, owned. Chance was an up-and-coming photographer for the same magazine at that time, so he knew I had in my contacts a variety of food manufacturers, agricultural specialists, and test kitchen chefs. He also knew I had old-fashioned resources, too, like ancient recipe books and food journals.

There had been a perpetual stream of emails from him asking me what I thought of this spice, or that vegetable, or a particular combination of ingredients. At one point, he'd even mentioned he'd found a unique hot pepper. One he'd never seen or tasted before and he'd wanted me to see what I could do recipe-wise with it. He was talking about the rocoto. One of the peppers that wound up killing him.

I wasn't sure if the pepper was a true lead, but I couldn't leave it alone. Besides, following up on a lead that would take me nowhere would be preferable to taking care of Chance's remains.

"I'm sure you find it funny, though, right Chance?" I asked him, wherever he was. "Me being responsible for the care of your body. You jerk." Once again I had to clench my eyes shut to keep the tears at bay.

Shrimp! I banged my head against the steering wheel. I needed to peel and de-vein some shrimp. Maybe even eat some. I had a feeling I'd be cooking a lot over the next couple of days and while there were some staples in Chance's kitchen, I knew I'd need more to work with.

I searched for *Fruit Bowl Grocer USVI* in the browser app on my phone. I had no idea how to get there from where I was, but I'd been there a few times before with Chance and knew I'd be able to get to his, that is my, home from there. Also, I knew the store was given a misnomer. They didn't just sell fruit. I could count on doing a full shop, load up on some beautiful seafood and check out the varieties of hot peppers they sold.

I entered the address into the Jeep's GPS unit and was told it was invalid. I wasn't surprised. What islanders call their streets is seldom what map makers call them. I stared hard at the GPS screen and scrolled around the image of the island until I thought I'd figured out where the neighborhood was for the grocer. I tapped on what appeared to be a main intersection there figuring once I neared it, things would look familiar enough for me to find it, or close enough to risk directions via landmarks given by an islander.

The navigation system brought me to a McDonald's but I could see the Fruit Bowl on the other side of it. I drove across the parking lot of the golden arches and through what I assumed was the access to the street. It wasn't. But the Jeep easily bounced over the sidewalk and down the curb.

"Now this is my kind of car," I said aloud. I'd never taken a curb that quickly before without that sickening crunch sound suggesting axle or frame damage. I crossed the street and turned into the parking lot of the Fruit Bowl, scraping the passenger's front corner panel against a light pole.

Inside the market I loaded up on shrimp and scallops before hitting the produce area. I cruised the hot pepper section first. The Fruit Bowl carried Scotch Bonnets, Habaneros, chilis, and jalapenos, as well as a few varieties I'd never seen before, but no rocoto.

I didn't get any peppers. I remembered seeing a plastic bag full of jalapenos in the giant refrigerator the night before. Obviously, Chance had planned on me making one of my specialties: bacon-wrapped, stuffed jalapenos. Maybe I still would, to honor his memory.

Back in the parking lot, I checked out the passenger's side scratch. As I thought, it was minor. But the little incident with the wall I had on my way to Butterworth's had dented the corner bumper and broken the parking light glass.

"Sorry, Chance," I whispered to him. "You know it wasn't intentional, eh buddy?" I ran my hand along the top of the as-yet undented front grill. It glinted in the sun showing off just how new it was. Curious, I got in, pressed the ignition button and looked at the odometer: 973.

Theoretically, it could take a long time to rack up mileage in a car on St. Thomas. The island is only thirty-two square miles and there aren't that many roads. I opened the glove box and dug out the registration papers to see how long it took him to reach just under a thousand. The answer: two months. He'd bought it back in February, around the same time I was fired and he'd asked me to marry him. Again Piper's phrase: *interesting circumstances* came to mind.

"Chance?" I shook my head and put the papers back in the glove box. "There's an innocent explanation, right? You weren't involved in something you shouldn't have been, right? I'm going to find a card or notice somewhere that says *Congratulations! You won first place in a nature photography contest.* Right? And the Jeep was the prize, right? AM I FREAKING RIGHT?"

The whirring of the air conditioner was the only response.

I put the Jeep in reverse and saw that the passenger mirror housing was moved out of position. I must have hit it when I scraped the pole. Unable to change it from the inside control, I got out to push the housing back into place.

I got back in the Jeep, pushed a few stray strands of hair out of my eyes and *Boom!* A large, tan palm struck the passenger window.

My body sparked. I tried to put the Jeep in reverse but wound up in neutral, gunning the engine.

"Ho!" a voice yelled and a man rounded the front of the Jeep. It was Charlie, the Rasta who'd picked me up at the airport.

Not knowing his intentions, I only opened the driver's window a few inches.

"Pretty Babylon gyul," he said as he approached. "Mine yoself. Yo toss be limin wi de big people an dey vexed."

"What?"

"Yo friend –"

"My friend is dead. What about him?"

He stared through the window slit into my eyes, clearly surprised to hear my news. He then opened his mouth but said nothing. Instead, he looked out toward the road.

"Hail up!" he called to a stripped down minivan and ran toward it. The van shrieked to a stop. He jumped in and was off before I was able to get the Jeep out of the parking spot.

Knowing I'd never be able to catch up with Charlie and his accomplice, I put the Jeep back in park and dumped my purse out on the passenger seat to find my phone. But as Piper's end rang, I realized I didn't want to tell him about seeing the Rasta yet. It would be better if I waited until I had a definite question or needed his help and then used the incident as barter. I tapped *End* and dropped it on the passenger seat.

It rang within a few seconds. The glowing screen told me it was Piper calling me back. I answered lest he worry and become curious enough to track me down.

"Is something wrong?" he asked.

"Why yes, I think there is." I sifted through my brain for something of substance to complain about. I once read that if you call attention to a problem, people will treat you like a figure of authority, someone who should be listened to. Practical experience had proven to me it worked about fifty percent of the time. "Why is no one at the Revenge Café looking for clues?" I asked.

"I had a team there until well past midnight last night and have a crew there now."

"Oh. Well then, OK." I clicked off thinking that fifty percent number was an overestimation.

I left the Fruit Bowl, exiting the lot from a proper lane and headed toward what was now my house. I drove slowly, hunched over the steering wheel, gripping it like my hands had been Super-Glued on as I bumped along the mountainous terrain.

Chance had chosen well when he bought the Grand Cherokee. I admired the way the Jeep responded to my correcting jerks—I had a tendency to drift right into on-coming traffic—and was confident in its ability to handle driving with two wheels on a shoulder that was uneven with the road. It takes me a while to figure out where a car begins and ends when I'm driving an unfamiliar one, so it was somewhat difficult for me to stay on the road, in my lane. Particularly when there were other people on the road driving, too.

"Eeee!" I yelled when a car passed me in the opposite direction. The road was walled and so narrow I instinctively sucked in my stomach as if that would make the Jeep skinnier too.

"Really, Chance?" I closed one eye and went around a hair-pin turn. "You had all that cash and instead of finding a place closer to town, you renovated one out in the sticks? Why?"

From what I understood, over half the population of St. Thomas lived in the south, in and around Charlotte Amalie, the only real city on the island. Where Chance lived, there were always more pelicans on the rocky beach and crabs in the tidal pools than people in sight. Occasionally locals would fish from the shore down the hill behind him and there was a walled-off salt pond nearby that sometimes saw human traffic, but otherwise no one was ever around.

Why had he insisted on staying in such a remote place?

When he'd first bought it, years ago, he told me it was because it was cheap and had a good view. So why did he stay? Judging by the amount he'd spent to remodel the house, he could have bought a very nice, new place in town, one close to his restaurant, maybe even within walking distance. And there are no bad views on St. Thomas.

I slammed on the breaks and swerved to avoid a large iguana sunning itself on a patch of blacktop. Chance had chosen to live out in a remote area as if he didn't want people noticing who came and went at his house.

Rounding another turn, going uphill, I nearly toppled a goat. Its rear end was in the street as it munched on a hedge.

"Chance!" I screamed and banged my palm on the steering wheel. "Why? Why all the way out here? Why so secluded?"

No answer, of course.

A short distance down the road I stopped for a feral pony to cross in front of me.

"A wild freaking pony? That's who your neighbors were? Iguanas, goats and ponies? No people? Come on, Chance! What were you hiding?"

And from whom? Could it be those big people Charlie spoke about?

I wasn't sure what the Rasta had meant. I only understood part of what he'd said. *Gyul* was girl. *Babylon* was referencing, in a not quite warm-and-fuzzy way, my homeland being the mainland United States. *Limin'* meant *socializing* or *hanging out* with someone. But who were the big people? Or what were they? And was *vexed* the same as *vexed?*

What kind of company was Chance keeping?

A car horn beeped behind me. I realized the pony was long gone and I was sitting there like the proverbial deer in the headlights, frozen in the middle of the road. I crept forward, spooked by the possibility that Chance had been keeping potentially dangerous secrets from me.

The driver behind me must have had to pee pretty badly. He kept right on my tail, his horn beeping an annoying form of Morse code for obscenities as if that would make me go faster. It didn't. I was more worried by the concept that Chance was hiding something or was hiding from someone. Because now that I owned what he used to own, maybe I was now hiding something too.

I finally turned onto his/my street. The driver behind me sped off, but not before thrusting his fist in the air and yelling swear words at me. I waved him off and slowed my speed to about five miles an hour, giving me a chance to really take stock of the neighborhood.

Only it wasn't a neighborhood. It was a rural road. And not another car approached me from either ahead or behind. Nor did I see another house.

I'd never really paid attention to his lack of neighbors before. Chance had been out there, all alone, in that house.

Did he need to be?

Chapter 8: Stick with Food

I put away the groceries and mixed up a marinade of lime juice, olive oil, garlic and minced jalapenos in a plastic bag. After pealing and deveining the shrimp, I dumped them in, sealed the bag and shook it to thoroughly saturate the krill before putting it all in the refrigerator.

Feeling somewhat settled, I propped my carryon on a desk in the guest room and unpacked my laptop, grooming essentials and a fresh set of clothes. In the bathroom, I gave myself a sponge bath, combed my hair and touched up my makeup. I changed into a pair of cargo-style cotton pants and a light-weight knit top. Both were pretty wrinkled from being in the luggage too long, but they felt cleaner than what I'd had on.

Somewhat refreshed, I headed back to the kitchen, plugged in my phone to charge, set up my laptop on the dining table and powered it on. I almost felt capable of doing whatever it was I needed to do.

"I'd prefer no more surprises, OK, Chance?" I said as I watched the Windows logo merge with my reflection on the screen. "The will was enough. And frankly, I'd love to learn everything was legal. That maybe you won the money in a lottery and was waiting to spring the news on me in person. OK?"

The little bugger continued to play the silent game.

I pulled the will out from my purse and placed it beside my computer. Instead of reading it, I made coffee. I wasn't procrastinating, I tried to tell myself. I really needed the caffeine.

My phone rang while the coffee brewed. Detective Piper was calling.

"Ms. Breen, we have downloaded all of Mr. Abbott's information from his cell phone and have dusted it for fingerprints. Would you like to have it?"

"It's one more reminder my friend is dead, why on earth would I *like* to have it?"

"I thought maybe it would be easier for you as you contact his friends and family. But I guess, since you were *engaged,* you know everyone your *friend* would want to have at his service? I'll just-"

"I'm sorry." I slammed my palm in to my forehead. "I really am. This is just hard, but yes, I'd like to have the phone." Really, I just wanted to find a number for Charlie.

"Where are you?"

"I am staying at Chance's house."

"Your house now," he said. "I'll bring it by shortly." And without giving me the opportunity to tell him not to, that I'd come get it, he hung up. Which was really fine with me, as I had had enough driving for the day but still, it was the principle. I wanted to feel more in control.

I had just plugged *St. Thomas USVI funeral homes* in Google when I heard Detective Piper's knock. The coffee in my cup hadn't even cooled enough to drink yet.

"That didn't take you long," I greeted him. "Did you know I was here before I told you?"

"No. I was over in Tutu Bay when I called." He walked past me despite the fact I hadn't asked him in.

"Someone in need of police services in Tutu?" I asked as he headed toward the dining area.

"No." He picked up the will from the table. "I was delivering a dog."

"A dog?" I drifted over to the back of the house and nonchalantly looked at the sideboard. The framed magazine was face down on the sideboard.

"A shelter mutt." He sat in a chair, kind enough not to take the one in front of my computer.

"You have the phone?" I asked.

"Yes." He leaned on one hip to pull Chance's cell out of his pants pocket. I spotted short, tan hairs on his navy blue trouser leg, giving credence to the idea he was doing something with a dog. He placed the phone on the table and pulled out a set of keys. "You may have these, too, which apparently you don't need." He raised his eyebrows at me. I remained silent. "They were also dusted for fingerprints. Only Mr. Abbott's were on them. Two go to the restaurant doors, one for the front and one for the rear. There's one to a post office box, a safe deposit box, and I'm guessing the others go to different doors inside the restaurant, this house and his Jeep."

"Probably," I said trying to hide my surprise over the P.O. box. I never knew Chance had one. I'd always sent mail directly to his house.

I picked up my coffee cup and took a sip while Piper glanced through the will.

"Hm," he said after a minute. He put the will back on the table, setting the phone on top of it.

"Did you learn something new?"

"From the will or the phone?"

"Both."

"We just downloaded the contents of the phone." He looked into my face. There was a quick sliver of something akin to appreciation in his eyes before they returned to being blank, piercing orbs. "You haven't read the will?"

"No." I slid into my chair disappointed by his unwillingness to tell me anything.

He met my eyes again. I was almost startled to find his face, while impassive, was not unkind. And handsome. Nicely chiseled jaw, narrow cheeks. I hadn't noticed how good looking he was at the station. Apparently his biceps had taken too much of my attention.

"Reading it, the will . . ." I looked into my cup instead of at Piper. "I don't know. Maybe if I don't read it, I don't have to accept that it is really Chance's will. That he is really dead." Even though I didn't invite them, tears welled up in my eyes. I sipped the coffee to force them back and hit the touchpad on my computer, making the screen saver go away to reveal the funeral home search results.

Piper stood and walked away from the table. I turned in my chair and watched him open and shut cabinet doors.

"Can I help you?" I asked.

"No, thanks. Just found them." He poured himself a mug of coffee and approached my chair.

"Many people use Davidsons's Funeral Home," he said, pointing to their listing on my search results. "You called anyone yet?"

"No." I clicked on their website.

He returned to his chair. "The forensics team is done with the restaurant. You can get in there if you want."

"Already?"

"It was a pretty clean murder. The only rooms disturbed were the main dining room and the kitchen."

"And I'm sure everything in those rooms had been thoroughly wiped down with a table cloth."

Piper grinned at me before sipping his coffee again. "I expect the office there will have all the information on his employees," he said. "You should call them to let them know about the memorial service. I can give you information to contact a DCT decon or crime scene clean-up company, but they are very expensive here and won't get to your place for several days, possibly weeks. You could try asking your employees for help cleaning so you can open it faster."

"I haven't even thought about opening it. I'm not sure if I will."

"Someone needs to."

"Why?"

"People depend on their jobs. You can always sell it later if you don't want it. But you should try to get it running until you do."

"Doesn't the health inspector or someone need to approve or deem it's safe? I mean, there was a dead body in the freezer."

"He wasn't alone in there. It was loaded with dead bodies."

The room spun on me. I gripped the table.

"Some of the best looking meat I've ever seen," Piper continued, grinning.

I rolled my eyes. "Was that necessary?"

He shrugged and sipped. "There was no blood, no bodily fluids, no potential for airborne pathogens. You can open as soon as you get the place cleaned out from the investigation and re-stock. You have some vegetables rotting in there, you know."

"I'm sure. But, honestly, who would want to eat there now?" I was really asking myself. Could I run the place alone? I had no idea how to do it. But I knew food. And I knew what I liked in a restaurant.

"Tourists will flock to it if you advertise it as the home of a mystery. Locals might be too superstitious, though," Piper said, oblivious to the conversation I was having with myself.

I stared at my monitor while the thought of running the restaurant filled my head. Could I still do it without Chance? Probably. He didn't have any applicable experience either. And besides, I was unemployed. The restaurant was my only option for income at the moment. Whether I *could* do it didn't really matter. I needed to at least try, didn't I?

"Do you know what else you need to do?" Piper asked.

I shook my head and returned my attention to him.

"Go through the contacts in his phone. You'll need to let everyone know he's gone. Go through his calendar there too and cancel any appointments. If there's a computer around here, do the same with it as well as the one in the restaurant." I typed his words into a Word document as he spoke. "Now that you own everything, you'll need to register the car and house in your name. You'll also need to alert his bank. There's information in the will about where his accounts are held. And since you have that key to the safe deposit box, you might want to see what's in it."

I looked up from my computer and squinted at him. His grin turned into a broad smile as he raised his eyebrows. "Of course you'll let the police know if there's anything of interest in it, right?" he asked.

"Without hesitation," I said with saccharine on my tongue.

He stood and picked up my half-full cup. "You take anything in this?"

Piper helped me finish the coffee, spouting out suggestions and directions on what to do and whom to contact. I was thankful for his help, and suspicious, too. Was he really doing it out of the goodness of his heart? Or did he have an ulterior motive? Like maybe one to make sure I didn't find out who killed Chance.

Eventually, he washed out his cup and returned to the table but didn't sit down.

"Listen," he said. "I checked you out. I know you've seen plenty of crime in the area. I'm sure you'll keep your head about you and not go out alone in town at night and you'll stay away from Back Street, right?"

"I'd planned on it." I walked him to the door.

"Good. Keep your doors locked all the time when you are home."

"Aye aye sir." I squeezed my hands together to keep from giving him a mock salute.

"Make sure you smile and greet everyone nicely when you go out."

"Yes, Daddy." I batted my eyes.

He sighed but grinned at me. "I'm just trying to keep you out of the line of fire."

"I appreciate it, really."

"You still have my card?"

"I put your info in my phone."

"Good. Feel free to call me if you need to go somewhere alone and it's night." He stepped outside and turned to look back at me. "I don't need two dead white people in my case load."

"Gee, I'll try not to add to your work pile." I shut the door.

Armed with the information I needed to arrange Chance's memorial, I pulled the bag of shrimp from the refrigerator and gave it a good shake to redistribute the marinade. Because I had to convince myself I wasn't procrastinating on making the arrangements, I told myself I was making sure I ate a decent meal that day. But I still couldn't call the funeral home. Instead, I cleaned and cut fresh greens, spun them dry and put them back in the fridge, next to the shrimp.

With nothing left to do with my food, I scrolled through Chance's contacts. There was no one named Charlie, Charles, Chuck or anything even remotely close to my Rasta driver's name. And apparently the police thought it important to delete his entire phone log.

Unable to come up with another distraction, I re-read the notes from Piper. He'd left something out.

"How do I call the morgue?" I asked as soon as he picked up his cell. "And don't you dare say with a telephone."

"I won't," he laughed. "But I will question your credentials as a journalist."

"My credentials are fine." Though as I said that, I realized he had a point. This was not unfamiliar territory for me. "Is there more than one morgue on this island?"

"No. Just the one at Schneider. I'm driving so I can't get the number for you off my phone and I don't have it memorized."

"That's probably a good thing." I clicked off and found the Roy Lester Schneider hospital website, typed *morgue* in their search engine and came up with zero results. I called the main desk and was transferred through. The line was answered before I was ready to say the words.

"I ... I need to discuss with you the, uh, the remains of Chancellor Abbott," I said.

"Who is dis?" the terse response came.

"I'm his ... I was his, uh fiancé. I'm responsible—"

"The body won't be ready fo' removal 'til Wednesday," came the rapid-fire interruption. "Have your funeral home director contact us 'bout transport. You can get his death certificate tomorrow. Tank you and have a nice day." *Click.*"

"That was relatively easy," I muttered and went back to Davidson's website, which listed all their contacts.

Within minutes, I had Chance's cremation arranged. I clicked on my calendar in my computer to enter the details the nice man at Davidson's gave me. That day's date was April 8. The memorial would take place on Sunday, the fourteenth, with a rent-a-reverend the funeral home would arrange for me. That was six days away. Six days to find people to attend.

Before hanging up from Davidson's, I agreed to come in the next day, Tuesday, to pick out an urn. I started to make a note in my calendar and I realized I'd be picking out an urn for my best friend's remains on April 9. The day that read *wedding/birthday* in my calendar.

A lump grew in my throat and tears blurred my eyes.

"No more crying, Breen!" I clenched my eyes shut. "You gotta stop this! No breaking down. Call Chance's family."

My fingers misbehaved and called Piper.

"Is the coroner's report in yet?" I asked as soon as he picked up.

"Why do you want to know?" I interpreted his answer to mean *yes.*

"Chester Butterworth told me the coroner suspected Chance . . . um," I cleared my throat, "that hot peppers were involved in . . . in . . ."

"I was unaware there was a public announcement," Piper said. "But yes, the report is in. The official cause of death is from heart failure consistent with toxic levels of capsaicin."

"Capsaicin," I repeated. "That's what makes peppers hot."

"Correct. How do you know about capsaicin?"

"I was a food writer before I went into crime."

"Food and crime," Piper mused. "Interesting combination."

"I'd rather just stick with food."

"I can understand that. So are we still in a tit-for-tat agreement?"

"Of course." I sat straighter in my seat, fingers hovering over the keyboard.

"A lethal dosage of capsaicin has not been established for humans," he said. "In mice, I just learned, it is forty-seven-point-two milligrams per kilogram of body weight. Abbott's ratio levels were double that."

"You don't really consider that privileged information do you? I could have researched that myself."

"I wasn't offering anything. I want information from you."

"About?"

"We spoke to your head chef."

"Harold, right?"

"Yes. He said Abbott had recently brought the peppers back from a trip to South America and wanted to experiment with them. We told him to keep them off the menu until he knows how much is too much."

"Good call."

"What can you tell me about Abbott's dealings in South America? Had he mentioned going there specifically for food? Or was he visiting for another reason?"

"Actually," I placed a hand on my forehead. "I didn't know he'd gone anywhere."

"Did your fiancé often travel without telling you?" Piper asked.

"Now do you really think I could answer that with certainty?" I slammed my hand on the table, not sure if I was angrier at Chance than I was annoyed by Piper. "Where, exactly, did he go? When?"

"I can't divulge details of the case with anyone outside the force yet." Which meant I owed him information before he'd say anything else.

Chapter 9: De Terrible News

I clicked off and walked over to the sideboard. The framed magazine still lay there, face down. Could I tell Piper about that? Not yet. I needed to at least locate Reggie Callwood and see what kind of ties might bind him to any current member of the police force, or even possibly to Piper himself. I put the frame in a drawer and returned to my computer where I dashed off a very short email to my cousin, Bob, who's a police officer in Hollywood, Florida.

Hey Bob,

I'm kind of unofficially working on an assignment in St. Thomas and need to get gossip on a local police detective here. Do you have any contacts out this way? Can you, without mentioning me, ask around to see if a Detective Matthew Piper, who is currently on the VIPD, is or was friendly with a Reginald Callwood, who used to be on the VIPD? I really appreciate any help you can give me.

I hit *send* and promised myself I'd get around to calling Chance's family as soon as I searched through the drawers and cabinets of the kitchen again. This time I was looking for his passport or travel receipts. I made myself believe I needed to strike while the iron was hot and that the sooner I could get that information to Piper, the sooner he'd tell me something else about the case.

I found nothing.

His bathroom and night stand came up empty, again, too.

On a table in the living area was only a stack of junk mail and magazines.

"Did you forget something?" Piper asked when I called him instead of anyone in Chance's phone. I could hear a dog barking in the background.

"Chance's passport."

"And you think I have it?"

"How do you know he went to South America?"

"Contrary to popular assumptions, we do actually follow similar protocols to what police on the mainland use. We checked out his recent credit card transactions."

"Are you sure you can't tell me where he went?" I wondered how to offer a *mea culpa* without looking like I'd done something wrong. "Maybe if I knew which part of South America, I could make a connection."

He didn't answer right away. "Peru," he eventually said. "Know why he might have gone there?"

"I can only guess he went for peppers. But I'm not sure." I clicked into Outlook on my computer.

"Is Peru famous for its peppers?"

"No, but . . ." I scrolled through the *sent* messages until I found the emails with *peppers* in the subject line. "About a month ago, Chance asked me if I could research a pepper variety for him. It has a couple names, one is rocoto."

"Aha."

"Right, but here's the coincidental part. It's also known as the Peruvian Death Pepper."

He laughed. "Are you making that up?"

"Honest and true. The scientific name is *capsicum pubescence.*"

"Pubescent?"

"*Pubescence.*" I spelled it for him. "It's Latin for hairy."

"That makes sense in an odd sort of way."

I laughed that time. It felt good to laugh. Actually, it felt good to know I could still laugh. "Anyway, the important part is, they can only be propagated in a narrow climate range. Peru is best suited for them. They are not commonly on market shelves anywhere else. So my guess is Chance went to Peru to get them." I spoke while I perused more emails.

"Why those peppers and not something else that would be easier to get? What's so special about them? Are they the hottest peppers in the world?"

"No. Though they're up there. Their Scoville Ranking, which is how the heat in peppers is scored, is pretty high. They come in anywhere from 100,000 to 350,000 heat units, which makes them much hotter than something like a jalapeno, which scores between 3,500 and 8,000 heat units. But they're the same level as Scotch

Bonnet and Habanero peppers, which are easier to find." I paused, unable to find any more related messages. "Maybe the novelty of saying *we have Peruvian Death Peppers* on the menu was what he was going for?"

"I could see that. You wouldn't happen to know if those peppers are sold on the black market, would you?"

"No, I don't think so."

"Know of any peppers that grow in England?" On his end I heard a shuffling noise, a dog whining and him shushing it.

"No. Want me to look it up?"

"Possibly."

"Why are you asking?"

"No reason."

"Did he go to England, too?"

"I'm not at liberty to discuss."

"Come on! Look what I just gave you! You can take it out in trade."

"You have more information for me?"

"Not yet."

"Then what can we trade?"

I looked around me, took in again Chance's beautiful kitchen, my beautiful kitchen.

"When I solve this case, I'll give you all the credit," I said, "and the recipe for that lobster stew."

"When you solve it based on the information I give you?"

"In part."

"Ha! This is all I'm giving you until you give me something else. And I don't cook, so you'll have to make the stew," he said. "He was in Peru for a couple days, about three weeks ago. From there, he went to London, where he also only spent a couple days before returning back to the island."

"London, England?"

"That would be the one."

"Bizarre."

"He was British citizen, wasn't he?"

"Yeah, but he hates, he hated, everything about England."

"Maybe you didn't know your fiancé that well after all."

Maybe I didn't. Had he visited his family in London? The family that I'd been avoiding?

I ended the call and glanced at the clock in the corner of my monitor. It was just after three. I went online and found the time in London was just after eight in the evening.

Chance's parents would probably be home. I should call, I told myself. *I need to call and tell them about Chance.* Then I said the words aloud.

"I should call his parents before it's too late at night there. Really, I should call now." My voice sounded too weak to do the job. "It is the right thing to do," I said louder and clearer.

But I wasn't so sure. The last time, the only time I saw his parents was for his brother's wedding. Chance was the wild child in a British upper crust family. The darling son was marrying a fellow aristocrat and Chance was expected to be there with an acceptable date. I was her.

After the wedding, I had the privilege of witnessing his father, Bertrand Abbott IV, telling Chance he never wanted to see him again. That Chance was a shame to his family and his family name. That he was a worthless human being.

But people seldom mean it when they say such things, right? Don't they always change their mind after they learn that person is dead?

And his mother had cried so hard during their argument. Surely she would want to know, or would she? Or would it only hurt her more?

Chance never spoke about him, them, to me again. Would he want them to know?

I picked up his cell phone. His father's contact information was the first in his database. Then I picked up my cell phone thinking it was time I tried my aunt again.

"Hello, dear," Aunt Maggie answered her cell with her happy, hurried, slightly nasal voice. "Babs told me about your friend. I've been waiting on your call all day. I would have called you but we all know you don't like to be rushed into your feelings."

"Thank you, I guess." I frowned as I opened the patio doors to step outside.

"You have good timing. I'm at a psychic fair. I mean a New Age fair. I keep forgetting that's what they're called these days. But, I'm between readings right now, so I have a few minutes to talk to you."

"Actually, Aunt Maggie, I think I need you to do a reading for me." The gorgeous view from the patio was refreshing. The beauty of the ocean, of seeing an uninhabited island that was part of the British Virgin Islands in the distance, made it easy to take for granted that Chance had kept the house and refurbished it to keep the view. The air was so pure I could even believe that maybe he had died in a crazy, accidental sex act like Butterworth thought. In fact, standing there staring out to sea, made me expect Aunt Maggie to tell me something that would make calling Chance's folks a quick and painless thing to do.

"From your friend?" she asked.

"Yes. He . . . His family . . . See, Chance left everything he owned to me."

"That was nice."

"I guess so. But that also means I'm responsible for his remains. I'm trying to figure out what to do about his . . . his memorial service. Can you help me?"

"Yes." I heard her inhale and waited for her to continue.

"So," I said after she was silent long enough for a pelican to fly across my line of sight and out of view. "I don't know what to do."

She remained quiet. I thought maybe she was in a trance or was doing whatever it was she did when she made contact with the dead. "I need to know, should I tell his parents?"

"Uh huh, yes, Tony, I'd like the tuna sandwich for lunch. Thank you, hon," she said to someone on her end. "Now then, Mandy," she said louder. "All your friend is willing to tell me right now is that he wants his parents to know and they can decide what they want to do about it."

"Are you sure, Aunt Maggie?" I walked back into the house. "I mean, you were just giving a food order—"

"Mediums are expert multitaskers." She laughed. "That's what I'm picking up from your friend. But he's also wanting you to know he'll be in direct contact soon."

"With who?"

"You. Who else?"

I ended the call and sat quietly at the kitchen table, waiting for Chance to do something. Maybe throw a book at me, burn the initials of the killer in the table, something, anything. But the wind continued to blow as usual outside the patio doors and the waves continued to crash down below, uninterrupted.

I picked up Chance's cell again and stared at the entry for his father, wondering if Aunt Maggie was wrong. She was listed in my cell as *Aunt Maggie.* My grandmother was still listed there as *Gram,* because I never had the heart to delete her after she'd died. I'd always assumed that if my mom had been alive when I got my first cell phone, I would have entered her as *Mom* and like my grandmother, I would have transferred her to each new phone I got.

In the name field for his father, Chance had typed: *Bertrand Abbott the Fourth.* Under title, he'd entered: *Pater Spurius.* I had to fight like hell not to use the phrase as an excuse to procrastinate by looking it up. Instead, I hit *call,* cringing as I realized too late that it was to his father's cell number. That meant I stood a good chance of him recognizing Chance's number on caller ID and ignoring it. Then I'd have to screw up the courage to call later because, again, I didn't think this was something I could leave in a message.

The phone rang several times before I heard a cold: "And what brings you calling?"

"Hello, Mr. Abbott?" I cleared my throat.

"Yes. Who is this?"

"This is Mandy Breen."

"Who?"

"Amanda Breen," I clarified. "I'm . . . I was a friend of Chance."

"Is he in jail?"

"No." I hated how he failed to notice I used the past tense. "He's in a morgue."

"Is this some kind of sick joke?"

"If only it were, Mr. Abbott, if only it were."

After filling Bertrand Abbott the Fourth in on Chance's death and memorial service, I told him to call the police station if he wanted more details. I read him Piper's contact information from his business card, omitting the cell number, and hung up. Since I was already in the A section of Chance's contacts, I scrolled to the next person, *Lydia Abiff.*

"Who calling from dis number?" a female Islander answered.

"Amanda Breen," I snipped back. "Is that any way to answer a phone?"

"Why you use Mr. Abbott's number?"

I pressed the heel of my free hand against my forehead and took a deep breath.

"I'm sorry," I said. "I am, or rather was, a friend of Chance Abbott and I'm—"

"Why you use his phone?"

"He . . . uh . . ." I sighed into the phone as tears pushed against my eyes. It'd be much easier to fight this woman instead of telling her why I was calling. "I have terrible news."

"I have heard de terrible news."

"Oh . . . well . . ." I faltered. Island gossip was quick, which meant not only was I making myself suffer even more, I was wasting my time. I had a feeling everyone who needed to know, already knew. So why was I intent on making these calls? Because Piper told me to.

Did he make the suggestion so I'd be sidetracked from following up on any leads?

"Why you call me?" the woman persisted on the other end of the phone.

"I'm calling everyone in Chance's contacts to let them know about the memorial service." I opened a new tab on my web browser as I voiced the words. What the hell was I thinking? If these calls were needed, they could certainly wait. The important one, to his family, was done. I needed to get back to the finding his killer.

"What about de memorial?"

"Huh?" I'd forgotten about her as I focused on punching Piper's name with one hand into the Google search bar.

"De memorial? What about it?"

"Oh, it will be on Sunday. His ashes will be spread in the harbor in front of his restaurant." I clicked off and set the phone down.

First I did a standard search and checked the images for photos of Piper and anyone he may have been keeping company with. He wasn't a very well known man. There were only a few shots that featured him and they were all from the VIPD's website. All were very official. All made him look like some kind of a hard-working, ethical, and morally strong (and good looking) badge-holder.

Unfortunately there weren't many hits for him in the web results, either. Again, he was featured heavily on the VIPD website. And the only other site associated with him that came up was the local ASPCA dog shelter, where he was lauded as a hero.

I went back into Intelius. From there, I took down his street address and the names of his neighbors. I was just writing down his ex-wife's name and phone number when Chance's cell phone rang.

Caller ID read: *Mum.* I almost threw up.

Chapter 10: You Have to Tink

"Answer it, Breen," I said out loud, staring at the phone. Both my hands stayed glued to the computer keyboard. "Answer it. She's hurting more than you."

I put the phone on speaker.

"This is Penelope Abbott," Chance's mother said. "I am . . . I was . . . Oh, is it true?"

"Yes, I'm so sorry. I really am. I—"

"It's not good. You should have told his father first. What am I to do now?"

"I just spoke to him. Isn't that how you—"

"No. I mean, yes. This is so difficult. What did Chance tell you?"

I picked up the phone and disabled the speaker function to listen to her directly. "I'm not sure if I know what you're talking about, Mrs. Abbott. What was Chance to tell me?"

"I still have some pieces. What should I do with them?"

"Pieces of what?" Eight? I couldn't help but wonder, though I had no idea what that phrase even meant.

"Unfortunately," her voice dropped to a whisper. "I cannot talk about this right now. Is there another number where I should call you?"

"I guess you could call—"

"Please!" she hissed. "Quickly."

I gave her my cell number and she hung up without confirming it.

I sat with the phone pressed against my face unable to let go of it. Clearly, Chance's mother was under the impression I knew something that I didn't know I knew. It was intriguing, to say the least. But not much help to me. I scrolled through the apps on Chance's phone. The police were thorough. They had deleted everything, including the search history on his web browser and any information he would have stored in his travel apps.

I set the phone down and resumed researching Piper. I couldn't risk trying to get gossip on him from anyone at the police station. I was too much of an outsider and had no idea where anyone's loyalties lay. So it seemed my next step should be to check out his neighbors and see what they had to say about him.

I typed in his address on Google earth and was just zooming into his neighborhood when someone knocked on the front door.

My heart slammed into a jackhammer dance. Unexpected knocks tended to do that to me. Invariably, my mind would flash through whatever crime-related current events were going on in the local community and I'd wonder if I were slated to be the next victim. I was pretty sure it was an occupational hazard from being a crime reporter. But today, my first reaction was to wonder if it was Chance's killer. Could it be Reggie Callwood? Could it be someone from Peru? Could it be whoever was the legal owner of all that cash that somehow fell into Chance's hands?

The knock pounded louder. *Why would anyone who wanted to kill me actually take the time to knock on the front door? They could easily go around back and step in through the open patio sliders.*

I crept to a front window and pinched the curtain aside just enough to get a good peak out. As if she knew I'd be looking for her there, an Islander woman, around fifty years old or so, in an orange paisley blouse and black skirt stood on the other side of the window, squinting in at me. Her braided hair was piled high on her head and held in place by a green scarf tied in a bow. An unlit, brown cigarette was tucked behind one ear.

I stepped over to the door and opened it.

"You de mainlander friend Mr. Abbott was expecting dis week?" she asked.

"Yes." I recognized the sound of her voice. Lydia Abiff had come to visit.

"I'm Mr. Abbott's housekeeper." She brushed past me as if I wasn't there and headed toward the kitchen. "I came to help you since you don't sound like you know what you doing."

"That could be a matter of opinion." I followed her over to the table, trying not to laugh. "But I think I got it all under control.

Who–"

"Where is his phone?" She spun around to face me. One hand was on her hip, her face scowled.

She was on the short and spindly side. Physically I could probably take her. But there was a force about her that made me want to give her anything she asked for. I picked the phone up from the table. She snatched it from me.

"Don't use dis no more. People will tink de jumbies are after dem and won't answer when dey see his number."

She scrolled through the names while I casually clicked out of Google Earth on my computer and shut down my web browser.

"You talk to his people at de restaurant?" she asked.

"I have other priorities right now." My voice disappointed me. It came out weak, almost apologetic.

"You need to do it now."

"I have it on my to-do list. I–"

She glared at me. I thought I even heard her growl. I took a tiny step back. "I was going to contact everyone on his cell phone first."

"I see." She sat down at the kitchen table. "Tell me 'bout his service again. I'll call de people in his phone. You go to de restaurant and call his people dere. Make sure you get dat place open soon."

"Ok, I guess I can call them."

"No guess. You will."

"Right, um–"

"And you still open on Wednesday, like Mr. Abbott wanted."

Chance and I had discussed that just last week. We'd decided we'd spend a couple of days working with the chef experimenting with foods and cocktails and then have a soft opening on Wednesday. If everything was running smoothly, an official grand opening was scheduled for the following weekend. I wanted to ask how she knew our plans, but when I looked at her glowering face, I changed my mind. I got the feeling people told her whatever she wanted them to tell her. Perhaps Chance had even asked her when he should open.

"Yes, OK. I guess we can still open."

"You need to." She eyed me the way someone eyes foul smelling chicken. "Too many bad tings happened dere in de past. De longer it sits idle, de more people gossip and de harder it will be to get it going again."

"What happened there in the past?" I wrote down all the information for the funeral on a piece of paper.

"Noting worse 'en wha' happen dere yesterday." She put the cigarette in her mouth, but didn't attempt to light it.

"Oh, well, I don't know if I'm going to keep it running, anyway." I handed her the paper. She didn't take it from me.

"Yes you will." She stood taller and stepped close to me. The tip of her cigarette was only about an inch from my chin. I half-way expected poisoned darts to shoot out of her eyes. Suddenly I wanted to apologize for something, anything, even for lying to the cafeteria lady back in primary school when I told her I was allergic to meatloaf. "Dat was Mr. Abbott's dream," she said. "You can't let it die wi' him. Now," she snatched the paper from me and sat down. "What your number?"

I gave her my cell phone number and picked up my purse and the keys Piper had left.

"You listen!" she yelled.

I halted too abruptly and bumped my head on the door I'd just opened.

"I meant wha' I said 'bout Mr. Abbott's dream. But you also got to tink about de people he hired to work dere. Dey need jobs. You have to tink about dem."

I got in the Jeep and headed toward Charlotte Amalie, decidedly not thinking about the people Chance had hired. I was at the wheel after all. I had to concentrate on what I was doing and keep my eye out for other people at wheels of their own.

St. Thomas is one of the most dangerous places to drive in the Caribbean. The roads, originally designed for horse and buggy traffic crisscrossing the mountainous terrain are exceedingly narrow and lack the luxury of guardrails in many places despite abutting jungle-covered cliffs. People drive in the left lane with cars made for the right. And few road signs match the maps and GPS systems, which means there are always a high number of tourists, often drunk tourists, perpetually lost. It can be a difficult and stressful place for even good drivers to navigate.

But somehow the gods of traffic smiled down on me that

afternoon because I arrived at the Revenge Café with only a scrape on the driver's side mirror as damage. I parked near the bottom of the steps and got out of the Jeep.

The last thing I wanted to do was re-enact entering that building. I almost called Piper to see if he'd meet me so I wouldn't have to do it alone. But I wasn't sure I'd want him hovering nearby. From an investigative standpoint, this could be the perfect time for me to wander around the restaurant and see if I could tell what the police removed from it, if anything.

From the standpoint of someone who's best friend had just been killed in there, though, it wasn't the perfect time for anything.

I tried to ignore that second point of view.

"I'm trained to be objective," I whispered to the bottom step. "I've been in worse situations before and made it through."

Even though I wasn't convinced that was a factual statement, I forced my feet to climb the stairs, walk down the walkway and stop at the door. Before I had time to think about what I was doing, I began testing keys in the lock. As I found one that fit, I heard the sound of dress heals striking the walkway behind me.

I turned and met a slightly sunburned, copper-headed woman in white capris and a lavender-flowered button-down blouse. Designer sunglasses held back her hair and she carried an equally high-end purse on her arm. Her posture and the tilt of her chin screamed elite American, probably from an old elite American family.

"I'm sorry," I said to her. "The restaurant isn't opened."

"I didn't think it would be," she said with a twang that told me she was from Texas or possibly Louisiana. "I'm to meet Chancellor Abbott here at five o'clock. Has he arrived?"

There are some uber-wealthy Americans who give all Americans a bad reputation. They have a sense of entitlement, a constant expectation that everybody else is on the ready, eager to fulfill their every wish and command. Unfortunately for Red, her first impression reeked of that snob appeal, a perfume that usually gave me a migraine.

"Chance will not be able to make it." I put my back to her and opened the door of the restaurant. A flashback to the first time I entered the building hit me like a blinding light, though it was dark inside.

"But we had an appointment," Red said.

I glanced at her over my shoulder. She obviously had no idea what had happened there just the day before. And I apparently, was going to have to tell her.

"Um, it's been cancelled." I stumbled inside.

"What do you mean? He didn't call." She was on my heels, in the entryway.

"Again, I'm sorry. He won't be here." I felt along the wall for a light switch and found none. I went to search the other side of the door. I still couldn't find a switch but the sun-baked former debutant acted like she owned the place, as she probably acted everywhere, and opened the wooden shutters. The late afternoon sun streamed in as if lighting up a path to the bar.

"Are you his partner?" she asked, almost giving the last word three syllables.

"Of sorts." I turned to face her, hands on hips. "Look, Chance . . . Chance was . . . Chance passed away last night."

"Oh my God!" Her hands flew to her cheeks in a gesture that was genuine enough for me to forgive, just a little, her snooty, one-percent attitude. "I'm so sorry!" She dragged me by the elbow to sit on a barstool. "How . . ." her eyes searched mine. "Oh hell," she said and rested her head in her hands, elbows on the bar.

I sat beside her, echoing her posture as it seemed the only natural response I could make. A mirror behind the bar proved just how pathetic we looked.

I took in her appearance. She was definitely older than I was, maybe around forty-five, and wore no wedding ring. Slender, but not very thin. And while she was attractive, she wasn't the bombshell type Chance typically favored whenever he wanted to get laid.

"So, what were you meeting Chance for, anyway?" I asked.

"It doesn't really matter, I guess." She sighed.

She sounded defeated, deflated. Like I probably would if I'd allow myself to stop researching, stop cooking, stop the manic attempt to keep busy and distracted from feeling anything ugly. I looked away from her and spotted a light switch beneath the mirror. "Anyway, is there something I can do for you?" I asked as I went around the bar to turn on the light above our heads.

"I'd love a strong drink right now."

"Got a particular hankering?"

"Well I'm in the islands, I guess rum would be good."

I found a bottle of aged Mount Gay and poured her a double shot.

"Is it too much to ask for a little lime?" she wanted to know.

I had no idea the Junior League type ever drank anything harder than a wine spritzer. The fact that she didn't ask for me to cut it with Coke-a-Cola made her rise enough in my estimation that I willingly hunted down fresh limes. I found them in a small refrigerator under the bar and then I found a bottle of water for myself.

"I hear it's never a good idea to drink alone," she drawled, touching her glass to my water bottle.

"I'll catch up when I finish this."

"Deal." She took a long drink. Didn't even wince at the burn.

"How did you know Chance?" I asked.

"I didn't." She removed the sunglasses from her head and tucked them in her purse. "I'd only met him a couple days ago. I'd come in response to a classified ad he'd posted."

"For a job?"

"Yes. I used to own some restaurants in Dallas." She snorted. "Actually, my ex-husband and I owned some restaurants in Dallas. He still does."

"So why are you here?" It was hard to meet her eyes with the sunlight glaring in from behind her. I took a few steps to the side to see her better.

"I had a little wild streak in college, came here during spring break and stayed. I supported myself tending bar until my daddy tracked me down and made me go back home to Alabama." She paused to drink. "Anyway, my life just recently changed and I thought I needed a fresh start. I had such fun memories here. Being free. Not expected to be some demure, quiet young woman I didn't want to be. Now that I am single once more, my boys are in college, and my daddy is dead, I wanted to come back and try again."

I frowned at her. "And Chance was looking for someone?"

"A general manager. He interviewed me and invited me to come back tonight to meet his partner and show me around."

"You live on island now?"

"I live at the Wyndham Resort right now." She put her head in the palm of her hand. "Would it be selfish of me to ask if you knew whether or not there was still a possibility of me getting job here?"

"You have experience running a restaurant or did you just co-own one?"

"I ran them. Several, at one time."

"Then you're hired." I reached my hand across the bar. "My name is Mandy Breen. I was Chance's partner and am now the official owner of the Revenge Café."

"Thank you so much. You have no idea what this means to me." She shook my hand. "I'm Ginger. Ginger Dillon."

"OK then, Ginger," I felt under the bar for the bottle of Mount Gay. "Let's find the office. I was told the first thing I need to do is call all the workers and let them know what's going on. As general manager, that seems like something you could help me with."

"Of course, honey. How soon are we opening up?"

Chapter 11: Got It Under Control

A familiar sound came to me in the darkness. I tried to reach toward it, but couldn't move my arms. Something was on them. My body was on them. The sound continued. I rolled over, freed an arm, and fell off an edge. Panic ripped through me. But only for a second. Because I landed and woke up.

I was on a tiled floor, part of my face was pressed against a rough, sisal rug. I could still hear the sound. A calypso tune. My cell phone was ringing.

I sat up, squeezed between a red sofa and a glass-topped coffee table, unable at first to figure out where I was. Though I easily recognized the nausea in my stomach, likewise the burning pain in my head. I needed water with lemon, aspirin, coffee, and for that God-damned phone to stop ringing.

By the time I found my cell on the floor outside the bathroom door, it had quieted. The call log read: *Ginger Dillon.* Apparently my new general manager was already up and at 'em. Which, I presumed, was a good thing. We had scheduled a full workforce to clean the restaurant and re-stock it later that Tuesday morning. That way we'd be sure to be open on Wednesday and Lydia Abiff would be happy. But first, I was to get my name on the bank accounts so that one day, hopefully soon, we could pay for said workforce and food.

I called her back.

"Hey there, sugar." She sounded like she was happy to be alive despite the fact I remembered her knocking back the drinks faster than I did last night. I had waited until I returned to Chance's place before I drank myself unconscious. "I'm so glad you made it home alive. Are you ready to get to work?"

"Almost," I mumbled. "I'll pick you up in an hour or so."

"I'll be in the hotel lobby, but take your time darlin'. I don't want you stressing at the wheel none." Seemed like I left an impression on her when I drove her back to the Wyndham.

I squeezed half a lemon into a glass of room-temp water and remembered it was my thirty-third birthday. "Cheers!" I said to the coffee pot and downed the water. I found aspirin in the cabinet housing the coffee cups and took two with another glass of lemon-water. At that point I felt capable of making a hang-over fixing breakfast of eggs and orange juice. I really wanted some coconut water but I didn't think I had it in me to tackle breaking open the coconut that was in the cabinet.

Relatively fortified, I did a full-on beauty regime but couldn't quite make myself look alert and perky. I dried my hair and clamped it together into a semi-messy, but cute, knot on top of my head. I hoped it would encourage people to look up there instead of at the circles under my eyes that, despite my valiant efforts to camouflage, remained evident. I stared at my reflection in the bathroom mirror and told myself I was ready to start my first day as a restaurateur. I bit my tongue to keep from adding a sarcastic "yeah, right."

I set the house alarm and stepped outside onto the front porch. I locked the door and squatted to pick up the conch shell.

"Hey buddy, listen," I said to Chance as I replaced the spare key in the shell, the way Chance always did. "I don't know exactly where to start finding out what happened to you. But everyone keeps telling me I have to get this restaurant open, so that's going to be my first focus, that and your memorial. If it looks like I'm not doing anything for you, don't hold it against me. I promise, as soon as I figure out what to do, I'll do it. But it sure would be nice if you did give me a sign or two."

I stood and turned around, holding my breath as I waited for a response. Nothing. The wind was normal. The birds were quiet. Not even an iguana moved.

"So is silence supposed to be a sign?" I asked him. "Not funny, Chance."

At the edge of the porch I ran my hand over the purple banister. All the trim on the house was purple, in stark contrast to the yellow wood siding. I loved the colors of that house. I was glad he hadn't repainted the outside when he completed the interior renovation.

I looked around, slowly, taking in the whole property. Chance had never spent any time in the yard, and it showed. Blooming cannas were half-eaten by insects. Overgrown crotons fought with the oleanders that nothing in the animal kingdom dared to touch. Some kind of unrecognizable flowering vine threatened to take over the various palms and other trees.

Whenever I'd visit Babs and Aunt Maggie, I truly enjoyed spending time in their well-tended yards and I'd yearn for one of my own. I had one now. Chance had given it to me. It needed some time and attention, but it had potential.

I found myself smiling at the feral grounds as I stepped off the porch and walked toward the Jeep. Yes, I could give it time and attention, I thought. And I could finally have a yard of my own. Along with my dream restaurant.

Just no best friend to share it with.

I managed to get to the Wyndham with only a few near misses, if you don't count bumping into a palm tree as I backed out of the driveway. It was my cousin Bob's fault. His call startled me. I almost answered but thought I'd let it go to voice mail in case it was birthday wishes, which it turned out to be. Not having the stomach for that kind of thing, I shut the ringer off on my phone before heading into town.

Ginger was dressed in Bermuda-style tan shorts and a crisp, white, button-down sleeveless shirt. Her hair was impeccably coifed and makeup done to perfection. Somehow she didn't have bags under her eyes.

"You know, I don't have a problem driving, sugar," she said when I stopped at an intersection where I had the right of way and no stop sign.

"I got it under control," I promised, inching half-way through then gunning across to the other side.

"OK, but–"

"Sh! I can't drive if someone's talking."

"Sorry, I forgot," she whispered.

We parked at the restaurant then walked the couple blocks between it and Chance's bank. There was one teller at the counter when we went in and no one else in sight.

"Hi," I said and inwardly cringed because I knew since I'd forgotten to say "Good morning" I was blatantly announcing I was an arrogant mainlander in need of being treated with more than the standard normal amount of rudeness. “I need to talk to someone about transferring bank accounts.”

The teller frowned at me. “Wa’kind?”

“I’m sorry?”

“Accounts? What kind of accounts?”

“Oh, personal and business and there’s a safe deposit box I need access to, too.”

She sipped from a plastic soda bottle and sighed before sliding off her stool and sauntering away.

“I see customer service hasn’t improved since back in the day,” Ginger said, watching the teller disappear behind a door.

“Guess not,” I laughed. “And island pace will always be the official way of marking time.”

“Don’t you worry none, honey,” she led me over to a sofa in the waiting area. “Our place will run right and run nice.”

“Is that our motto?”

“Good Lord, no!” She waved her hand. “We'll have to come up with something better than that. You know anything about restaurants?”

“I can order off a menu like a professional.”

“Good thing you found me.”

“Right,” I nodded and struggled to keep my head upright, even though I had a feeling it would be nice and comfy to rest it on the back of the sofa. It had been a long time since I’d had a hangover. I love alcohol in most forms. I love the taste, the relaxed sensation of having just enough. But I also know it’s very easy for me to allow it to block out my world whenever the need should arise. And the previous night, that need apparently did just that.

I had returned to the house intent on seeing what else I could find on Reggie Callwood and to get the names of Piper’s neighbors. But the house had seemed too empty for me to concentrate. And the loneliness too intense, too deep for me to feel comfortable sober.

Already buzzed after drinking with Ginger while we made the calls at the restaurant, it was very easy to talk myself into drinking a little more when I got back while I ate my shrimp and salad for dinner. Then, too full to cook something else, I drank myself unconscious to keep from crying and missing Chance.

But alcohol is tricky. Sometimes when you go to bed drunk, your blood sugar crashes in the middle of the night and you wake up with nothing to do but stare at the ceiling unable to think about anything other than the reasons that made you get drunk to begin with. I woke around two-thirty in the morning, got up, powered on my laptop, but still couldn't concentrate on anything other than how it didn't feel right that I was there without Chance. To keep from getting lost in grief, from risking being overwhelmed by loneliness, I kept myself busy cooking and drinking some more, which makes it somewhat difficult to type on a computer.

It wasn't behavior I was particularly proud of. But I told myself, I could do it that one night, that maybe it was necessary for my grieving, and that I'd do better tonight. I'd stay sober and find a way to finish the research and prepare myself to go running around the island to interview people.

The teller re-appeared. I stood. Ginger rose with me. We waited like hungry puppies for the woman to acknowledge us again. She didn't. She went to her stool without even glancing our way.

"Did I tell you about the Moko Jumbie campaign and customer service pledge the Chamber of Commerce did here a few years ago?" I asked Ginger in a loud voice.

The teller glanced over at me and rolled her eyes, obviously getting my hint. "Someone will be out to speak to you as soon as they can," she hollered and looked down at the cell phone in her hand.

Ginger and I returned to our sofa.

"What was that?" Ginger asked.

"A couple of years ago the Chamber did their best to improve customer service on the island. They created TV commercials and print ads featuring Moko Jumbies who went around teaching people about good customer service. The campaign encouraged everyone to make a service pledge to treat their customers better."

"Good to know," she pulled her cell phone from her purse and started tapping on it. "Where do we get a Mocko what?"

"Moko Jumbie," I spelled out the words for her. "Ever see those street performers or dancers on stilts?"

She nodded.

"They are Moko Jumbies. They are tall so that they can look out for jumbies, or evil spirits, and scare them away. In this case, they scare away the bad service jumbies."

"Aha," she continued tapping. "Useful. We should hire a few for our opening weekend."

"Good idea," I nodded. We sat quietly and watched the people on the other side of the bank window walk up and down the road. One man just stood there with his hands in his pockets, staring at the bank building, as if he had nothing better to do.

Ginger eventually found an emery board in her handbag and tackled her nails. When she was done, she returned it to her purse, snapped it shut and stood up.

"Suppose we can find a Moko Jumbie to help us out here?" she asked me, loudly.

I looked at the teller. With an exaggerated groan, she dragged herself off the stool again and disappeared. She came back a few minutes later with a man and pointed at us.

"Yes, what is it?" he yelled across the bank. We approached him and explained why we were there.

As it happened, Ginger was the only one who could find any satisfaction that day. She was able to open an account, but I needed to return with certified copies of the death certificate and the will before I could get access to anything in the bank related to Chance or the restaurant. I promised to come back the next day and then waited for nearly an hour while Ginger opened a personal account and made arrangements to transfer funds into it. I noticed her driver's license listed her home as being in Dallas, Texas, and her full name was Ginger Cassia Dillon.

"What did your mother do for a living?" I asked Ginger as we walked back to the restaurant.

"Breathe," Ginger said and put on her sunglasses. "Though she smoked like a fiend until it became passé. Why?"

I glanced at her as we crossed the street. "Your name is Ginger Cassia. Cassia is Greek for—"

"Cinnamon." She nodded, staring straight ahead.

"I thought maybe your mom was a baker."

"Ha! No, honey she craved spicy cookies when she was pregnant with me." She turned her head to look at me as we walked. "She wanted to name me Cookie, but when I was born with red hair, she changed her mind."

"I think I'd prefer Ginger over Cookie."

"I do. But what I don't understand is that somehow my brother was called Charles Joseph even though she craved beef jerky with him. Seems to me that name would have suited him just fine."

A few of the restaurant employees were already at the Revenge Café waiting for us when we got back. When we had called everyone the night before, Ginger suggested we promise the crew time-and-a-half pay if they'd help clean the place despite the fact that we had no idea how much money we had in the restaurant accounts. I let everyone in, counting seventeen people as they passed by. I wondered how much each one made per hour and I hoped there were enough funds in a coffer somewhere that could cover it.

After they all entered, another person showed up: Lydia Abiff, the helpful, albeit daunting, housekeeper.

Ginger and I introduced ourselves and she took down their names. I had no idea what to do next and was happy Ginger stepped up to the plate and divided responsibilities among the crowd. Within a few minutes she had organized the cleanup effort and everyone got underway, except for Lydia Abiff.

"You and I will speak," she said to me.

"Yes ma'am."

She took my elbow, led me out the entrance doors and down the walkway. We stood at the top of the steps leading to the parking lot. I couldn't help but notice that if by chance we both fell, I was the only one in position to tumble down the stairs.

"My son is Harold, your head cook," she said. She stood with one hand on her hip, the other, with the first two fingers squeezing the filter of a lit cigarette, was on the railing, barring me from running for shelter in the restaurant. "He got himself a worthless wife and three children. You know how I know she worthless?"

"No." I swallowed.

"Because dey all live wi' me. I would appreciate it if one day dey didn't."

"I will do my best to keep this restaurant running."

"Good. Dat's what I wanted to hear." She took a drag off her cigarette and pointed the lit end at me. I leaned back from it. "I will be clearing out Mr. Abbott's personal items on Thursday." She exhaled smoke as she spoke. It curled between us. "You don't need his clothing but people at de shelter do."

I hadn't even thought about having to deal with his clothing, but now that she mentioned it, I realized I had no desire to touch anything of his as personal as his underwear.

"OK, come whenever you need to." I smiled.

"Of course I will." She nodded. I stepped aside, letting her pass me to go down the stairs, then I went back into the restaurant.

I grabbed my purse and found Ginger hovering at the bar, speaking with Lydia's son, our chef, Harold.

"Hey there, sugar," Ginger smiled at me.

"I think I'll head over to the morgue," I said. "To, you know, take care of that, uh, that . . ."

"Thing." She squeezed my hand. "You take your time honey. We'll be here when you get back."

"OK, do you need anything else from me?"

"Nope. It's all good in here."

I went out again and down the stairs to the parking lot. Once in the Jeep, I looked up the hospital on my phone then plugged in the address on the GPS unit. I love having a GPS tell me where to go. It's like having my own private God in the car looking out for me. They always come with a soothing voice that only tells me where to turn, in plenty of time, and never chastises or sounds angry when it needs to recalibrate each and every time I miss my turn.

The GPS god took me through the old narrow city streets of Charlotte Amalie. I drove by beautiful Colonial-style stucco buildings, wooden shacks, roadside markets and too many people walking too close to the street. Part of my driving problems, aside from the constant terror that some vehicle is going to blindside and kill me, is that I'm never sure where to look and if something's a potential problem. My eyes dart around so much and so quickly that I often don't realize someone's stopping in front of me until I almost (actually sometimes do) bump into them. Sometimes cars seem to appear in the lane next to me so suddenly, that my reflexes jerk the steering wheel in the opposite direction before I have a chance to see if the traffic is clear.

One of my former therapists had once told me that if the human brain changes focus more than seven times in one hour, it creates the same fight-or-flight chemical reaction in the body as being faced head-on with a dangerous threat. I can't pull out of a parking space without changing focus more than seven times. Trust me, I've tried. So even if I don't have an accident when I drive, I still wind up being panic stricken most of the time when I arrive wherever I'm going. With or without a GPS god to guide me.

All of that explains why, despite the fact I remained in my lane, most of the time, and didn't hit a single object, unless sideswiping a hedge counts, I toyed with the idea of stopping by the ER in the hospital to have my vital signs checked. I could feel my heart beating everywhere in my body. I was sure that was a sign of dangerously high blood pressure. But I was too afraid to find out it was a sign of something worse. Suddenly the morgue was somewhere I wanted to be.

"Nice, Ms. Breen," said a surprisingly kind female coroner. Unfortunately, Talkative Terry wasn't in. "Davidson's is a very reputable funeral home. You chose well. I'm sure this was not easy for you."

"Thank you, it's not."

"All we need from you is your signature on these forms." She handed me a pen. "I've highlighted where you need to sign. Basically, you are swearing you are legally responsible for the care of the body."

"I was talking to Detective Piper yesterday," I said as I finished signing. "He mentioned the official death certificate stated the cause of death was capsaicin from hot peppers."

"Yes. I'll be right back. Please wait here." She turned around and left the room.

I wondered if she would have told Butterworth more.

"Here is a copy of the death certificate," she said when she came back again. "You will need this as you settle his affairs."

I left the calm, serene environment of the morgue and made my way back to the sunlit and chaotic streets of Charlotte Amalie. The next stop would be Davidson's Funeral Home, to pick out an urn.

Back in the Jeep, I plugged in the address for the funeral home and was told it was invalid. I checked my phone again, clicked on the map feature there to copy and paste the address in. The map suggested I go to the center of town, but the street names didn't match what I'd plugged in. I really didn't want to call Davidson's. I knew they'd give me Islander-style directions based on landmarks that only made sense to people who'd lived there their entire lives.

I dialed Chester Butterworth, hoping he'd meant it when he said to call if I needed anything.

Chapter 12: Our Own Brand of Weirdness

Butterworth didn't know the street address of Davidson's Funeral Home, but he knew how to get there. Instead of me taking directions from him, I encouraged him to go with me so I wouldn't be alone when I picked out the urn. Of course he was delighted be of service.

En route to his office, I scraped against a tree in order not to hit a bicyclist after I'd over-corrected when I drifted to the right again.

Butterworth was waiting for me, sitting cross legged on the rock rubble across from his office, staring at the screen on his cell phone.

"Aw, you scratched your paint," he said in greeting. He ran his finger along the scratch on the driver's side, bent over to look at the broken light and grimaced at the passenger's door. "I know a good body repairman. I'll get you a card."

"Thanks, will he work on a retainer?"

"I'm not sure." He flipped on the radio. I quickly shut it off.

"I'm sorry. I can't drive when there's noise in my car." He nodded as if I made sense. "Anyway, thanks for coming with me." I took a deep breath and pressed the gas pedal, slowly heading up the hill, hugging the left side of the road.

"It's my pleasure," he said then bounced around and grabbed my wrist, making me jerk the steering wheel, pull sharply into the oncoming lane and almost hit a car going past me. "It's not really my pleasure, but you know, it is my uh, my something."

"Right." I dodged back into my lane.

After a few blocks, I remembered I had no idea where I was going.

"So you know where Davidson's Funeral Home is, right?" I stopped at the top of the hill.

"Yes." He had pulled the sun visor down and over to one side and was moving his head around as if to get it in the shadow.

"Am I going the right way?"

He stopped dodging his head and frowned out the windshield. "No. Not at all."

I explained my car rules: no talking except to give directions with plenty of lead time. He promised we'd be at Davidson's in ten minutes. It took twenty-five for me.

In the funeral home lot, Butterworth ripped out of the car and bounded over to my side before I had even reached for the door handle. I stepped out, let him slam the door behind me, and was about to apologize for my inept driving skills, but he had already raced up the steps and opened the front door. He bounced on the balls of his feet as I walked by.

The receptionist ushered us to a room at the rear of the building where an older gentleman greeted me.

"Ms. Breen," he said. "I am Richard Davidson. We spoke yesterday on the phone. Again, I am so sorry for your loss."

"Thank you." I was grateful for his calm presence. It almost balanced out Butterworth's energy. "I'm not really sure what to do." I paused to clear my throat, not so much because it felt blocked, but to get Butterworth's attention. He was browsing the caskets on display, opening the lids and standing on tiptoe to stick his head inside the ones where you could just open one half of the top. He didn't respond but Davidson didn't seem to mind him, so I continued. "See Chance, well, we never really discussed this sort of thing."

"That's perfectly natural at your age, and understandable."

Davidson touched my arm and guided me to an alcove where urns were on display. Butterworth retrieved his sunglasses from inside a coffin and followed us over.

"From what I understand," Davidson said. "You will not be keeping the ashes in your home, but scattering them. Is that correct?"

"Yes."

"It's really a good thing he's getting burned," Butterworth piped in. He picked up an urn with an Asian motif and tipped it over to look at the bottom as if expecting to see a price tag. "I couldn't imagine having a viewing with that eye, could you?"

"What do you mean?" I asked.

"We have ways of making the deceased resemble their old, living selves," Davidson said. With the reflexes of a prize fighter, he caught a black urn Butterworth elbowed and gently replaced it on a pedestal.

"Really? Did you get a look at that thing?" Butterworth's voice was excited. "You could have fixed that?"

"The body has not arrived yet, but yes. If Ms. Breen wanted a viewing, we could probably make the eye presentable." Davidson turned his attention to me. "Did you wish to have a viewing?"

"Oh God, no." I could picture only Butterworth and me, and possibly Lydia Abiff watching over me to make sure I did whatever it was I needed to do, in an otherwise empty room staring at Chance's body. "But, Chester, what are you talking about?"

He stopped squinting into a long urn as if it were a telescope to look at me. "You didn't get a peep of that shiner?"

"What? Was there something wrong with his eye? What happened?"

He raced over to me, cradling the urn in one arm like a football. "The night before he was killed, a woman threw a stiletto at him and got him right in the eyeball."

"A stiletto shoe? Who was she?"

"Oh love! No one for you to be upset about!" Butterworth waved his free hand at me and passed the urn to Davidson. "She was aiming for her fiancé and missed."

"Who was she?" I repeated

"Some bride-to-be." He went back to perusing the urns. "Apparently Chance was originally supposed to photograph their wedding, but he had given up the photography business before their day. He found someone else to do it, but somehow still managed to be involved with getting a stripper for—"

"Excuse me, Ms. Breen," Davidson redirected me. "I don't mean to hurry you, but . . ."

"No, you're right. I'm sorry." I tried to blink away the image of Chance's blue face with one eye swollen shut. "Please, let's continue."

Soon I had chosen something called a keepsake urn. It was black and white marble and very small, designed to hold only a few of his ashes. I figured after I disbursed his ashes in the harbor, I'd secrete it in the restaurant, unless his family wanted it. If they showed up.

Outside, Butterworth said I could just return him to the restaurant. He said he lived nearby and would walk home from there.

"You know, I owe you an apology," I said to him when I parked at the Revenge Café. I saw a red welt forming on his forehead. I was sure it was from when I slammed on the breaks because I incorrectly thought someone was about to pull in front of me and his head bounced against the dash board. "I'm so sorry for that ride. Really, I am. I get nervous when I'm in cars."

"We all have our own brand of weirdness, love." He patted my back. "Nothing to apologize for."

"Still, can I offer you a drink or something? I'm not sure what there is to eat in the restaurant, but I noticed the bar is well stocked."

He quickly agreed and followed me to the stone steps, where we met the two girls I'd seen in the lot the day before. I stopped to speak with them.

"Can I help you?" I asked, making the blond girl jump.

"Uh, hey," her friend said. The friend had funky colored hair. I couldn't decide if it was burgundy, red or purple. "Like, we're supposed to be working here."

Neither one was looking at me or Chester, who was already at the top of the stairs thumbing through his phone screen. They were eyeing each other as if searching for clues for what to do next. They were attractive in a way. Probably, once they were considered very pretty but they looked hardened for their age now. They couldn't have been more than twenty-five years old. Both had faces like tan leather and both were skinny, very very skinny, as in crack-head skinny. I thought they sounded as if they were from the mainland, but they hadn't spoken enough syllables for me to be sure.

"In the restaurant?" I asked.

"Um, like yeah." The blond's eyes bugged out at me but I had a feeling she couldn't quite get me in focus.

"Did you get a call last night?"

The question was too difficult for her to understand enough to formulate an answer. She gripped the magenta-headed woman by the arm.

"Why would we?" Miss Magenta said.

"I'd called all the employees to help clean up."

"Oh, no. We weren't, like, you know, um, employed here." The blond said and blinked. "Yet."

"Right," her friend interjected.

"OK," I drawled out the syllables. "Why don't you come in when we open, then? That way you can fill out an application and—"

"Right. Like we're supposed to work here," Blondie insisted.

"Right. Like we open tomorrow." I overemphasized *like*. "Excuse me." I headed up the stairs toward Butterworth. Their appearance only increased my worry that the Revenge Café was a popular druggie stop-and-shop.

Butterworth and I entered the restaurant and found an argument brewing.

"I'm telling y'all, if you want this place to continue staying in business and paying you a paycheck, if you want to keep your jobs, we have to be open on weekends," Ginger yelled. "Good Lord, Mandy. I'm so glad to see you. Will you explain to everyone how important it is for a restaurant to be open on the weekends?"

"Um, yes." I turned in a circle to look at everyone. "It's important for a restaurant to be open on weekends." Someone had found all the light switches and the place dazzled more than the sun.

"What's going on in here?" I struggled not to shield my eyes with my hand.

"Excuse me, Ms. Breen?" A thin, older man approached me.

"Roger, right?" I asked, squinting at him. He nodded, eyes wide. He'd obviously been in there long enough to be used to the light. "Call me Mandy."

"Very well, Miss Mandy," he said. "I been working here in de kitchen for almost tirty years. I seen dis restaurant change owners 'probly a dozen time. I know dis place. And I know I ain't working here on de weekends."

I stumbled over to the bar and sat on a stool. "Can you tell me why?"

"De place is haunted," a woman said.

"Did we meet?" I asked.

"No, I'm Florence Baa. I waitress here." Hers was a head I hadn't counted earlier. I feared I'd have to take out a line of credit to pay them all.

"How long have you worked here?" I asked.

"Eight year." She came over to stand in front of me. "I tell you, de place is haunted."

"By Chance?"

"I know who might be haunting this place," Butterworth chirped. I'd forgotten he was there and was almost startled to hear his voice. I looked over at him. He was gazing at Ginger like she'd been painted on a half shell.

"Um, Chester, have a seat," I said and patted the stool beside me. "What are you talking about?"

"It's probably the Russian consulate's wife." Butterworth continued to gawk at Ginger as he sat down on the stool nearest her, not on the one I'd patted. "She was one of the people who died here. But she's just one. She might not be the only ghost."

"Do you know how to get rid of her, sugar?" Ginger asked him with a bewildered yet amused smile on her face.

"Maybe," he beamed at her.

"Chester, this is Ginger, Ginger Dillon," I said. "She's our general manager. And Ginger, this is Chester Butterworth. He's the restaurant's attorney."

"Oh, I'm not an attorney, love," Chester said, wiping his hands on his shorts before shaking Ginger's. "I just give legal advice."

"What's the difference?" I asked. I was sure my face now resembled Ginger's, at least as far as the bewilderment went. I wasn't amused by the prospect that I'd planned on taking legal advice from someone who wasn't an attorney.

"Well, I went to law school and I'm good at researching so I can help people figure out their way in the legal waters."

"Did you graduate law school?" Ginger asked.

"Of course, love. That was the easy part." He beamed at her, his eyes soft.

"Well then, why aren't you a lawyer?" she asked.

"I'm not a member of a bar or anything. I have a problem taking tests and it kind of hurts the ego when you keep trying and keep failing, yes?"

"Ye-es, I think so." I was a little nauseous, and I knew it wasn't from my hangover. "Can you excuse me? I just remembered I need to talk to someone."

I went to the office and sat down at the desk to dig my phone out of my purse.

Piper picked up on the first ring.

"Butterworth's not an attorney," I greeted him.

"Yes, I know."

"But Chance used his, his services or whatever."

"Apparently so."

"Do you think there's a possibility that he didn't legally buy the restaurant? Or that...." I stopped when I heard Piper laughing. "What's so funny?"

"If Chester Butterworth helped him, it's all good. The papers might be smudged with chocolate or torn and wrinkled, but I can promise you it was all legal."

I hung up, leaned back in the chair and realized it was my first time being in the office alone. I searched through it looking for anything I could consider a clue. First I browsed Chance's computer. He had a brand new Apple that held little other than the contact information on the employees. There were no emails and when I went online, I saw his browsing history had been deleted.

I tried accessing his account from the bank's online site. But I couldn't figure out his login ID and passwords. After three failed attempts a message on the screen alerted me to the fact that I could only try from the same computer three times with inaccurate information before being locked out for twenty-four hours.

After the file cabinet drawers came up empty, literally, I decided either someone had already been in and thoroughly cleaned out the place or he wasn't hiding anything in his office. I needed to barter some kind of information with Piper to see whose fingerprints were found in there.

I went back out into the dining area where almost everyone had left but Butterworth, who was sitting at the bar watching Ginger and Harold go over a shopping list. I listened to them prattle on about ingredients and menus, making final decisions on what we'd need for the next day to open. I had no idea how they would pay for the food, but since they didn't ask me for any money, I took for granted they had already worked that out and I kept my mouth shut.

"Harold, before you go," I asked him when they were done. "Do you think I could take a few oranges home with me?" I had a hankering for something citrusy and sweet.

"Miss Breen–"

"Mandy."

"Miss Mandy, dis is your restaurant. You can take whatever you want."

"I gotta get used to that." Then on a whim I asked: "So, do we have any honey?"

"Yes! Dis way." I followed him through the kitchen, keeping my eyes averted from the freezer door. He stopped at a cabinet and pulled out a jar. "Dis honey here comes from a farm out in Estate Bordeaux, on de western side of de island. Pure, Caribbean honey. It's very good. I get it from de Farmer's Market in town."

"Did you buy all the food?"

"Almost." He leveled his eyes at me. "But not dose peppers. Mr. Abbott bought dem himself."

"Yes, I'm sure." I smiled at him. "But, uh, were you familiar with the particular peppers that . . . well that . . ."

He lowered his head. "Only de habanero. Never saw de udder one before. But we still have some of dem."

"You can throw them away." I said. "Let's stick to what we know well, OK?"

Chapter 13: Constant Attention

Chance's house was eerily quiet when I returned to it early Tuesday evening, which almost struck me as funny. After all, if Chance had still been alive and maybe just down on the beach or out on a photo shoot, it would have been as quiet, but I wouldn't have called it eerily quiet. Depending on my day, it would have been blissfully quiet, peacefully quiet, maybe even cool and dark. But he was not simply out there somewhere, he was dead. So the place was eerily quiet. It made me uncomfortable. And it made me feel lonely. Very, very lonely.

So lonely that I wasn't even sure why I insisted on staying there, except that it was free and technically now I owned it. So why wouldn't I?

"So, uh, a sign would be good," I said to Chance as I headed into the kitchen. "If you sent it already, I'm sorry but I missed it."

He must have been out haunting someone else.

I knew I needed to tackle the computer and finish up whatever internet research I could do. But I was also hungry and, again, very, very lonely. I'd never cooked my way out of loneliness that felt this deep before. Unsure whether or not I had the ability, I plugged along anyway since I had no other skills to help myself.

I opened the refrigerator and took stock of the inventory. What would keep the lonely boogie monster away?

I needed to make something that required constant attention. That required my eye, non-stop. Something I could easily burn or destroy if for one second I was distracted.

Scallops would be perfect.

I could do some kind of glaze with the oranges and honey. Maybe even spice it up with a little of the sriracha I'd spotted in Chance's cupboard.

No, it's in my cupboard, I reminded myself as I reached for the bottle. Then I said it out loud: "It's in my cupboard." I had to fight like hell to resist cringing. Maybe I needed rum.

With a full rocks glass on the counter nearby, I revisited the conversation I had had with Harold while I squeezed the oranges. I found it very odd that he'd kept the peppers that had killed his former boss. And not only his former boss, but the former boss of his mother.

Once the orange juice was ready, I had to figure out what to do with it. I was now thinking that indeed, a glaze of some kind would be good, made with the honey and juice. But it would need something to counter all that sweetness. I zested a lemon and had started on a lime when someone pounded on the door. I froze.

Potentially terrorizing ideas raged through my head. The pounding repeated.

"Ms. Breen! Are you there?" Detective Piper was knocking.

I opened the door and let him in.

"Is everything OK?" I asked as he walked by me.

"I was wondering the same thing. That's why I'm here." He took long, slow steps and perused the house. I watched him ever-so-casually glance in the guest room where my open suitcase was still set up on a chair.

"I don't understand."

He turned to grin at me. "I got used to hearing from you frequently. So after only one call today, I was worried. I'd been calling you repeatedly but your line keeps going to voice mail."

"Right. Sorry. My ringer was off. Why were you calling me? Did you find something?"

"No." He resumed his search, glancing in the bathroom. "Since it was to be your big day, I thought I'd make sure you were okay."

"Excuse me?"

"Your wedding day." He looked at me again. Maybe it was because I stepped between him and Chance's room, where the bed remained neatly made presumably by Mrs. Abiff, and I shut the door.

"Oh yes, that." I cleared my throat. "Are you looking for decorating ideas?"

"Never know when inspiration will hit." He grinned and walked into the kitchen area. "Am I interrupting dinner?"

"Not yet." I joined him at the counter.

"Looks good," he said, peering at the foods I'd laid out.

"I'm playing with a recipe. Trying to create a citrusy-sweet something to have with my scallops."

"Sounds good too." He picked up the bottle of sriracha and read the ingredients.

I turned on a burner and poured honey and the freshly-squeezed orange juice into a pan. He didn't move. I thought I'd wait him out to see if I could get the real reason why he came.

I stirred in the lemon and lime zest and took the bottle of sriracha from him.

"You like peppers, huh?" he asked, watching me squirt a good amount of sriracha into the pan.

"I like a little heat in my food. But not enough for my meals to hurt me." I stirred the pot and leaned against the counter. "Speaking of peppers, did you know Chance's housekeeper is the mother of the restaurant's head chef?"

"Lydia Abiff?"

"Yes."

"I did."

"Don't you find *that* an interesting set of circumstances?"

"They were both at a very popular wedding on Sunday afternoon. Both have several alibis."

"Oh."

"Besides, I don't think killing someone like that is Lydia Abiff's style." He grinned at me. "Have you spent much time with her?"

"No. I find her a bit intimidating."

"You should." He wandered around the dining table, not seeming to notice the bare spot on the sideboard where the frame once was.

"So why are you really here?" I picked up my glass and followed him.

"As I said, I was checking on you."

"Nice of you to worry." I took a long drink of the rum and set it down on the table. "But I'm fine. You can go now."

"All right then." He took his keys out of his pocket. "Don't hesitate to call if you need anything."

"I won't." I walked toward the door. He followed. But when I caught sight of a pair of my shoes by the coffee table, I remembered

Butterworth's stiletto story.

"Actually, wait." I turned around, too abruptly. He bumped into me and quickly stepped back.

"Sorry," he said.

"That's OK." I took a deep breath and stared at his chest. The man clearly worked out. "Why didn't you tell me about Chance's eye?"

"How did you find out about it?"

"Chester Butterworth told me."

"What did he say?"

"That a woman threw a stiletto and hit him in the eye."

"Then I didn't need to tell you about it, after all."

"No." I crossed my arms in front of my chest. "That's not good enough. You were holding out information. Why?"

"You need to check that sauce?" He nodded toward the kitchen.

"It's a glaze and yes, I should check it. Don't you dare leave."

"I won't. In fact I'd be happy to stay for a taste test."

He led the way back to the kitchen providing me with ample opportunity to appreciate the time he obviously spent at the gym doing squats.

I'd never been so grateful to have something almost boil over before. It was much easier for me to focus on my glaze than acknowledge the fact that I found Piper attractive. I don't do well in those situations–those situations that involve attractive men. Usually if I'm drawn to them for any reason, they're bad news.

My glaze was bubbling and I didn't want that. I only wanted to warm it up. I turned the heat down to low, stirring quickly to keep it from sticking to the sides of the pot. Once satisfied that it was still okay, I turned on the broiler and retrieved my glass from the table.

"I'm waiting," I said to him after taking a sip. I pulled the scallops and butter from the refrigerator and set them on the counter. "Why didn't you tell me?"

"A couple of reasons. First, and most important, you're holding out information on me." He picked up my glass and sniffed.

"The bottle is in there." I pointed the garlic crusher I'd just taken out of the drawer toward the cabinet where the rum was housed. "Why do you think I'm holding out something?" I resumed crushing.

"I'm good at what I do, Ms. Breen." I heard him drop ice cubes in a glass and hoped he'd refill mine while he was at it. "I could tell when I spoke to you Sunday afternoon. You are keeping something from me. And it's not that you killed Abbott."

Instead of answering him, I focused on watching the butter melt into the olive oil in a cast iron skillet. I couldn't tell him I wrote that article and Chance took the pictures, not yet. Not until I knew for sure he wasn't connected to that whole scene in some way.

But I couldn't see why the circumstances around Chance and me getting married would have any bearing on the case. I *could* easily see how it would look like Chance was trying to hide something by not going through proper channels and that I was in cahoots with him. Of course by not coming clean, I would appear even guiltier if it came out later. I glanced at Piper. He stuck his finger in the glaze and tasted.

"Needs more heat," he said.

Like hell! I scowled at him and took a spoon from a drawer to taste it myself. Unfortunately he was right. I gave the glaze another, longer squirt of the sriracha.

"Whether or not you tell me, I'm sticking around to taste those scallops." He folded his arms over his chest. "So why not give us something to talk about?"

"Fine, here it is." I crushed the garlic, scraped it into the butter and oil mixture and took a deep inhale of the delicious aroma before I continued. "All I'm holding out is the real reason I was marrying Chance."

Piper took a sip of his drink and leaned his backside against the counter next to the stove. I salted and peppered the scallops and tried not to think of said backside. It was hard to concentrate on the frying pan and it occurred to me that maybe I shouldn't be around him when I drank.

"Mr. Abbott wasn't the love of your life?" he asked.

I snorted. "God, no. Chance was my best friend. But we weren't lovers."

"I'm sure it's hard to bond with people when you're not easily forthcoming with information."

"*Touche'.*" I smirked. "Anyway, he had some minor skirmishes on his legal record. Mostly on the mainland." I shook my head. I was getting buzzed and needed to cook the scallops before I drank too much to do it properly. They only needed a minute on each side, then a minute under the broiler covered with the glaze. Too much rum makes me forget how long a minute is. So does thinking about tight rear ends.

"Like?" Piper asked.

"He got arrested once for a barroom brawl with a Lesbian." Piper raised his eyebrows at me. "They were fighting over a stripper they'd both been flirting with."

He grinned.

"Another time, was on the anniversary of Freddy Mercury's death. He got drunk, sat on a bench in Miami Beach and belted out *God Save the Queen* until he was arrested for disturbing the peace. I think a few other times it was for possessing small amounts of pot." I lay the scallops in the pan.

"Probably a good thing he wasn't the love of your life."

"Probably." I paused thinking that I'd never dabbled with much better. And the only one I'd ever considered to be the love of my life, Malcolm, was the worst one of all. "When he wanted to become an American citizen, he thought those little issues would be a barrier. So he asked me if I'd marry him and make him a citizen that way." I flipped over the scallops.

"And you agreed because?"

"It really didn't seem like a bad idea when he asked. I'd just lost my job with the TV station and part of the deal with him was that I'd get half the restaurant in exchange. I'd always wanted to own a restaurant. And I was between therapists at the time, so I had no one to help me counter him."

"Between therapists?"

"I used to do a lot of therapy."

"Do I want to know why?"

"Probably not."

"Then I won't ask." He frowned and sipped his rum. "But you have to explain why he'd leave everything he owned to you if the marriage wasn't supposed to last 'til death do you part."

"I honestly don't know." I turned off the heat under the scallops pan. "That part doesn't make sense to me either, except that maybe he chose me for lack of anyone else."

"No family?"

"None who would admit to it." I spooned the glaze over the scallops.

"I'm not sure if I'm buying that explanation for the will, but it does explain a few other things." Piper said while he watched me.

"Like?" I placed the pan under the broiler and stood up.

"I found it odd you were going to marry a man you hadn't physically seen in a year. One that had been traveling around the world without you knowing. One you called a 'friend,' even in an emergency to the dispatcher. And one that you only felt comfortable enough with to set up camp in the smaller bedroom, the guest room." He waved his hand toward the bedrooms.

I gave him what I hoped was an innocent smile and opened the oven door to remove the scallops.

"Now it all makes sense." He returned my smile.

I drizzled more glaze over the scallops and tried to lie to myself that his smile was unattractive. "It might, but it doesn't tell us anything about who killed him and why," I said.

"You're right, it doesn't. But it does put you in a more positive light."

"If what I'm saying is true," I teased.

"Again, I'm good at what I do."

"Yeah? So am I." I stabbed a piece of scallop with a fork. "Taste this." I handed it to him knowing I was probably under the influence, otherwise I wouldn't have teased. Nor would I have offered the food. I have yet to meet a man who didn't fall for my cooking. It was usually good enough for them to forget about my driving issues, therapy addiction, and all my other flaws.

He nodded his head at me as he chewed. "Good stuff."

I divvied up the scallops and gave us both a few slices of dumb bread, a Virgin Island staple I love. I could have asked him to leave. I owed him nothing, but he had yet to tell me about the stiletto incident. And, I knew once he left, I'd feel lonely again.

I led him to the table where my laptop was still set up.

"I wasn't expecting any guests, otherwise, I'd have made a salad or some kind of vegetable," I said.

"Vegetables are overrated," he grinned. "And I wasn't expecting a meal. I just wanted a taste. I love scallops." He took another bite. "But feel free to let me know the next time you make these."

"No. I won't. Unless you come clean about the stiletto." I swallowed. The scallops were cooked to perfection: crisp outside, tender and almost creamy inside.

"Not much to tell, really. Abbott apparently arranged for a stripper at a bachelor's party. The groom-to-be was fondling the stripper. The bride-to-be stumbled in and saw him. She threw her shoe at her fiancé and hit yours instead."

"That's it?"

"That's it." He chewed. I pulled his plate away.

"Not good enough. You owe me more."

Piper threw his head back and laughed.

"What about everything I gave you yesterday?" he asked.

"Still not enough. Butterworth has given me more."

He laughed again. "I can't really tell you much except that the time of death that the coroner was able to estimate is right around the time estimated by you: about an hour and a half before your plane landed. Also, along with Abbott and you, there were at least two other people in that kitchen that day."

I slumped in my chair for a second before scooting his plate back to him again. If he was telling me the truth, which I suspected he was, he deserved to have his scallops back. If nothing else, to keep him interested in telling me more when he could.

"I take it you've interviewed all the restaurant employees?" I asked.

"Just about all of them were at the same wedding the chef and Lydia Abiff were at. None were in that day. Most everyone had been in on Saturday stocking supplies and setting up. And the baker had delivered a cake he'd made at home, presumably your wedding cake, that day too." Piper took a drink.

"The baker?" I remembered a conversation I'd had with Ginger before leaving the restaurant. "Did you speak to the baker?"

"I did."

"He quit on us. He told Harold to tell us. Don't you think that's suspicious?"

"Maybe. We'll follow up on it. But I'm not surprised. He kept ranting about how something evil was in that building. I don't think he had anything to do with it. I think he's afraid of spirits at your restaurant."

"Yes, well, we do have a ghost."

He gave me a lopsided grin as he chewed. "So your friend has company?"

"Apparently."

Piper stood and took his plate and glass to the kitchen sink. I started to follow, but someone knocked on the door.

"You expecting company?" Piper asked.

"No." Grateful he was there for back up, I edged toward the door. I opened it and was greeted by a large bouquet of flowers.

"Dere a Mandy Breen here?" the delivery man asked.

"I'm Mandy Breen," I answered.

He handed me a clipboard. "Sign dis please. Sorry I'm late. I couldn't find dis place so good."

"No worries." We exchanged the clipboard and flowers. I shut the door and took the bouquet to the kitchen table.

"Wedding flowers?" Piper asked.

"I don't think so. But, God!" I put my hand on my head. "I'm guessing I should have called a judge or someone to cancel today." I looked at him. "Chance was to make all the arrangements. I have no idea what was supposed to happen."

"I'm sure you'll be getting the bills soon enough." Piper took the card out of the flowers. It wasn't in an envelope, so the message from Chance was obvious to him and me when he handed it to me: *Happy Birthday! A full decade! Here's to another ten years!*

"A birthday decade?" Piper asked.

I turned the card around to see if anything was on the back. It was blank.

"Um, oh my God." I dropped the card. "Actually he was wrong."

"About?"

Tears built pressure beneath my eyes. I sniffed. "About no one I love dying on me." I took my glass into the kitchen and set it on the counter while I cut a fresh lime. "What to hear something bizarre?"

"Always." His eyes were serious, watching me as I filled my glass with fresh ice.

"My dad left when I was two. He's presumed to be dead. My mom died when I was twelve. My kid sister, Maddie, and my grandmother passed when I was twenty-two." I squeezed the lime into the glass and topped it off with rum. "I once joked with Chance about how maybe my something-two years were cursed. He remembered that when he proposed and suggested today's date. We were supposed to celebrate the wedding, the new restaurant, and everyone I loved still being alive. I turned thirty-three today." I took a long swallow as Piper walked toward me, in silence.

I put the glass down, too weak to even hold it up. Piper started to say something, but caught himself. Instead, he lifted his hand toward my head at what seemed like a quick speed. With reflexes that should have been too dusty to work, I slapped his arm away.

I ran away from him back toward the open area. Ready to bolt out the door.

He took one step and stopped. My blood coursed through my veins so hard, I almost looked at my arms to see if my pulse was visible.

"You have white stuff from the flowers in your hair," he said, after staring at me for what felt like a full rotation of the earth.

"What?" I had heard his words but their meaning wasn't clear.

"There are little, white flowers in your hair." He made another step toward me, hands wide open. "I was going to wipe them out. That's all I was doing."

I blinked at him, willing my body to calm down as I reached up and ran a hand over my hair. I pulled away a few pieces of white baby's breath flowers.

"I see." I crushed the tiny blossoms in my hand and squeezed my eyes shut. I opened them and saw he had yet to move. "Look. I think it's time for you to leave."

"Sure. I have some dogs I need to feed anyway," Piper said. He took as wide a berth as possible going past me. I remained motionless. At the door he turned and paused.

"I wasn't trying to hurt you, Mandy."

"I know."

He paused. "Good. Well, thank you for the scallops."

I nodded, unable yet to move.

He went out. I moved then. I locked the door. Checked to be sure the patio door was locked. Set the alarm. Then knocked myself out with more rum because I had too many painful thoughts going on in my awake, sober brain.

Chapter 14: The Absurdity of It

"So, about that grand opening idea of yours," I said to Ginger on Wednesday morning. We were camped at the bank on the same sofa where we'd sat the day before. We'd been waiting for nearly ten minutes although, once again, we were the only customers to be found in the building.

"Wasn't that your idea to begin with?" She rounded a fingernail with an emery board.

"Well, um, yes, in theory. Kind of. Partly." I shifted in my seat so I could put my elbow on the back of the couch and rest my head on my hand.

I was a little hung over again. That made it two nights in a row that I'd gone to bed drunk off my ass instead of making myself get control of what was going on inside my head. I knew it wasn't a healthy way of dealing with my life and I promised myself I wouldn't do it again. Though I was still working on how I would be able to keep that promise. For the first time in over a decade, I had no psychologist to call.

"Well, sugar," Ginger tucked her emery board back into her purse and looked at me. "Can you tell me what is kind of almost in theory with your original opening plan?"

"The part about having our soft opening today at lunch and then a grand opening this weekend."

"We're still going through with that."

"Right, well, that part about paying people time and a half on weekends until we get the ghost thing sorted out—"

"It was the only way to get anyone to come in. We can't be the only restaurant on the island closed on Saturdays and Sundays. We'll be out of business within a month if we tried that."

"I know. But, um, what if we don't have the money to cover it?"

"What? How much do we have?"

"I really don't know."

Ginger stared at me.

"Chance was handling all that." I scratched the back of my head. "I wasn't involved in the pre-opening part of the business. Chance found the location, hired everyone, did the design and set up for the place, and then asked me to be his partner."

"I see."

"I only landed here the day he, uh, you know."

"So you only know how much money you'd given him for your share. Is that what you're saying?"

"In a sense." I blew out a long sigh and looked at the people outside the window. Like the day before, pedestrians walked back and forth along the sidewalk, on their way to whatever was important in their lives. The scene would have been hypnotizing except for the fact that I thought a slim man leaning against a street lamp on the opposite side of the street was someone I'd seen there the day before. His face was shaved and he wore clean clothes. He wasn't a homeless man begging on the streets. And clearly he was staring into the bank building.

"In what sense, honey? Is there something you're not telling me?" Ginger asked.

"Lots." I crossed my legs at the knee and leaned toward her, looking her in the eye. "This is going to sound weird. But, uh, I didn't give Chance any money for my part of the restaurant."

"What did you give him?"

"A promise to marry him so he could become an American citizen."

Ginger's blue eyes remained locked on mine for a full minute. Then a smile spread across her face and her body began to shake with laughter.

"Good Lord, honey. I was hoping my life would be more adventurous once I got here. Sounds like you're going to make that happen." She pulled a tissue out of her purse and wiped tears from her eyes.

"I'm relieved to hear you say that, but, uh, what if we don't have enough money?"

"We'll just get creative and make sure we get the place packed full as soon as possible. Otherwise, Harold's mamma is gonna put a hurtin' of some kind on us." Ginger's head turned to look behind the sofa.

"So you find her scary too, huh?" I followed her lead and saw the teller pointing us out to a very tall woman.

"A little. Chester told me she's Obeah."

"Are you serious?" Obeah, a form of folk magic not unlike Voodoo in Haiti, is supposed to be illegal in the Virgin Islands. I wasn't surprised that something illegal was happening there, something illegal always seems to be happening everywhere. What surprised me is that Lydia's day job was as a housekeeper. That and I got the feeling Detective Piper knew about her off-hours occupation. His exact words from the night before now carried a double entendre: *I don't think killing someone like that is Lydia Abiff's style.* "Does Chester know her?"

"Of course he does. Honey, he knows everyone in the Caribbean."

"Oh, I thought it was just on the island."

She laughed. "Well anyway, he said Lydia's a good one."

"What does that mean?"

"That she doesn't do harm. She only fixes things."

"I think I see, but when did you talk to Butterworth about her?" I was pretty sure I'd only been blacked out one night since she'd met him.

Before she could answer the tall woman approached us.

"Good morning," she said. "Can I help you?"

Ginger and I stood up.

"I'm Amanda Breen," I extended my hand to her. She took it, barely, and we made an almost perceptible shake. "I was in yesterday to change over the bank accounts from my deceased business partner."

"That's what I've been told," the woman said.

"I didn't have what I needed yesterday, but I have the will and death certificate today. So I'd like to change over the accounts."

"You'll need to come back tomorrow."

"I don't understand."

"You need to have Vincent help you."

"But–"

"He's the one who deals with transferring accounts."

"Where is he now?"

"Off island, I guess." She shrugged and walked away.

"Well that's island style for you," Ginger said. "No hurries. No worries."

"Right. For her." I was tempted to tackle the tall woman but I didn't think I'd win. "What are we going to do? What am I going to tell Lydia Abiff? Do you know she left a voice mail for me yesterday reminding me payday is Friday and she'd appreciate it if Harold got paid."

"He will." Ginger giggled. "We'll figure it out. Right now, though, all we can do is get that soft opening going for lunch and hopefully earn some money." She pulled her sunglasses out of her purse. "Here's a thought: why don't we give a discount for cash customers for a little while? If nothing else, we can hand out envelopes of green paper on payday."

We left the bank, walking toward the restaurant. She prattled on with ideas to increase income. I nodded and mumbled assurances, unable to pay close attention. The slim man was still standing outside when we'd exited the bank. He'd put on sunglasses so I couldn't tell for sure, but because he'd shifted his position, enabling himself to continue looking in our direction, I suspected he was watching us as long as he could.

Back at the Revenge Café, Ginger immediately went into the kitchen to chat up Harold. A few of the other kitchen staff were busy in there with him. A hostess, the bartender and some wait persons were fluttering around on the dining floor. It was around ten thirty in the morning. We had about a half hour before we were to put a *NOW OPEN* sign out on the road and then serve a buffet lunch to anyone who happened to wander in.

I watched everyone in action, waiting for inspiration to strike and tell me what I could do. After nothing came to me, I retreated to the office and re-searched through Chance's computer. No new leads. And still none in the few bits of paper lying around.

I did find a pile of mail that looked like it needed to be sorted. In it there was nothing that seemed to scream *evidence* at me, though when I ripped open an invoice for bathroom sanitation supplies, for some reason it dawned on me, a couple of days too late, that I should probably get to that post office box, too. Why hadn't I thought of that before? Oh yeah, I'd been drunk.

Florence Baa knocked on the door frame.

"Hi," I said. "Come on in."

She remained standing in the doorway. "Did you know that we are supposed to get paid on Friday?" she asked.

"Yes." I smiled at her. "No worries. We'll take care of it."

She nodded in response. Her face didn't seem to believe me.

As soon as she left, Ginger popped her head in the door distracting me from slamming mine into a wall.

"Mandy, honey," she said. "It's eleven o'clock sugar. The buffet is set up. Why don't you join us for a little lunch?"

My kitchen crew with Harold at the helm had pulled together a scrumptious smorgasbord of island fare and tourist staples. Representing the tastes of St. Thomas was a variety of seafood, including conch fritters and chowder, a cornmeal-based dish called fungi, sugar cakes, and killaloo, a fish and okra stew. Among the mainland, tourist fare was chicken wings with jerk seasoning that were prepared so that the bones pointed upright and the meat was pealed back. I filled a plate with the finger foods, intent on going back for a bowl of stew as a second course.

"Francis has some great ideas for house drinks, including this here punch," Ginger said, clinking her glass to Francis Frazer's, the bartender. "I sent out the menu for this week and next to get copied, but I think we should change it up a couple times a month to keep things interesting. What do you think?"

"Sounds good." I sat next to her and picked up a chicken wing by the bone, marveling at the sheer genius of preparing it that way. You could eat it without getting your fingers messy.

"But we'll keep most of what's here as staples dat people can count on each time dey come to de island," Harold said.

"Sure," I bit the chicken.

"And I was thinking–" Ginger was interrupted by a crash.

Chester Butterworth had arrived. His foot had caught on a chair leg; he stumbled and pulled over a table as he fell.

Francis and I ran over to help him up.

"Are you alright, Chester?" I asked.

"Of course, love!" He smoothed down his cargo shorts, and pulled on the hem of his shirt, I heard the sound of a small tear. "Sorry about that. I hope nothing is broken." He stood straight and tall. I could clearly see a round bruise on his forehead from our car ride together, but didn't see any new signs of other physical damage from his fall.

A few other staff members had already swooped in to clean up the glass from the vase and set the table upright.

I led him to where we were eating. "Congratulations. You are our first customer. We're open, just barely, but we—"

"Wonderful! I wasn't planning on eating, but of course I'll have a bite. I came by to drop off that card to the auto body shop I promised you." He stopped to search his pockets. After the shorts came up empty, he found the card in his shirt pocket and handed it to me. There looked to be a fresh food stain on it.

"Oh, thank you." I could barely refrain from wiping the card off with a napkin before putting it into my pocket. "Why don't you have a seat?"

"Ginger!" His smile was so bright we could have dimmed the overhead lights as he walked to her. "How are you, love?" He sat in my former chair, next to her.

I pulled another chair up to the table for myself.

"I'm fine Chester. Good to see you again." She seemed genuinely pleased to see him.

He popped one of the conch fritters from my plate into his mouth. "Delicious," he said to her.

"Oh that's all Harold's doing."

Chester picked up my glass of punch and *cheered* Harold with it in the air before sipping.

I returned to the buffet table to re-load a lunch for myself. This time, I started with the killaloo stew. Francis winked at me as he poured me a fresh punch when I returned.

Butterworth chatted with everyone at the table, of course knowing them all by name. *Why hadn't Chance ever introduced me to him?* As I thought about it, I realized Chance had never introduced me to anyone on island. Every time I'd stayed with him while working, we'd go about our respective business during the day and then meet up at his place in the evenings for dinner and drinks. Except for the time I wrote that magazine story.

Chance had taken time off photographing his brides and grooms to help me with it. We brainstormed and fed off each other's ideas, spent every waking moment together, and created a brilliant article.

It was like old times for us, like when we worked for Malcolm, only better because Malcolm wasn't hovering over us to keep an eye on me. Chance had wanted to do more work with me, but I didn't need a photographer after that. I landed the job with the TV station and began spending more time in front of the camera instead of beside one.

Regardless, Chance and I had spent quite a bit of time together on St. Thomas. Why didn't he ever introduce me to anyone? Why did I never notice that before?

Did I introduce him to anyone when he'd visited me in Florida? I drank my punch and thought about it. No. I never had. Somehow when we were together, we didn't need anyone else around. We never ran out of things to talk about, laugh about, or eat.

My eyes drifted to the kitchen. I hadn't been able to spend much time in there since I took on ownership of the restaurant. Frankly, I couldn't understand why I wasn't grossed out by the fact that we were eating in the building where Chance had been murdered.

Instead, I realized, though I was sad, I was still somehow at peace with the absurdity of it. I looked at the faces around my table: Harold, Francis, Ginger, Butterworth, and Cassandra, the sous chef. They looked at home, too. And none of them seemed to act like I didn't belong there.

Could that be my sign from Chance? That I belonged here?

My cell phone rang. It quit by the time I dug it out of my purse that was under Butterworth's chair. Caller ID read *unknown number* but whoever had called left a voice mail. I took my bowl of stew and a fresh glass of punch and retreated to the office.

Seated at the desk, I listened to the message.

"Hello," a female with a British accent said. "This is Penelope Abbott, Chance's mother. Please call me. I need to speak with you."

Chapter 15: Warning Bells

I dialed the number Chance's mother left. The call went to voice mail.

I hung up and dialed Piper.

"I just got the strangest call," I said and told him about Penelope Abbott. "I'd spoken to his dad earlier in the week and got the impression he wasn't coming for the funeral. I gave him your number for details about the investigation. Has he called you?"

"No." He cleared his throat. "I'm glad *you* called me, though."

"Really? Why?" *Did he like my backside?* I dropped my spoon and literally slapped myself in the forehead.

"The woman who threw the stiletto at Abbott was just in asking if anyone knew anything about his funeral arrangements."

"What?"

"She wants to attend."

"But . . ." Warning bells blared in my head.

"I wasn't here when she came in," he continued. "The officer at the information desk suggested she contact you. I wanted to give you a head's up."

"Thank you."

"You're welcome, and I'm sure you'll let me know if anything interesting transpires in the course of your conversation with her, right?"

"Of course." I hung up without saying good bye. I took a long drink of the punch, convinced he hadn't noticed my backside at all. Which was a good thing, I told myself as I hit redial.

"So we're back to normal?" he answered the line.

"What?"

"Frequent calls?"

"Don't take it personally. You're just all I got right now." And besides, it wasn't like I was flirting or anything.

"I'm listening."

"It has nothing to do with Chance's case."

"Are you cooking scallops again tonight?"

"No." Though the idea had its merits. "I've been seeing a couple of women hanging around the parking lot here at the restaurant. Probably early twenties. Both are white. A blond and a, I'm not sure. The other has reddish-purplish hair."

"A freak of nature?"

"A freak of something." I swallowed the last bite of my stew. "I tried to talk to them but I think they were too spaced out to hold a conversation. Can you check with your narc guys and see if they've noticed an increase in dealing activity around here? I don't want my restaurant to turn into a hotspot for that crowd."

"Will do." He hung up.

I frowned at my empty bowl and wished I'd brought more food into the office with me.

"Oh," I said out loud as I realized I was hiding and recognized the irony in my behavior: I had just decided I belonged out there, with the people on the other side of the office door, and then I found a reason to ensconce myself away from them. I sighed as I stood.

One of the reasons Aunt Maggie and Babs had encouraged my move to St. Thomas was they thought real life would be better therapy than anything I'd tried before. I almost called Babs to tell her she was right, but that would have kept me at the desk, behind the closed door. Instead, I dragged myself back out into the room with the people.

We had a few customers at the buffet and more were being shown where to sit. Seemed possible that we'd at least make enough to pay the dishwasher for the day.

"Mandy," Ginger said when I returned to our table. "You should hear what Chester is saying. He knows all about this building and the ghosts. He's quite the history buff!"

Chester blushed. Although, it might have been alcohol causing the red flush. He had a couple empties on the table before him. Apparently they'd moved on from the punch and had been taste testing cocktails.

"Oh? Can he help us get rid of her so we have nothing to fear on the weekends?" I asked.

"We working on it, Miss Mandy," Francis said filling a glass with the latest drink for me.

I accepted it and sat at the table next to him. Someone had placed a large platter of sugar cakes on our table. Sugar and alcohol, what more does a girl need for lunch? I dropped a few pieces on my plate and looked up when the door opened. Another customer had come in. Someone I knew. Someone who made me lose my appetite for the sugar part of my meal.

"Hello!" the slender and well-dressed Islander man called out as I stood up. "Well, well, well. I didn't expect to find you here, Miss Mandy Breen." Reggie Callwood smiled like a moray eel.

"Isn't there an old expression how one should expect the unexpected?" I asked him. Or maybe I was asking myself. "Are you here for lunch?"

He laughed as he made his way toward me. "Not exactly, my dear."

We met halfway between the table and the door.

"Then why, exactly, are you here?" I was trembling inside. I kept eye contact with him even though I really wanted to glance down to see if I was trembling outside too. I was also mentally kicking myself in the ass. If I'd been able to keep my head in the right place and been able to stay sober in the evenings, I'd know exactly where Reggie lived. By now, I should have found his home, spoken to his neighbors, found out where he worked, what bars he frequented, maybe even whether or not he and Piper were friends. But, no, I'd been unconscious on Chance's red sofa.

"I don't know if you're aware, but I'm not with the police anymore. I've moved on." His eyes dropped from my face. I crossed my arms in front of my chest and jutted out my chin.

"Where did you move to?" I asked.

"You could say I'm in real estate now. I have a partner I'm helping find properties in the Virgin Islands to purchase."

"Nothing's for sale here." Sometimes when a man stares at my chest, I am tempted to bend over and blatantly stare at his crotch just to see how he'd react. But I wasn't tempted with Reggie. He'd probably get turned on by it. His eyes reminded me of a man I'd once watched as he enjoyed, too much, choosing which lobster he wanted to eat from a tank.

"And how would lovely Mandy, the reporter, know that?" he taunted. "Is she covering the opening for a story?"

"She would know because she's the owner."

The news clearly startled him. His eyes popped up to mine and he took a tiny step back. Before he was able to reply, Ginger interrupted us.

"Good afternoon." She greeted him with an extended hand. "I'm Ginger Dillon." He shook it, without taking his eyes off me. "I'm the general manager here and just wanted to let you know you're free to browse the buffet table. We'll be open from breakfast through dinner beginning tomorrow with a full menu. And you should be sure to tell all your friends to come this Friday night for our first grand soiree. Can I show you a table now?"

It was almost a funny question coming from her at that moment because she had taken him by the elbow and had turned him around to face the exit.

"No, thank you. I'll come back another time," Reggie said. Ginger returned him to the door and deposited him outside.

"Thank you!" I took her arm and walked her back to our table.

"Chester told me he was bad news," she said.

"Do you know him?" I asked Butterworth.

"Love!" He waved his hand in the air, a paper napkin stuck to it. "Every one. Just ask me about anyone."

"You said you knew Matthew Piper." I didn't want to, but I stared at a spot of chutney on his chin.

"Yes, of course." He tried to scrape the napkin off his hand.

"How long has he been with the VIPD?" I braved dabbing at his chin with a clean, cloth napkin.

"Thank you!" He winked at me. "He's been here a couple of years. He came over from St. Croix after a major internal affairs investigation forced the firing of most of the police force on island, including Reggie there."

"I see. And what do you think of him?"

"What do you mean?"

"Is he trustworthy?"

"Who?"

"Piper!"

"The man is kind to dogs." Butterworth peeled off the last of the stuck napkin, wiped his hand on his shorts and nodded once at me.

"Of course he's trustworthy."

We somehow managed to have a straggling of customers come in all afternoon. Ginger was pleased with the turn out. Said we'd *done good* for a place with no advertising. She seemed to be everywhere at once—helping in the kitchen, helping on the restaurant floor, chatting Butterworth up at the bar.

I floundered around as much as I could. I even did a little table bussing until I dropped a stack of dishes when I smashed into Cassandra. Thankfully it was after she'd closed the oven door and not before, when she was putting in a giant casserole.

"Sugar, I think we got everything under control in the kitchen," Ginger said. "You can finish up whatever you need to in the office or mingle with our customers if you'd like.

I retreated to the office and spun around in the chair until I heard my phone ding with a new email. The message was finally a response from my cousin, Bob.

Sorry, I missed you on your birthday. Hope you had a blast. I couldn't get much info on your Piper man. Seems to be a good guy. He's in good standing with the VIPD. He went to college in Miami for criminal justice and has an impeccable record there. I found no connection with him and Reginald Callwood. I did see Callwood was fired from the VIPD after an internal affairs investigation found evidence that a few officers in the department were in the drug smuggling trade. Charges had been brought against him, but he got off with some kind of a plea deal. Let me know if I can be of more help.

Interesting. Not very helpful, but interesting.

Ginger came in, saw me in front of the computer and mentioned she wished it wasn't a Mac. She wanted to do some internet shopping.

"I have a Windows-based laptop at home," I said. "You're welcome to use it. And you know what? I made a boat load of stuffed jalapenos when I couldn't sleep last night. Too many just for me. Why don't you come home with me? You can help me eat them and use my computer."

She hesitated. I worried I came across as too needy.

"Sure thing, sugar," she eventually said. "It'll give us a chance to talk marketing, anyway."

Later, outside in the early evening, she hesitated again to say a quick prayer and make the sign of the cross before she opened the Jeep door.

"I'll just sit in the back seat, honey." She climbed into the Jeep. "That way I won't be tempted to take the wheel from you."

"I appreciate it," I said. "But don't worry. I got it all under control. It's the other drivers who are nuts."

"Right." She buckled her seatbelt tightly and pulled out her cell phone. "But I got my ride home taken care of."

We made it safely to my place and Ginger immediately logged on the internet from my computer still set up on the dining table. She said she was going to order a few pieces of equipment for the restaurant, at her expense.

I fired up the grill and pulled the stuffed bacon-wrapped jalapenos out of the refrigerator. I'd made them in the middle of the night when my blood sugar had crashed, again, and I'd woken up. They were filled with cheeses and breadcrumbs. Some had chopped scallions and cilantro, too. They were all beauties.

"That looks like something we could put on the menu," Ginger said as she opened the patio door for me.

"I think we should have a bacon day once a week," I replied. "Everything on the menu could be made to include bacon somehow." I stepped outside to lay the peppers on the grill.

"Not all ideas are good ones," she called through the open door. "But don't be afraid to run any by me."

I came back in the house as Chance's cell phone rang from where Lydia had left it plugged in on the kitchen counter. I stared at it. Caller ID read: *unknown.* I pushed the *call* button to answer when I remembered, at the last second, that I didn't know his password to retrieve any messages.

"This is Chance Abbott's phone," I answered.

"This is Evie Schwartz," the voice on the other end said. "I'm calling about my photographs."

"I'm sorry . . . I . . . uh, well, there was an accident."

"What? That was my son's Bar Mitzvah! You cannot just re-do a destination Bar Mitzvah! Those are the only pictures. If I don't receive my photographs—"

"I'm sorry, but Mr. Abbott is dead."

"Oh! Oh . . . oh."

"Yes." What else was there to say?

"Well, about those pictures," she started.

"I'll see what I can find. Where can I send them?" I took down her information and realized there was something else I'd been too stewed by alcohol to notice. Where the hell were his cameras?

Chapter 16: Just Now Noticing

While Ginger continued to research equipment, whatever the hell that meant, and the peppers heated on the grill, I tore through Chance's bedroom.

Nothing was under the bed. The drawers in his dresser held only clothing, and the nightstand just a little baggie of pot and some condoms. I was almost frantic when I hit the closet. I ripped clothes off hangers and dove through boxes. I was so obsessed with my search I didn't notice anyone entering the room.

When the closet was bone bare, I heard a man speak to me.

"These are really good. You should serve them in the restaurant."

Piper was in the room, eating one of my peppers.

"Have you already searched the house?" I asked from the floor.

"No, but it looks like you're doing a thorough job." He took the last bite of one of my jalapenos. "Something missing?"

"Yes!" I stood up and shook a dress shirt off my leg. "He was a photographer. Look around, see any cameras?"

His eyes scanned the room. "It's a little hard to tell with the mess in here."

I stormed passed him to the kitchen. Ginger had piled a platter with the peppers. She was on the phone out on the patio.

"You just now noticing the cameras are missing?" Piper followed me to the counter.

"Yes."

"You been here for how long?"

"Long enough to notice before now." I took a couple small plates from a cabinet and set them on the counter. "I've been a little drunk."

"Is that a normal habit?" He loaded some peppers onto a plate and handed it to me before loading one up for himself.

"No, just whenever it's handy."

He stopped to look at me. I couldn't help but think: *How many peppers can Piper plate if Piper could plate peppers?*

"I hope you don't mind me letting him in," Ginger said as she re-entered. "He showed me his badge and all. I was in the middle of an order."

"No worries, Detective Piper and I are becoming good friends." I took a bottle of water from the refrigerator.

"Who's she?" Piper asked.

"I'm the general manager at the restaurant," Ginger said, offering him her hand. "Ginger Dillon."

"Detective Matt Piper." They shook and he turned to me. "She staying here?"

"No, I'm at the Wyndham right now." Ginger answered as she loaded a plate.

"Did you bring her with you?" Piper asked me.

"No. Chance was interviewing her for a job before I even arrived." I closed my eyes and shook my head. "But that doesn't matter. He's loaded with cameras. Those cameras should be here, somewhere."

"And they're not at the restaurant?"

"No."

"How did he process the pictures?"

"He'd moved to digital a long time ago."

"Which suggests he should have a computer around here, too, right?"

"Ugh!" I held my forehead. "I can't believe I hadn't thought about all that before now."

"Thought about what?" Ginger asked.

"That someone took Chance's photography equipment." I nibbled a pepper.

"I don't understand," she said. "Was he doing his own ad campaigns for the restaurant?"

"You know, I need to make some calls myself," I said instead of explaining. I stood up from the table. Piper stood, too. "In private," I added.

I took my plate of peppers, bottle of water and cell phone out to the patio. I sat down at the table and called Aunt Maggie.

"How are you, dear? I'm so glad you called. Babs and I have been thinking about you non-stop, but we know you don't like us to nag you with our concern."

"I don't consider it nagging, Aunt Maggie."

"Yes you do. But we know you love us for it nonetheless. Are you holding up all right? Do you need any help?"

"I think I need guidance. Can you check with Chance for me? Could you ask him where his cameras are?"

She paused before answering. "He doesn't want you to find them."

"Oh for crying out loud! Really? Well, can you ask him who killed him?"

"Killed him? I was under the impression it was an accident."

"What?"

She was quiet again. "Dear, it was an accident."

"Aunt Maggie, that's not possible. His hands were tied behind his back—"

"He's coming through clear and strong. Two people were involved. They didn't mean for him to die."

"What? Who are they?"

She remained silent long enough for me to finish a whole pepper.

"You know dear, he's enjoying your search too much to give me anything more."

I punched *end* and swirled around in my chair, tempted to throw my cell through the sliding glass doors.

"Could you be just a little more frustrating, Chance?"

Silence. He must have still been chatting it up with my Aunt Maggie.

I went back inside.

"Mandy, honey." Ginger smiled at me. "Those were damn good." She took her plate to the sink to rinse it. Piper was still enjoying my peppers at the table. "But we'll have to talk about marketing another time. I need the powder room now so I can tidy up before Chester gets here. Where is it?"

"Through that door." I pointed. "But wait . . . Chester Butterworth?"

"Yes." She slung her purse on her shoulder.

"Why's he picking you up?" I shook my head to try to clear it.

"We're going to dinner together."

"As in a date?"

"Yes, as in a date." She laughed as I walked toward her. "What else, sugar?"

"But . . . but . . . You're an upper-class Southern Bell. He's a border-line destitute Peter Pan." I was only a few inches away from her and had to use all my strength to keep from gripping her wrists and/or slapping her face. I didn't want my new general manager to be so flighty as to think Butterworth was a good catch.

"That's not quite right, sugar."

"You can't go out with him!"

"Mandy, honey, you might be signing my paycheck one day but that doesn't mean you can tell me who to date."

"It's just that he's . . . you . . ." In lieu of slapping some sense into her, I pulled my hair back into a pony tail. "You just met him two days ago."

"Right." She stared in my eyes.

"You didn't have enough time to get to know him."

"We've been together just about every spare minute."

"What?" I glanced over at Piper. "Do you know him? Is she safe with him? How does she know her body won't be consumed by sharks before anyone reports her as missing?"

"Oh, so that's your problem!" Ginger laughed. "I get it now. You got trust issues, huh?" She patted me on the arm and headed toward the restroom. "Thank you, honey. I'll take that as a sign of affection." She stopped at the door. "But don't you worry none. I promise not to go skinny dipping with him tonight."

Butterworth arrived soon after, blushing a little at the door like he was sixteen. They left. I shut the door behind them and turned to find Piper grinning at me from the kitchen table.

"What are you laughing at?" I asked him.

"You really think Butterworth is dangerous?" He picked up both our empty plates and put them in the sink.

"I honestly don't know. But better safe than sorry, right? Isn't that what a good police officer would advise?"

"Chester Butterworth can be dangerous. I'll give you that." Piper nodded. "But not in the way you're thinking. I wouldn't ask him to turn off a light switch that was next to the on-off button of a life support machine. But he's not maliciously dangerous."

I snorted a laugh. He returned to his chair at the table, stretched out his legs in front of him, and clasped his hands behind his head.

"Those were some fine peppers," he said. His barroom eyes rested easily on mine and I knew I had to stop feeding him. Otherwise he'd be over every night, things would progress from the kitchen to the bedroom. And that might put me back in therapy.

"Thanks, but I'm not cooking anything else." I crossed my arms. "Did I ask you why you came here tonight?"

"Nope." He grinned and waited.

I tilted my head and huffed. "Fine, you win." I returned to my seat at the table. "Why did you come here tonight?"

"Thought I'd check in on you."

"And you think I need checking on because?"

He twisted his lips to one side, eventually forming a lopsided grin. "OK, so I'm not checking in on *you.* I'm checking in on what you're doing."

"What do you mean?"

"You told me you were intent on finding the murderer. I'd like to know what you have, or what you know that you think I don't."

So I was wrong about what those barroom eyes had been saying.

"Sounds like you're the one with the trust issues," I said.

"Has nothing to do with trust. This isn't my first rodeo. I've been a detective long enough to know that there are a limited number of reasons for people to get involved in finding a murderer."

"And those reasons are?" I got up from my chair to retrieve another bottle of water from the refrigerator.

"Sometimes, people think they're a suspect when they're not and so they're desperate to find the real perpetrator. I don't think you're one of them. Sometimes, they think they know who the murderer is and want to protect them from the police, which again, I don't think is the case. And finally, sometimes they're aware of information that the police aren't, information that for some reason they may not want to share."

I returned to the table but didn't sit down. Instead, I stood behind my chair and rolled the water bottle around in my hands.

He raised his eyebrows at me. "I think you're in category number three."

"Actually," I squeezed the bottle. "I have another reason."

"Let's hear it."

I rolled the bottle faster. Perhaps I was drumming up nerve. "Let's just say," I said slowly, "from back in my reporter days, I learned that not all officially assigned personnel are as trustworthy as they should be. Maybe I don't feel comfortable letting them be the only ones on the case. Maybe I don't trust them enough to actually find the killer."

"I took an oath when I took this job."

"So did Reggie Callwood."

He shrugged. "Reggie's a different kind of man than me. How do you know him?"

"He was on the police force when I covered some stories here." I tossed the water bottle back and forth between my hands waiting, just waiting for him to spin something positive about Reggie. "And coincidentally, he came in the restaurant today looking to buy the place."

"Really?" He straightened in his chair and wrinkled his brow.

"Really."

"Hm. Well, like I said, I'm a different kind of man than he is." Piper leaned forward, resting his elbows on his knees and looking at me from under his brow. "I've been a police officer for fifteen years and have an impeccable record."

"Says the police department whose records are not quite impeccable but look like it."

"That's in the past."

"How am I to know that?"

"Do your research."

"I started."

"And what have you found so far?" He leaned back in his chair again, relaxed and composed, as if he had nothing to hide.

"Nothing, yet. Except for Butterworth saying you must be a good guy because you're kind to dogs."

Piper erupted in laughter.

"What's up with that anyway?" I asked, finally sitting down and opening my water bottle. I liked his response to the subject of Callwood enough that I could let it go, for now. "You and dogs?"

"I like dogs all right. But my boys love dogs."

"Your boys?"

"I got two sons who I only see every other weekend and for summer breaks. One of them did a school project about the animal shelters here always being at capacity. So we foster dogs now and I helped him start a program to find adoptive families for them. It gives me something to share with my kid and it keeps him out of trouble."

"Oh." I stared at his chest as he reclined in his chair. It looked powerful and yet soft. I caught myself doing the math, trying to figure out how long it had been since I leaned my head against a chest. The answer suggested the loneliness would be palpable after he left.

"God, I need a real drink." I stood to find the rum.

"I thought that wasn't normal for you." He stood too and met me at the counter. "Or is it a handy time?"

"Staying in a drunken stupor isn't normal for me." I found the rum bottle and was disturbed by the rather small amount in it. "But right now, it might be handy. I'm either going to get drunk or I'll start crying." I tried to look at his eyes, but all I could see at close range was his chest, his broad and welcoming chest. He was standing so near that it seemed if I just bowed my head, it would touch him. I tested the theory and my head did, indeed, touch his chest.

"How about you try to just keep both at a minimum?" He put one arm around me, stiffly, as if following protocol.

"Good idea." I straightened up and shook off his arm. He got two glasses from the cupboard and filled them with more ice than I would have. But then again, I hadn't planned on sharing either. I poured us both drinks anyway, emptying the rum bottle.

We returned to the kitchen table.

"So do you think it's a coincidence that Callwood would come in talking about buying properties so soon after the owner, that is, Chance, passed?" I asked.

He fingered his drink on the table. "I think so. The murder made the local news and Callwood's probably still connected to precinct gossip but I don't see how either of those things could have told him who owned the property."

I nodded and sipped.

"When did Abbott propose to you?" Piper changed the subject. "Did he actually propose?"

"He made the proposition a couple of months ago. In February. Why?"

"He was busy that month."

"What do you mean?"

"He did a lot of things in February."

"Like, for example . . ."

"Buy that Jeep, in cash," Piper said. "Paid off this house, in cash. Put a down payment on the restaurant, in cash."

That little shit! He was obviously in the midst of some major trouble and asked me to join in without warning. Good thing he was already dead or I'd have to kill him myself. I stood up, took both our glasses from the table and emptied them in the sink.

"When did he pay it off?" I leaned against the counter and watched Piper walk toward me.

"The Friday before you landed." He stopped within close enough range that his chest could have been inviting again, but I wasn't even tempted. I was too angry at Chance for starting this damned mess and at Piper for not telling me about his financial transactions before.

"So why the hell didn't you tell me this already? I still can't get access to his accounts at the bank."

"You're holding out information from me, remember? What is it?"

Chapter 17: Suspicious Without Cause?

I kicked Piper out and went to bed relatively sober. But I was hungry again and, although I was tired as hell, I just couldn't sleep. I kept wondering where Butterworth took Ginger and what they'd eaten.

My mind refused any attempt to discipline it. Thoughts bounced around like exploding popcorn kernels inside my brain. I needed to know what had happened to Chance. I needed to know his death wasn't my fault. I needed to know I wasn't next in line.

Most of all, I needed a viable lead. Or a real suspect. Or a specific incident I could connect to something else.

And then there was Aunt Maggie insisting that it was an accident. What kind of medium was she?

I got out of bed and headed back to the kitchen. I needed to do something physical this time. I didn't need to be too busy to ignore how lonely I was, I needed catharsis for my angst.

Nothing I had bought from the Fruit Bowl seemed labor intensive enough, but I spied the coconut in the pantry. I shook it and heard a little milk sloshing inside. It was still good.

But I couldn't find anything to break it open in any of the drawers or cupboards.

"Then again, Chance, why on earth would you have a hammer? A hammer is something a responsible home owner would own. I'm sure all the freaking nails holding up your pictures were pounded in by some woman's shoe." I made a slow circle in the middle of the kitchen unable to come up with another place to look for tools.

None were in the bathroom cabinets either, but there were plenty of towels. I was going to have to go old school.

I retrieved the coconut from the kitchen, wrapped a towel around it, and smashed it as hard as I could against the tile floor in the bathroom.

"Oh, my, God!" I grinned at the lumpy wet towel. The relief was almost orgasmic.

Back in the kitchen I pulled a chair over to the counter so I could sit and do the tedious work of prying the meat from the husk and then peeling off the skin. It gave me a chance to go over what I knew and did not know about Chance's murder. I spoke out loud to force myself into keeping the wheels turning in my head while also preventing me from drinking anything.

"What I know for sure is . . ." I paused and wiped the vegetable peeler I was using on a paper towel. "One: Chance is dead. Two: he met Ginger a couple of days before he died. Three: he was impaled by a stiletto the night before he was killed. Four: Reggie Callwood is interested in buying the restaurant property. Oh!" I sat up straighter and continued. "The property that may or may not be an illegal drug contact spot."

I stood and rinsed my hands as I thought about how coincidental it was that Callwood, someone who had been in a drug ring in the past, was wanting to purchase my restaurant, a place I suspected was a convenient spot to pedal drugs.

I turned on the oven and let it pre-heat while I sliced the coconut into the smallest pieces possible, which I then spread out onto a baking sheet, sprinkled with salt and put in the oven.

While my coconut baked, I poured a glass of wine, promised myself it would be the only one, and sat down at my computer. Ginger had left the internet browser up. I nosed around the history and discovered yet another coincidence. Ms. Ginger Dillon had purchased cameras from my computer.

I finished the glass of wine as I continued to follow her use of my machine. Aside from camera browsing, she'd also visited several Facebook pages. Most of them were of women in Dallas posting pictures and blurbs about their latest shopping sprees, social functions, and their extraordinarily intellectually advanced, beautiful, graceful and talented children. She'd stopped by only one man's page, that of Darren Dillon. He looked to be in his mid-forties and had "restaurant owner" in his bio. Not much word-wise was on his wall, but there were plenty of photographs of him and a scantily-clad woman about half his age sitting on his lap, often drinking shots at a bar, always showing off her artificially-induced cleavage. He had a medical bandage taped between his brows in the most recent pic and seemed to have a large one on his left hand.

Ginger hadn't commented on anyone's page. I tried to find one on her, but although there were several Ginger Dillons listed, none had her middle name nor did any look like her.

I logged in to Intelius and found Ginger had herself a police record. An interesting, but short, police record.

Thursday morning all scheduled employees showed up for work happy to be there. A few tourists showed up for breakfast, too. They must not have had far to travel as they all arrived before I did. But they weren't the only ones to make it there alive. The two strung out women who I'd suspected were buying drugs in the parking lot were speaking with Ginger when I came in.

I got myself a cup of coffee from the kitchen and cornered my new general manager and her suspicious friends.

"Hi there," I said, a little too loudly. "What's going on here?"

"These young women are under the impression you told them they could work here," Ginger said. "Did you, sugar?" Her face exemplified that unnamed talent of a true southern bell. On the surface, she was poised with a polite smile, but there was a tilt to her head and a lift to her eyebrows that clearly told me I'd have hell to pay if the women were telling the truth.

"Actually, I met them Tuesday and they told me they were supposed to work here. I thought perhaps they were confused since we hadn't called them in to help clean." I turned to the women. Blondie had a hand on her hip and looked pissed. Her friend was too dazed to show expression. "Did you apply for a job?" I asked.

"Uh, no," insisted the blond. "Chance told us we could be hostesses. Why would we have to apply?"

"Oh, I see." I nodded my head. "I get it now." Chance had probably met them in a bar and they took him seriously about some kind of an offer. "Well, Chance is, um . . ."

"He's no longer in the position to make hiring decisions," Ginger rubbed my back as she finished my sentence. "If you'd like a job, you can fill out an application and we'll call you if we have a need for you."

"But – But! He promised we'd have a job!" Blondie said.

Magenta seemed to wake up. Her eyes fluttered with a rapid blink. "No, wait. It's all cool," she said and tugged at the blond's arm. "All cool. C'mon Amy." She tugged her friend away.

Ginger and I watched the women meander out of the restaurant.

"Good Lord, is that the kind of company Mr. Abbott usually kept?" she asked.

"Only when it was late at night and there was no other young lovely at the bar to take home," I answered.

"Sad, really, to watch them." Ginger shook her head. "But good riddance. We don't need hopped up hussies with purple hair around here."

"Amen. But would you call that color purple?"

"I'm not sure. I just hope she wasn't charged full price for it."

"I'm thinking I want to call it magenta. Doesn't it sound more fun to say you once met someone with magenta hair?"

"It sure does." She laughed.

We continued staring at the girls until they sauntered down the steps out of sight.

Yet again, I had no idea what to do with myself. I went into the office, sat down at the desk and drummed my fingers on it until my cell phone jangled its Carribean beat. It was Lydia Abiff.

"What you do to his room?" she demanded before I even finished saying *hello*.

"Excuse me?"

"Mr. Abbott's bedroom!" she yelled. "What you do to it?"

"Oh, uh," I'd forgotten to clean it is what I did. "I was uh, looking for Chance's cameras. Have you seen them?"

"No! But dat no excuse to make a mess like dis." Her patient, slow talk she used with non-Islanders was gone. "Rass won' rample it no mo'. Yuh check?"

"Um, yes." I was pretty sure I'd just promised never to make a mess like that again. Or maybe it was that I'd give her my first born. She clicked off before I could clarify.

Thinking maybe I'd spent enough time in there, I headed out to the restaurant area. The thin crowd was down to just a few diners, including a couple women sitting in a booth by a window, eating with their eyes darting around the room as if worried they'd be seen by someone.

Butterworth was sitting on a barstool, chatting with Ginger.

"Hello," I said to the two of them.

"Hey there, sugar," Ginger said. "Chester and me are making big plans." She filled a coffee cup and handed it to me.

"Really? For what?"

"Taking care of that ghost."

"Oh, good." I eyed Chester. "You got any experience in that department?"

"Not at all," Chester bounced on his seat to look directly at me. "But it's a thrilling prospect, isn't it?" His face beamed. In fact, his smile was so eager that I had to lie and pretend to agree with him.

"Absolutely!" I took a sip of coffee.

"Won't it be wonderful to find out who they are, what they're all about?" He waved his hand in the air, knocking over his own coffee.

"And it will certainly be a wonderful, historical story for our restaurant," Ginger said, mopping up the spill. "We promo it right and it'll help get and keep tourists interested in the place."

"Right." My stomach churned as she pinched his chin and smiled at him. I spun around and leaned my back on the bar. We were down to only two sets of customers. One of those rare, elderly couples who still seem to be happy despite being together a long time and the two nervous women.

"OK Chester," I tapped Butterworth on the arm. "Who's who time, again. Who are the women eating in the booth by the windows?"

He turned around and openly ogled the women, as did Ginger. One of them couldn't help but notice and whispered into her companion's ear. They both stared back at Chester.

I stood to go speak with them before we scared them off.

"Hello," I said as I approached their booth. The thinner one jumped in her seat. "I'm Mandy Breen, owner of the Revenge Café. Thank you for coming. I hope you enjoyed your breakfast. We've only recently opened and we appreciate you giving us a try."

Neither woman said anything at first; they were too busy making eyes at each other. There was a slight resemblance. Aside from their dark, wavy hair, both had high cheekbones, narrow chins, and blue eyes. The thinner one was dressed fashionably, but conservatively, in a pale pink sheath and pearls. The chubby one wore khaki slacks and a black tank top.

"Thank you for coming," I tried again.

"Oh, it's the least we could do," the thin one said.

"The least you could do?" I smiled, aiming for it to be encouraging.

"I'm Tiffany Alexander," she said. "And this is my cousin, Tiffany Shrock."

The cousin put her glass down. "Most people call her Tiff-one and me Tiff-two."

"I see," I lied.

"Our mothers were very competitive sisters," Tiff-one continued the explanation.

"Right, so what made you decide to come in for breakfast?"

"I was the one, who . . . oh!" Tiff-one perked up. "Did you say you owned this restaurant?"

"Yes."

"I thought, well, there was a man who owned . . ." Tiff-one looked at her cousin with such insecurity, I wanted to help her.

"Were you in partnership with that Chance Abbott guy?" Tiff-two asked.

"Well, um, yes." My smile was starting to hurt my cheeks. "How did you know him?"

"I didn't." Tiff-two looked at her thinner cousin, not with *I'm here for you, I have your back* on her face, but with *For Christ's sake, will you do something right for a change?*

"I'm the one, who, you know," Tiff-one looked down at her plate. "I'm afraid I'm the one who blinded him."

"With the stiletto?" I asked.

She nodded. "It wasn't intentional."

Tiff-two sighed. "The men were having the bachelor's party at the same time we were having the bachelorette's," she explained. "I think everyone had too much to drink when the two parties crossed paths."

"I never thought Jeff would be the kind to even want a stripper at his party," Tiff-one came in. "I was just so shocked and, well, disappointed in him. I didn't know what to do. But I had my shoes in my hands because I couldn't walk in them anymore and . . . I was aiming at Jeff! Honest!"

"I'm sure."

"I really didn't mean to hurt him."

"Of course not," I assured her. "Those kinds of things can

happen to anyone."

"I am so very sorry," she said, her eyes glistening. "Honestly."

"Right, well, I hope it didn't destroy your wedding plans."

"We decided to put it on hold. I forgave Jeff, but ... I don't know. It just seemed like a bad omen for our marriage."

"I understand." I glanced at Tiff-two, who was clearly enjoying her meal. "How long will you be on island? Perhaps after a few more days of paradise, you'll be able to get a clear perspective on the whole situation."

"That's what I'm trying to do now," Tiff-one said. "I was supposed to leave tomorrow. But I think I'm going to stay longer. One of the reasons we were getting married here is because my cousin," Tiff-two's pace of eating quickened, "accepted a job teaching at the university. She's moving here and we'd be separated geographically for the first time."

Tiff-one looked upset over the prospect. Tiff-two's hand moved faster. Replace the plate of food with a stiff drink, and I could see myself in her these days. I wondered if she was a problem cooker too.

"Maybe this was a sign for me to not get married but stay close to my cousin for a little while longer."

Tiff-two sucked down her orange juice.

"Anyway, I'm sure there are plenty of other things you could be doing today," I said. "I appreciate your taking the time to experiment with our restaurant. And I hope you both come back." I turned to go.

"Do they know how he died?" Tiff-one asked, surprising Tiff-two as well as me. Tiff-two actually took time off from chewing to stare at her cousin, but I knew why she'd asked.

"Not from a shoe blinding him," I smiled.

"I'm so relieved."

"I'm sure you are." I walked away. She was odd but not a suspect. I wanted to call Piper and tell him about their visit. But I was beginning to think I was calling him too frequently. Actually, I was beginning to think I was inventing reasons to call him.

Chapter 18: Chance Encounter

I floundered around the restaurant constantly peaking at my watch, trying to bide my time before I thought I could leave without looking like I was abandoning my crew. But then it happened again. I slammed into a young woman who'd just finished bussing a table and made her tray drop in a loud crash.

"Sugar, is the bank open yet?" Ginger asked while we cleaned up my mess.

I walked to the main post office first. Armed with the death certificate and the will, I was ready for anything they could throw at me. But they didn't really care what kind of proof I had that the post office box was now mine. I was at the wrong place. Chance's P.O. Box was in the Tutu post office, not the one closest to his restaurant. Nor was it anywhere in a direct line between his house and the restaurant. Not that anything was in a direct line on that island.

"If I didn't know better, I'd think you were one masochistic bastard, Chance," I mumbled under my breath as I glanced at the directions the postal employee gave me. He told me the GPS wouldn't recognize the address as valid so he gave me traditional St. Thomian-style directions, which included going left at a large mango tree, right at a yellow house, and then driving a long while until I had to turn right again before I saw the old lady who sells the best cassavas and pumpkins. If I saw her, I should stop and get new directions after I bought some cassavas and pumpkins.

I sat in the Jeep scrolling through images in my phone, looking for mango tree pictures. Nothing came through clear enough to recognize so I drove until I found a woman walking beneath a pink parasol and asked her what a mango tree looked like. She was courteous enough not to say I'd recognize it by the mango fruit hanging from it.

I never saw an old lady selling any produce, but I did get pulled over by a police officer. I sat with my heart in my throat, knees shaking and stomach a deep pit while the man took down the license plate number and ran my driver's license information.

"I'm sorry ma'am," he said, after forcing me to walk a straight line then stand on one foot and touch my nose with my eyes closed. "But we're not used to seeing people drive that speed when they're sober." He handed me a piece of paper.

"I'm getting a ticket?"

"Yes. You can't drive that slowly on the main roads. You can cause an accident."

"What? It's legal to drive around this island with an open container of booze in the cup holder and yet I get a ticket for driving too slowly?"

"I don't make the laws, ma'am. I just enforce them." He tipped his head at me. "Oh and, you have fifteen days after coming into the receipt of a bequeathed vehicle to get it registered in your name. You might want to get that taken care of soon. Have a good day."

I climbed back in the Jeep awe-struck. A ticket for going too slowly? That was a first for me.

I turned the car on and realized I should have asked him to re-direct me to the post office. But then I realized I was on the backside of Blackbeard's Castle. I'd never been there. Nor had I been to Bluebeard's, which was just down the road. I'd always wanted to go. I'd always wondered if the two hirsute pirates were really one in the same, but had never taken the time to find out.

I pulled into the parking lot of Blackbeard's Castle. Not because I thought now was the perfect time to learn more about him, but because I had a sudden urge to call my aunt, someone who will tell you sudden urges must always be obeyed. I parked and went, like a proper tourist, toward the Castle, which is really just a tower now and part of a hotel resort.

April isn't even close to the height of tourist season on St. Thomas. Which might explain why I was the only one climbing the tower that day. I reached the top and looked out over Fort Christian while I dialed my psychic aunt in total privacy.

"How are you my dear?" she answered. "I've been thinking about you all morning."

"Really? Why?"

"Well, let's see. Your best friend just died. Your birthday just passed and I know you have issues with it. You're starting a new life on a tiny island where you don't know anyone. You haven't been in touch with Babs and you only ignore her when you're upset. You're right. There's absolutely no reason why you wouldn't be doing OK."

"I am doing OK." I smiled into the distance.

"No you're not. Now, tell me your biggest trouble."

"Aside from me not knowing who killed Chance, I'm guessing it's that I don't know whom to trust."

"That's nothing new, dear. You've been that way for years. What's your second biggest trouble?"

"I can't get access to the bank accounts that Chance had, so I don't know if I can pay the employees in the restaurant."

"Nope. Can't help with that one. What's next on your list?"

The view was amazing but the tower was otherwise anticlimactic. "Well, I guess that would be the ghost who's haunting the restaurant."

"I knew I could help with something. Tell me about it."

"I don't really know much. The employees all think it's someone who makes bad things happen on the weekends and are reluctant to work then."

"What bad has happened there?"

"Aside from Chance being killed, I've heard something about it burning down, but I don't really know what else."

"I see."

I headed back down the steps. "So what do I tell them?" My voice echoed off the round walls.

"Who?"

"The employees."

"What do you want to tell them?"

"That they have nothing to worry about. I mean, there are no ghosts at the restaurant, are there?"

"Of course there are! There are ghosts everywhere."

I stepped out into the sunshine again, relishing the warmth and brightness as I stood at the top of the steps leading down to the resort pool. A few tourists baked in lounge chairs and floated in the water. Didn't seem like there were any ghosts around them.

"What do they want?" I was in the white jeans and white silk blouse that was supposed to be my wedding outfit. Pretending to be a guest sitting poolside didn't make sense. I headed the opposite way and found a bench in the courtyard area where I sat facing a statue of a pirate who looked suspiciously like Johnny Depp.

"The ghost wants what most ghosts want. Revenge."

"Revenge?"

"Yes, revenge. Boring I know. But unfortunately that's what most ghosts want."

"On who?"

"People who are now ghosts in other places, usually." I heard her sip a beverage.

"That's not telling me much."

"Sorry my dear, but wait. Are you there, at the restaurant, now?"

"No, I'm at Blackbeard's Castle."

"Really?"

"Yes, why?" An iguana scrambled across the courtyard behind the statue.

"Why are you there?"

"I'm a fan of Johnny Depp." I followed the iguana, stepping onto the grass.

"When are you going to learn you can't lie to me?"

"I've been to this island several times and have never seen the castle?"

"Try again."

"I have always wondered if Blackbeard was the same person as Bluebeard?" The iguana took me up the hill, back toward the hotel.

"Again, why are you there?"

"The roads are too crazy here. I was on my way to a post office and got pulled over near this place. It seemed like a good idea to stop and call you." I lost sight of the reptile and headed toward another bench.

"I see. I'm sorry, but I'm not so sure about the ghosts at your restaurant. You'll need to call me from there on them."

"Fine."

"But, I'm thinking your friend wanted you to visit the ghosts where you are now, which is why he told you to stop there."

"I thought I was still waiting to hear from him."

"There's a message for you at that castle, Amanda. Hang around until you get it."

"Let me guess," I said, staring at a plaque cemented in the

ground by the bench. "It has something to do with revenge?"

"Maybe you already got it."

I clicked off from Aunt Maggie and stared at the name of Blackbeard's ship: the Queen Anne's Revenge. According to the plaque, most of the time Blackbeard carried textiles and cocoa aboard her and periodically the hairy—pubescent?—pirate's mighty boat was fortunate enough to be laden down with gold and silver coin minted in Mexico and Peru. There was no mention as to whether or not he was the same man as Bluebeard.

If Aunt Maggie was right, Chance wanted to tell me something about revenge. What about it? Was someone seeking revenge on him? He on them? Did he want me to get revenge on someone for him? Was this the place where he got the name for the restaurant? And there was the mention of Peru. Did he want me to take revenge on the person who fed him the peppers?

"Why can't your messages be clearer?" I asked a little too loudly. A few tourists who'd walked by gave me a startled glance. I pointed to my phone and smiled innocently at them.

I gave up on the post office for the day and drove to detective Piper's house. Doing my best to drive the speed limit, I followed the lit up route my GPS god was finally kind enough to provide. Piper lived near the back of a dead-end lane in the western part of the city. His street was short; there were only six houses on it. And not a single person answered a door when I knocked, which I hoped meant that they were not home. Because if they really were there, and maybe peaking out a side window, they'd be witness to me accidentally knocking over a mailbox when I tried to turn around. I did my best to right it again, propping several rocks at its base to help keep it upright.

I returned to the Revenge Café parked in the lot and walked to the bank. About half way there, I realized a familiar, slim profile was following me.

The slim man remained outside the bank while I went in and found my luck was changing: not only was Vincent on island, he was in his office. I waited for him in what I now considered my usual spot: on the sofa were I had a good view of the activity on the street. The slim man had taken up his usual spot, too. I called Piper and asked him to meet me at the bank.

"Your call is good timing," Piper said from his end. "I think I might have something you'd be interested in seeing."

He arrived before Vincent came out to greet me.

"You have something I might want to see?" I asked.

"I do," he said sitting on the sofa next to me. "But first, why did you call me?"

I turned sideways on the sofa to face him directly. "Look, but don't be obvious, out the window. Do you see the skinny guy in the tan pants with the red and white striped shirt?"

Piper tilted his head to scratch his chin. His eyes slid over to the people outside.

"Leaning against a lamp post?"

"Yes, that's him. Know him?"

"No. Should I?" His eyes came back to mine again. Their deep, brown color seemed to pull me into them. I actually found myself leaning toward him more.

"Um." I straightened up and tried to remember why he was there. I don't *do* relationships. I don't fall for anybody anymore. I had to be misreading myself, if that's at all possible. After my last break up, I promised myself I'd only do the occasional one-night kind of thing if I felt the need. But I didn't think I felt that need right now. And Piper didn't seem like a one-night kind of man. What was drawing me to him?

"What is it, Mandy?" He put his hand on my arm. "Did that man say anything to you?"

That's why I called him! I inhaled and shot my eyes to the side to see the slim man still standing there.

"No. This might sound crazy, but I think he's following me." I glanced in Piper's face. He was looking, but not obviously, at the man outside. "I've come to this bank every day this week and he's been there, watching me. Today I walked over from the café and he followed me."

"Maybe he finds you pretty." He slid his eyes back to me and grinned. A butterfly wing in the dust of my stomach attempted to flutter. I imagined a combat-booted foot stomping it back down.

"Excuse me." It was Vincent. "What is it you need?"

Perhaps it was because Piper was with me, I'm not sure, but I was able to put my name on the signature cards in a New York minute.

"While I print out copies of the statements for the last two months, is there anything else I can do for you?" Vincent asked.

"Can I get access to the safe deposit box? I have a key." I held it up.

"Of course. Follow me." I did as I was told, with Piper on my heels.

Vincent took us to the vault where he produced a key that he used alongside mine. Together, we pulled out the box. He then escorted us to a private booth.

"You know," I said to Piper once Vincent was out of earshot. "I think this proves I don't have trust issues. I could kick you out right now." Though, the real reason I was glad he was there is that I was a little afraid of what the contents of that box might be: a computer disk with damaging information? Camera memory cards with incriminating pictures? Ancient secret recipes he'd been stealing to use in the restaurant? More peppers? Zombie dust?

"Yes, you could kick me out. But then again, you'd be mad at yourself because I'd leave without showing you what I have."

And there was that.

"You'd bring it to my house tonight anyway," I said.

"How do you know?" He sat on a folding chair beside me.

"You'd get hungry at some point."

"Are you procrastinating for a reason?"

I slid into the free chair. He was right. I was procrastinating. But I didn't see any reason to confirm that for him.

I opened the box. It held only a folded piece of paper. I smoothed it out and read:

Mandy, my dear:

You know how I always said I can act like an adult and be responsible whenever it was necessary? I believe I'm proving my point now. I rather have the feeling I'm in over my head and I may not make it out of the water alive.

Chances are, if you're reading this, I'm at the Great Tiki Bar in the sky. But no worries, my dear, I had one hell of a ride here and have no regrets other than I never got to see you blossom. If nothing else, I hope you learn from me. My only wish is that you finally become comfortable in that beautiful skin of yours so that you allow yourself to be free to enjoy life.

Remember, we're all going to die at some point. Whether you go young or old, which would you rather look back on: a life of fear and inhibition or a life of joy and good times?

The restaurant was our dream. Who knows? Maybe I'm not in the kind of danger I suspect I am. In which case, maybe I'm reading this letter to you over margaritas at the Revenge Café's bar. Maybe we're toasting our new joint adventure and laughing at me behaving like a big boy without it being necessary.

But instead, if you're reading this by yourself in the bank vault, please know that I made sure nothing could point back to you. I only wanted to give you a push in the right direction. Follow your dream, Mandy babe.

I have always loved you but knew better than to tell you.

Chance.

p.s., if you need anything from me, look in my cloud. ChanceEncounter. Never2L8.

Chapter 19: Trying to Make Sense

I stared at the letter and turned it over to see the back. There was no date anywhere.

"Is that Abbott's handwriting?" Piper asked.

"Yes."

"What does it say?"

Without responding I handed the note to Piper and watched his face while he read it.

"Sounds like you were the love of *his* life," Piper said.

"I never knew."

"Yeah, I get the feeling you keep people at arm's length." Piper returned the letter to me.

I kept quiet.

"What do you think that bit at the end means?" he asked. "The part that looks like code?"

"It's his company name and slogan."

"Why put that on such a personal note?"

"I have no idea."

"Are you all right?" he asked.

I shook my head.

"Take your time." He put his hand on my shoulder. "We don't have to hurry out of here."

I wanted badly to lean against him. To press my face into his neck and breathe, inhaling him as deeply as I could.

Instead, I closed my eyes and tilted my head back against the chair more confused than ever.

"Now what do I do?" I asked the ceiling when I opened my eyes.

"Regarding?" Piper answered.

I wasn't sure at first. But after a minute to prioritize, I looked at him. "About Chance. I have no leads, no new clues. I don't know where to look. I'm wondering if Callwood is somehow involved but I can't find a direct connection. What do you think?"

"I don't know about Reggie. But I have something that probably belonged to Abbott," he said. "I'd like you to see it and maybe help me with it."

"What is it?" I folded the letter and stuffed it in my purse.

He hesitated again. "It's something one of my men found this morning. Right now it's in my car."

"We can go." I stood up. "I think I should probably get back to the restaurant anyway."

We exited the bank. Piper headed over to an unmarked police SUV.

"I'm going to walk. It's only a few blocks," I said to him.

"That's a good idea. I'll walk with you and we'll see what your friend does." He opened the door and pulled out a white, plastic shopping bag. "But we'll wait until we're inside your restaurant, in privacy, to look at this."

"What is it?"

"You'll see soon enough." We headed toward the restaurant.

After a few paces, he cleared his throat. "Other than this, the only lead I haven't personally followed up on yet, is finding your Rastafarian driver."

"Oh, yes, him." I ran my hand through my hair.

"Yes, him. A couple of my men went to Duffy's and of course no one knew a Rasta named Charlie there."

"Of course?"

"They were uniformed men."

"I see. Um, did I tell you I saw him again?"

"I knew it." Piper stopped walking and partially turned, grabbing my arm. "I knew you were still holding out something." I saw his eyes slide behind us. I glanced too and saw the slim man had left his lamp post and, without question, was following us.

"It wasn't intentional. I totally forgot." We resumed walking away from the bank. I filled Piper in on meeting Charlie at the Fruit Bowl. He explained that *big people* was slang for important or powerful people and confirmed *vex* meant *very angry.* So theoretically, I now knew what the Rasta had said: Chance had been social with important people and now those people were angry. I just didn't know what that actually meant.

"Would Callwood be considered a big person?" I asked.

"I guess it would depend on who you were talking to." Piper stopped walking at the base of the steps to the restaurant and held the bag toward me. "Go on in. Take this into the restaurant and open it in the privacy of your office."

"What's in it?" I reached for the bag, but he didn't let go.

"You'll see when you open it."

"You're right. Why waste my powers of ESP to see it now?"

He grinned. "It's a camera."

"What?" I tried to pull it away. He tugged it out of my hands and swung it back behind him, making me lean against him as I tried to grab it again. He smelled good. So good, I wanted to rub my face against his chest.

"Wait till you're inside," Piper said. "Since we don't know who killed him yet, you may not want just anybody seeing what's in this bag."

"Oh, right." His pectorals peeked out at me from the V-neck of his pullover. I finally understood how men felt when they couldn't raise their eyes above my collarbones.

"I'm going to talk to your friend, now." He released the bag and stepped away from me. "I'll come in to see you when I'm done."

Inside the restaurant, Ginger and Butterworth were sitting next to each other at the bar, heads bent close. I waved hello to Francis as I sped past. In the office I dropped the bank statements on my desk. Their importance paled in comparison to the camera, which felt portentously heavy in the bag. As if weighted somehow with news I needed to learn before I discovered anything else.

I watched my arms and hands. It seemed they belonged to a robot and not to me as they opened the bag. They lifted out the camera and set it on my desk. A tiny label on the bottom read: *Chance Encounters: Don't Wait Til It's 2L8. Make your memories now.*

I clicked it on. The display panel lit up with pictures of a restaurant or bar that was not the Revenge Café. I scrolled through, disappointed, thinking perhaps the pictures were of another location Chance had wanted to buy.

"My team found it among a bunch of other photography

equipment in a second-hand thrift store this morning," Piper startled me. He sat in a chair on the other side of the desk. "It was mixed in with several other pieces of equipment. Only a few had labels like that on them. We dusted it for prints."

"And?"

"Unfortunately, the place cleans everything with those anti-bacterial wipes. Not many prints were to be found and what was found were only of the workers in the store."

"Where did it come from?"

"The woman who sold it to us wasn't sure. Said a man dumped them on Saturday, claiming he didn't need them anymore. He didn't even take a receipt for charity deductions."

"Sounds like something Chance would do."

He reached across the desk with his palm facing upward. "I need to take it back and download the images. But I want you to see something first." I gave him the camera.

"Did you get all the equipment?" I asked. "Were there other cameras?"

"There were more, but we only took what had labels on them."

"Right. And Chance probably got bored with the job and never got around to finishing the task of identifying his equipment." I sighed. "He wasn't real good with responsibility."

"Well, even if he did I'm not sure it would help much. We couldn't confiscate this equipment, we had to buy it. He never filed a report that anything was stolen." He scrolled through the photos as he spoke. "There's no proof that the store didn't get them from anyone but him, so we may not be able to use it as evidence against anybody for stealing it. However," he stopped on a picture and looked up at me. "On the other cameras we took, the pictures were all of weddings and parties. This one had a different subject. It looked like he was trying to get photographs of a few particular people without them knowing." He handed the camera back to me. "Do you know these men?"

I looked at the image and heard myself gasp.

"I'll take that as a yes," Piper said.

I didn't, couldn't respond.

"Mandy?"

"I know one of them." I cleared my throat, unable to go on. Piper came around behind me and bent down to look over my shoulder.

"Which one?" he asked, his voice soft, close to my ear.

I pointed to a man sitting at a table, a glass of wine in one hand, laughing. He was handsome, young-looking for his age, which I knew was forty-seven. Although he was casually dressed, I also knew his clothes had been purchased by a private shopper and custom tailored for him.

After a few minutes I tested to see if my vocal chords still worked. "His name is Malcolm Wenner. He's the owner of several magazines. All food, travel and antiquities related. Chance and I used to work for him."

"Is that all you can tell me about him?"

I put the camera back on the desk. Which wasn't good enough. I put it back in the plastic bag, tied it shut with a double knot, paused, then moved it to the other side of the desk.

"Chance and I met when we worked as a photo-journalist duo for him, Malcolm. He had just one magazine at the time." I closed my eyes and took a long breath. "I was, uh, involved with him for a long while. We broke up when Chance gave me proof that Malcolm was sleeping with other women. We were fired then."

Piper returned to the chair on the other side of my desk. "And you still don't think you have a trust issue?"

"I don't. I'm just cautious." I opened my eyes in time to see him grin.

"I guess you haven't seen him since?" he asked.

I shook my head.

"What about Abbott? Has he been in contact with him?"

"I'm not sure." I pinched my forehead together and blew out a loud sigh. Piper sat quiet, waiting for me to continue. "Up until today, this minute, I would have said for sure, *no.* But, now I don't know what to think."

"What did you both do after you were fired?"

"Chance couldn't get another job on the mainland, so he started his special event business here. Another photog friend got him set up. I kept trying to write about food but it didn't pay me enough to eat. I didn't want to leave Florida, and the only job I could get there was covering crime in the Caribbean for the Ft. Lauderdale Sun. I wasn't exactly qualified at the time, but I had print media experience, was inquisitive, and no one else wanted the job. That's how I came to write about crime and food. Eventually I was able to land the gig as a TV investigative reporter."

"Did you ever work for one of Wenner's competitors?"

"No. Not really. I still occasionally freelance a food column but I sell to several publications. I don't think he could want revenge on me for that. Not enough to kill my best friend."

"How long has it been since you left him?"

"Probably five or six years ago." Actually, it was really six years and two months. If I thought it mattered, I could have given him the exact number of days. I would just need a few minutes to figure out which months had thirty-one.

He picked up the bag. "Do you think it's possible your old boyfriend knew that Abbott was in love with you?"

"No! I mean, I didn't even know."

"What kind of man is your ex-?"

"Meaning?"

"Is he the kind to be patient while he plots revenge?"

"That is one way you could describe Malcolm." The hollow feeling in my stomach gave way to a heavy weight pulling me down. Piper came around to my side of the desk and leaned against the edge.

"Listen," he took my hand. "I know it might be tough, but if you could call anyone, maybe old co-workers or other people from the magazines and ask if they'd seen the two of them together, or had heard anything recently. That could be helpful for the case."

"Right. I'll see what I can do." I stood up, effectively pulling my hand from his. I knew I couldn't do two things. One: I couldn't let him touch my hand like that for very long and control myself. Two: I couldn't talk to anyone remotely connected to Malcolm, even if it helped the case.

"I can probably give this to you later today," he said, holding up the bag with the camera. "As I said, we still need to download images. But if there's any reason why you would like to have it, it's yours."

I nodded, though there was no reason why I'd like to have it.

"And, uh ..."

"Uh?" I asked, pretending my insides weren't ready to pour out all over the place.

"I started to tell you I have yet to follow up on your Rasta."

"Oh, right." I'd forgotten all about him again.

"You said he invited you to join him at Duffy's right?"

"Yes, why?" The question seemed trivial and pointless given the possibility that Malcolm could have killed Chance because of me.

"It seems odd he'd go there as a customer. Most of the Rastas here are farmers on the west side of the island. Duffy's is on the east, over near Red Hook. When my men were there, they met a Rasta who works there, but his name isn't Charlie. I think I'd like you to see him, see if he's your driver. Why don't we go there and have dinner tonight?"

"OK." I said without any of his words really registering.

"Good. I'll pick you up around six-thirty, then." He left. I watched him go through the door, unintentionally making room for cogent thought. Why couldn't we go to Duffy's now? Had Piper just invited me out on a date?

Chapter 20: Something Better

"Mandy, honey," Ginger said when I ran out to the bar. "You won't believe this. Look what Chester brought in." She pulled a glass from the rack. "You drinking today?"

"Just a little." I was almost proud of myself that she didn't just assume I was drinking. Similarly, I hoped she wouldn't think *just a little* actually meant *just a little.* The idea that I may be going on a date with Piper was a good enough reason to have a drink. But coupling that with the idea that Malcolm might have killed Chance, rather suggested I needed more than just a little.

"Good, 'cause Francis created another something special." She turned around to retrieve a pitcher.

I took a stool by Butterworth. A pile of wrinkled and torn papers lay before him on the bar.

"Mandy, love," he said. "I found my notes on the history of your estate here."

"My what?"

"Your estate. Villa Olga. Remember I said I had the whole history in my research?" Butterworth tried to tap his unruly pile into order, a few pieces slid to the floor.

I vaguely remembered him saying he had more to tell us about our ghost whenever he could find his notes, which apparently he'd kept hidden in a rat's nest. I wasn't sure I was in the right frame of mind to hear and comprehend it, nor was I even sure whether or not I cared about any of it. And I still wasn't clear on why he was such an expert. Regardless, I was now determined to let him enlighten me on the full history of the estate. He was my only option for diversion, unless I guzzled rum.

"When these islands were still part of a Danish colony," Butterworth started, his fingers frittered through the pages, though he was looking at me. "The very land where this here restaurant now stands was the first to have a building. The governor, Jurgen Iverson, himself built it, well his slaves actually, for himself and his first wife Birgitte. She hated living here. It was a bit hotter and wilder than what she was used to in Denmark, as you would guess, yes?"

"I would guess." I gratefully accepted the drink from Ginger and sipped Francis's something special. It was under named. "What the hell is this?" I asked Ginger.

"We're still working on a name, sugar," she said. "Like it?"

"Love it. Stick with Something Special for the name until we come up with something better. Ooo! That's it. Let's call it Something Better." I slugged back a larger swallow. "So is that who you think is haunting this place?" I asked Butterworth.

"Birgitte could indeed be the ghost," Butterworth said. "She was the first on record to die here when her home caught fire in the middle of the night. Some believe it was an arsonist's attempt to kill her Jurgen, because he ruled with an iron fist." Butterworth's foot worked hard to keep his leg bouncing while his fingers shredded napkins. The napkin bits littered the area around him like snowflakes. I glanced down at them, briefly wondering who was going to clean it up, but then an image of Malcolm unconscious, with broken white bits of porcelain surrounding him popped into my head. I looked into Butterworth's eyes again.

"So then," he continued, "long after Iverson left, a wealthy Russian bought the land to use as a water station for ships coming in. The Russians decided to make it their consulate and that's when it was named Villa Olga, after the aristocratic wife of the Russian consulate."

"I see." I sipped.

"He wasn't exactly faithful to her and had several affairs." I watched Butterworth shuffle through his pages until he found the notes he wanted to shove in my face. I peered at a wrinkled and stained page of indecipherable handwriting and could clearly see Malcolm, unconscious at my feet while I held the bottom of an expensive vase in my hands. "It's believed she got mad and, when she had had enough, she set the place afire when he and his mistress were sleeping. The true tragedy is that only the wife herself was killed." Butterworth slid backwards off his bar stool and leaned his hands against it, as if ensuring it stayed on the floor.

"Wow," I said because I really had no idea what else to say and he looked like he was waiting on something to come from me.

"Yes," Ginger said. "Two fires leading to the deaths of two women."

"Right." Butterworth just couldn't contain himself. He paced in circles as he continued the history-lesson-cum-circus-act. "In the late 1800s when this island was *the* place for the world's first super-wealthy tycoons, a brothel was built here. Would you believe it was set on fire by a love-smitten fellow?"

"Um, yes I would believe," I said, the alcohol in the Something Better finally melting my nerves. "I mean, why not? There seems to be a lack of creativity when it comes to killing people around here."

"You're funny, honey," Ginger clinked her Something Better against mine.

"And then," Butterworth went on, "once the U.S. took ownership, a gambling house was built out of the ruins, which was later used as a quarantine station during World War II, where many a men died here. And finally, in the early 1980s an arsonist set the place ablaze."

"Anyone die then?" I asked

"Not that it's been reported."

"I see." I finished my drink and let out a sigh for more reasons than Butterworth and Ginger were aware of. "Now what do we do with all this information?"

"We're still working on that part," Ginger said. She refilled my glass and I decided to call the drink lunch. She also poured another one for herself and Butterworth, which made him sit down again. We drank in silence as I glanced over Butterworth's notes.

"Why do you have all this?" I asked him.

"My family has been in these islands since the mid-1600s. I grew up with ancient stories and local folk lore around me. I love it and can't get enough of it."

"Chester really wanted to be a history professor, but his daddy wanted him to go to law school," Ginger piped in.

"Well, it's a good thing you wound up here," I said to him.

"Had no other place to go, really. I can't give legal advice on the British islands. They have stricter laws about that there." He beamed at Ginger. "Though I'm happy to be here now."

"And how long have you been here then?" I asked.

"Over a decade." He slurped his drink, a little dribbled out the corner of his mouth.

"So you meant it then when you said you knew everyone on the island?"

"Just about."

"Do you know a Rastafarian named Charlie?"

He laughed, spitting out his Something Better in a spray.

"What's so funny?" Ginger asked, wiping his chin and the bar, clearing off the soggy napkin shreds. I couldn't help but feel it was a terrible waste of the booze but I was refined enough not to lick it up.

"There are no Rastas named *Charlie.*" He ducked his head and grinned like a school boy. "*Charlie* is Rasta slang for penis."

Which explained Piper's reaction when I told him. I groaned, slumped before my drink and for some reason remembered I owned the place. "So, uh, Ginger, how's business?"

"Not bad for a place with no marketing to date."

"I got a copy of the bank statements. They're in the bin on my desk. Should we go over them?"

"We can, but you know what? I gotta go shopping. Did I tell you I invited an entire cruise ship to come to dinner tomorrow night for our grand soiree?"

"What? Can we seat that many?"

"Not everyone, of course, but the whole ship won't come. Besides, it is one of the smaller vessels. We just better be all prettified for the ones who do show. Do you have yourself a nice cocktail dress?"

"I don't even have a set of clean clothes for tomorrow."

"Then let's go spend some money."

"But shouldn't we make sure we can pay everyone?"

"Honey, what difference is it going to make between now and tomorrow morning? We'll go over the statements in the morning when we can count in the cash we get tonight. Sound good?"

"I guess so."

"Good. Now then, lunch is covered, but I'll need to be back before the evening shift starts."

I went into the office to get my purse and noted she'd said nothing about whether or not I needed to be there for anything that evening.

"So did you need me here tonight?" I asked when I returned to the bar. "I, um, actually have, you know, um plans."

"That's alright, sugar. You don't have to be here every night. So tell me, will you be checking out the competition with that strong silent man?" She came around the bar and kissed Butterworth on the cheek. I had to avert my eyes.

"Who?"

"That police detective who has the hots for you." She looped her arm in mine and led me out.

Ginger led me away from the restaurant, toward a duty-free shopping district. We travelled only about a half block before I saw the slim man was following us. I set my purse down on a street vendor's cart to rummage for my cell phone. Piper answered at the first ring.

"That camera threw me off my game." I said. "Did you talk to Slim?"

"I did. But you should know that already since you're apparently on a first-name basis."

"It's not a time to joke. He's still following me."

"Go talk to him. He's trying to get brave enough to talk to you."

"What?"

"He wants a job."

"Why hasn't he approached me directly?"

"When you talk to him, you'll understand."

I clicked off and headed directly toward the man, pulling Ginger along with me, in case he and Piper were working together on something sinister I didn't know about.

"Good Afternoon," I said to him. "I just spoke with Police Detective Matthew Piper. He suggested I talk to you."

"Th- th -thank you." He cast his eyes to the ground.

"Is there something I can help you with?"

"I - I n-n-n-need a j-j-j-ob. I-I-I am a b-b-baker."

"A baker?" I asked, looking at Ginger. "We need a baker right?"

"We do indeed. Ours hasn't shown up for work since the uh . . . the incident." Ginger batted her southern bell pretty blues at him. "Can you do pastries, sugar?"

"Y-y-yes." His eyes widened. "But—" he pulled his left hand out of his pocket. He was missing two fingers and his arm was just noticeably shorter than his right arm. "I-I am good. I promise."

"I'm sure you are," I said. "Ginger, should he come in tomorrow morning?"

"Be there by nine o'clock, but you know after tomorrow you'll have to be in hours earlier than that."

"Yes ma'am." His smile lit up the Caribbean.

"Great, we'll see you then." I smiled back at him.

"So, was it that soft heart of yours that ended up causing you those trust issues?" Ginger asked after he walked away.

"I got a normal heart and I don't have trust issues. I'm just cautious."

"Uh huh."

We'd turned back around and headed toward the shops again.

"Then, does this mean you think I'm safe with Chester as long as I'm cautious?" she asked, stopping to window shop a boutique.

"You might be safe. I just don't see how you're a good match. I mean, he doesn't seem like your type."

"And you know me so well, do you?" She entered the shop and headed right to a clerk. "Good afternoon. That red number in the window. Do you have that in a four?"

The woman eyed Ginger up and down, her upper lip lifted into a slight snarl.

"It's not for me honey," Ginger said. "It's for her."

"Oh, yes." The woman left to go to the back.

"Apparently," I said. "I know you as well as you know me, seeing's how you just picked out a dress I'd never wear."

"Until you see how good you look in it, trust me."

"So maybe I'm right about Chester?"

"You know why I'm here, honey?" She leaned into a mirror and fluffed her hair.

"For a fresh start, isn't that what you said?" I browsed a rack of lacy tank tops on sale.

"Yes, and though it's the truth, that's only what I was telling strangers. You wanna hear the whole truth?" She turned to face me.

"Only if it's not going to make me regret hiring you. I like having someone around who knows what she's doing."

"Ha! Well, look closely at me, at my face. What do you see?"

I stared hard at her. "I see you."

"And what do I look like?"

"A pretty, red-haired, blue-eyed woman of about forty."

"Good to know." She grinned and turned her focus to a rack of dresses that might have been beach cover-ups. I couldn't tell which. "The day I decided to come back to St. Thomas was on my forty-fifth birthday. My mamma had sent me a card with a 5,000 dollar gift certificate to a plastic surgeon. She thought the frown line in my forehead was too deep and that I wouldn't be able to get myself a new man as good as my ex-husband unless I got myself fixed."

"Ouch." I pulled a few of the dresses off the rack.

"Yes, that's what I thought at first. Then I thought about when and how I got that damned frown line. And you know what? I got it when I agreed to be a good little girl and marry a man my mamma approved of and have a couple of ungrateful kids. While I slaved my ass off running those damn restaurants, he was screwing around, having a good time with cocktail waitresses. And did he get a frown line? No." She slammed her hand down on a display shelf making a wedge-healed shoe wobble. I grabbed it before it fell.

"I got myself drunk but good that day. Went to our, *his* restaurant and next thing I knew, I was arrested. I don't know. I lost my mind for a few minutes and tried to give my husband a frown line of his own with a paring knife." I flashed back to the photo of him on his Facebook page and winced. "Yeah, well, he wasn't hurt that bad. Anyway, the last time I remembered not frowning all the time was when I was here. And I didn't want to frown anymore."

"I think I understand," I said taking the dress from the clerk. "Thank you and do you have these shoes in a seven?" I handed her the wedge shoe. "But, Chester? He's, well, he's a mess."

"I know." Ginger smiled at me and pulled another dress off a rack. "Good this is an eight, it should fit." She held it before her in front of a full-length mirror. "Chester reminds me of my boys when they were toddlers and too young to talk back or be disrespectful. Every time they looked at me, they usually had food on their faces, but they would look at me with true love and adoration. I want that again without having to change diapers."

She folded the dress over her arm. "But you know what? He's so intelligent. He knows all about art and history. His parents are both dead. He inherited everything from them. He's filthy rich, but do you know what he does with his money? He gives it to organizations that do Caribbean research: genealogical, art, history and culture.

He wants to help save the richness and beauty of the people here. He could be out blowing all that cash on himself and pissing it away. Isn't that something?"

I guessed so.

She convinced me to buy the red dress and I convinced myself to buy the wedge shoes and a couple of the casual dresses that may have been beech coverups. At another store I picked up some cargo shorts and tops.

Ginger seemed perfectly at home and comfortable in her skin the entire afternoon. I kept thinking I was borrowing someone else's life. I hadn't been that kind of female for years: the kind who went out with girlfriends, confiding secrets, talking about men. Not since I met Malcolm, and I had met him when I was too young. I mostly ate alone and shopped alone now. It's a little hard to keep friends when you perpetually hide their car keys.

Chapter 21: Almost Makes Sense

Lydia was still at the house that Thursday evening when Piper came to pick me up. I heard his knock on the door but she beat me to it and let him in.

"Hi," I said from the guestroom doorway. "I'm almost ready."

"Take your time," he answered.

I went to the sofa to sit while I buckled the straps on my new wedge heeled sandals. I was also wearing one of the new sundresses, hoping I wasn't sending the wrong message. I still wasn't sure if it was really a beach cover up, or even if there was a difference. In Florida, it wouldn't be a big deal. In the Caribbean, where people dressed a little more conservatively, the dress might be telling Piper (and Lydia) I was on the fast, loose and easy side.

Shod, I stood and caught his eyes scan my body, quickly, as if he wanted to do it without me noticing.

"You look nice," he said, staring out the front window.

"Thanks." I approached him trying to make myself relaxed enough to banter. In the heels, I was almost eye-to-eye with him. "You do to, even with the extra fur." He wore a black button-down shirt with a pair of dark jeans. Tiny white hairs littered his chest and shoulders. I wiped them off. "Must be a giant of a dog."

"Nah," he grinned. "He's just a puppy. Likes to be in my arms. I guess he feels safe there."

I could only imagine. And it was too easy to imagine how it would feel in his arms. I had to step away.

"I think we're leaving now," I called to Lydia. "Mrs. Abiff?"

"Out h'ye."

Piper followed me to the front door. Lydia was outside pouring rice in a pile by the porch steps.

"Dere," she said and straightened up. Her eyes gave me a critical once over, but she didn't spit or do anything that would suggest she didn't approve. "Now listen. Dere's an ill wind here. You leave dat broom be." She pointed, with a cigarette in her hand, to an upside down broom beside the door. "And pretend you don't see dis rice. I'm doing whatever I can to keep de jumbies away from you. Don't you go working against me by accident. You understand?"

"I think so." I glanced back at Piper. He gave me a curt nod. "Um, Mrs. Abiff. I don't know much about jumbies but are they like ghosts?"

She looked me hard in the eyes. "Why?"

"I was wondering. The people at the restaurant don't want to work on weekends. There are ghosts doing bad things there then."

"And?" She squinted against the curl of cigarette smoke that blew up toward her face.

"And I was wondering if a broom and rice would work at the restaurant, too."

"Ha!" she threw her head back and laughed. "Dose kinds of ghosts work different den jumbies. You got to find out what dey want. You know, I told Mr. Abbott I'd take care of his ghosts if he wanted me to."

"Yeah? Why didn't he take you up on it?"

"He said he was more scared of crazy Peruvians den ghosts."

Chills went down my spine.

"What did he mean?" Piper asked. His hand was on the middle of my back, which may have been the cause of the chills.

"How would I know?" She turned to walk toward her car. "I never understood his English too good." She opened her car door and yelled at me before shutting it: "I'll get wi' dat red-haired lady 'bout de ghosts."

I almost felt sorry for the ghosts.

I made sure the patio doors were locked, set the alarm, and locked the front door behind me, testing it to be sure. Then I went around to the back to test the patio door, to be certain it was locked too.

"Anything else happen I should know about?" Piper asked holding the door to his SUV open.

"No, why?" I didn't get in.

"You always that secure?"

I laughed. "No, but Mrs. Abiff made me nervous."

"You don't trust her, either?"

"I do trust her! I don't trust the jumbies. She didn't put a broom by the back door."

"That almost makes sense." He nodded his head. "So why aren't you getting in the car?"

"I, uh, I was hoping I could drive."

He tilted his head and raised his eyebrows. "You got control issues, too?"

"No. I'm nervous in cars."

"I remember that."

"I'm less nervous when I drive."

He shut the door to his truck and walked over to the Jeep. "You know your back bumper is loose?" he asked.

"Yeah, I had some trouble backing out of a spot by the sea wall at the restaurant." I climbed in the driver's seat. "I got stuck on the guard rail," I finished when he got in.

"You got stuck ... How did that happen?" He clicked his seatbelt buckled.

"It takes me a while to get used to new cars. I'm still trying to figure out where the Jeep actually ends."

"I see." He pulled on the seatbelt as if to test it.

I drove to the end of the driveway. "What's the address?" My hand hovered in front of the GPS screen.

"I don't know. I can tell you how to get there."

I cleared my throat. "OK then. Well. So." I paused and gave him my most glamorous smile. "The thing is: I need quiet while I drive. You can tell me when I need to turn. But that's all you can say. And give me fair warning. Got it?"

"I don't mind driving."

"I'm sure. But I mind less if I'm driving."

He knit his brow. "I'll be quiet except for when you need directions."

"Good." I waited for several minutes and after not seeing any cars, I darted out onto the road. I could feel Piper staring at me while I drove. It made me more nervous, but I couldn't tell him that until I was able to stop.

"You're staring at me. That's creeping me a little," I said as soon as I stopped at the main road.

"Because you're scaring me. You alright?"

"Yes."

"OK. Go left here and I'll try not to look at you."

"Thank you."

I took a deep breath and turned left, reminding myself to keep to the left side of the road. There was a *thud* when the front, driver's tire went off the road. I jerked the wheel, getting the Jeep back in the lane with a lurch and slowly accelerated to a safe, for me, speed.

A car came around a bend toward us, taking up more than its fair share of the road. I held my breath and swerved to the left. Piper clutched the dash with both hands to keep upright.

"You sure you're okay?" he asked.

"Yes! Don't talk." I stopped at an intersection.

"You see all right?"

"What do you mean?"

"You don't have a stop sign."

"I know. But people run through intersections all the time."

I inched half-way through the intersection and sped across the rest of the way, slowing back to a safe speed when I was on the other side. Another car came by in the opposite direction and I swerved again to avoid hitting it.

"Have you had your depth perception checked?" he asked. "Why are you swerving out of the way like that?"

"They were almost in my lane." I slowed even more so I could talk and drive at the same time.

"They weren't even close to your lane."

"Shh."

"They were on my side. You didn't need to swerve."

"SHH!"

I continued down the mountain road and entered an area where homes abutted the street. Several other roads crossed over. I couldn't quite keep my breathing quiet as I forced myself not to stop at each intersection.

At one point I thought a car was about to run a stop sign. I slammed on the breaks. Piper's knees crashed into the glove box.

"Jesus!" he yelled. "What the hell are you doing?"

"Stopping."

"Why?"

"I thought that car was going to run the sign. I was trying to avoid hitting him."

"Usually you can tell a car is about to stop because it slows down. Didn't you notice it slowing?"

"No, I just saw it for the first time at the intersection."

"You have to look ahead, you know."

"I can't do that."

"Why?"

"That would cause long-term paranoia. I'd rather deal with spurts of short-term stress."

"You serious?"

"As a heart attack."

A horn behind me honked.

I crept forward.

"Are you the person who was ticketed for driving too slowly this morning?"

I nodded.

"I thought that was just a joke going around the precinct."

"I TOLD YOU NOT TO TALK WHEN I DRIVE!" I yelled, almost going off the road because I can't control a car and yell at the same time.

"Pull over now!"

I did as I was told.

"As someone who promised to serve and protect the public, I cannot let you continue driving to Duffy's."

"Just why not?"

"It's too dangerous. Get out of the driver's seat."

"What?"

"If you can't handle this road, there's no way in hell you can handle Smith Bay Road all the way down to Red Hook. And I've got two boys and several dogs who need me to live a little while longer. Get out."

I stayed in my seat as he came around to the driver's side and opened the door.

"Do you really think I'm the danger? Look at these lunatics!" I pointed to the road.

"You mean all the cars driving the speed limit and staying in their lanes?"

I watched the traffic for several seconds.

"It never looks like that way when I'm driving," I finally said.

"Have you thought about a defensive driving course?"

"Isn't that what I've been doing?"

"Not at all." He tugged at the seat belt. "Undo it."

I unclicked the buckle and got out, hesitating to move out of the doorway.

"I have a perfect driving record," he said.

"And the longer it remains perfect, the more the odds increase that you'll be in an accident."

"How's your record look?"

I tried to stare him down. He won. I trudged over to the passenger side and got in

He sat and adjusted the driver's seat before moving back onto the road. I gripped the seat belt.

"You all right?" he asked after a few seconds of quiet.

"Of course." Though really, my forehead was already tingling and I was short of breath.

"Really?"

I cleared my throat.

"My kid sister and grandmother were killed when I was driving through an intersection, on a green light. We were slammed by a drunk driver."

"I'm sorry."

"My mom was killed when a semi-truck hit a patch of slippery, wet highway and crashed into her."

"Again, I'm sorry."

"Yeah, well, we all had perfect driving records until both accidents happened." I fought back tears. I didn't want to ruin my makeup.

"Mandy," he reached out and tugged at my arm until I let go of the seat belt. His fingers traveled down its length to hold my hand. "I get your point, and I don't mean to sound harsh, but people die every day in all sorts of ways. You can't protect yourself from them all and when you over protect, you can just as easily cause harm."

I knew all about overprotection. Malcolm had nearly smothered the life out of me with overprotection.

"Right." I said and gasped as a car turned onto the road in front of us.

"Why don't you close your eyes and try to relax?" Piper said, squeezing my hand.

Chapter 22: Duffy's Love Shack

I followed Piper's orders and rode to Duffy's with my eyes clenched shut. With no inhibitions, I practiced the therapeutic deep breathing exercises, too, as we drove all the way down to the southeast part of the island to an area that's almost a town called Red Hook. The blind exercise proved effective as an anti-anxiety measure, but it may have worked too well because I think I dozed a little. When we pulled into the lot, he rubbed my arm, gently, and brought me out of some kind of non-awake state.

"Good thing I'm not a drooler," I joked and shook my head. "I'm sorry. I haven't slept more than a couple of hours a night all week. I guess it's catching up with me."

"I don't mind. You're a better passenger when you sleep."

We stepped out of the car and I laughed. Duffy's full name was Duffy's Love Shack. "Charlie" had offered to take me to a love shack. Finally I understood Piper's reaction back in the interrogation room. And *shack* was the appropriate term: the restaurant literally looked like a green shack had fallen from the sky and landed in the middle of a parking lot.

We sat at a table outside in the lamplight where we had a good view of just about everyone dining there and milling about at the nearby shopping strip.

Piper and I ordered drinks and crowd watched in a comfortable silence while we waited for them to arrive. It would have been very pleasant if it weren't for the fact that I was so damned tired. I stifled a yawn.

"I'm boring you already?" he asked, leaning forward when our drinks came.

"Again, I'm sorry. I'm just tired. Did I mention I haven't been sleeping?"

"Yeah. Considering the circumstances, it's probably normal."

"Right, well, at least I was sober all night last night." Mildly buzzed from the wine, would have been more accurate. But I wasn't drunk, which was the important part. I didn't pass out from the alcohol.

"Which seems pretty healthy. What were you doing?"

"Researching."

"What?"

"Ginger, Callwood," I tilted my chin. "You."

"What did you find out about your general manager?" He swigged his beer.

"Not much. Seems like she is who she says she is. A divorced former restaurateur." I sipped my drink: a rum punch, not straight rum because I was trying to pace myself. "One weird thing, though. Recently she'd been arrested for disorderly conduct and assault but the charges were dropped."

"I saw that too."

"You checked her out?"

"How bad at my job do you think I am? I ran a report on her first thing this morning."

"I never said you were bad. I just wasn't sure if I was being paranoid. You know, some people say I have trust issues."

"Yeah, I heard that, too." He grinned. "I'm guessing that's why you were checking me out."

"Could be."

"The disorderly conduct charge was when she got drunk in her ex-husband's bar." Piper said. "He was the target of the assault, too."

"Ah, well he probably deserved it."

"He's a man, so he must be guilty, is that it?" His eyes mocked and challenged me.

"Not necessarily." I chuckled. "But I saw his Facebook page. He's been keeping company with very skinny, silicon-injected things young enough to be Ginger's daughter."

"Who he may have met after they split, right?"

"Possibly, but I don't think so."

"Whatever happened to innocent until proven guilty?"

"Looked guilty to me." I folded my arms over my chest. "Though, perhaps a divorced *man* would have a different perspective."

"I can't speak for anyone's marriage but my own. And my wife was clearly to blame."

"Of course she is." I burst out laughing. "You're too perfect, as every man is, right? I understand. Your ex-wife and Eve are sorority sisters. Meanwhile, you and innocent Adam are like this." I held up my fore and middle fingers, twisted together and pointed to one of them with my other hand. "This one is you."

"My wife told me I was too hands off in our marriage and that she wanted more involvement." He leaned back in his chair and spread his hands wide open. "Before I could even interpret what that meant, I found her in the arms of another."

"Ooo. I'm sorry."

"Nothing to be sorry for now. We're both happier people now. But I think it shows she was clearly to blame."

"And you being aloof and arrogant had nothing to do with it?" I couldn't help myself. One of my former therapists would have told me I was unconsciously trying to destroy any chance of bonding with him by seeing how far I could push him. But I was pretty sure I was just having fun, maybe even flirting.

"I am not aloof and arrogant." He picked up his beer.

"Then what are you?"

"I'm cool headed and confident." He clinked my glass. "Your nerves calm after that drive?"

I laughed and let him change the subject. "Yes, I'm fine now."

"Have you thought about getting some help for that, that, fear or whatever that you're going to wreck?"

"It's called amaxophobia. And I have tried therapy several times. But you have to drive to go to therapy and then it's really painful once you get there." I took a long drink. "Denial hurts less."

"But think rationally, people die—"

"All the time. I know." I put my glass down and leaned my arms on the table. "And, rationally, with my record, I guess I shouldn't expect anyone to die now for another ten years, so you'd think I'd relax."

"What do you mean?"

"Now that I'm thirty-three, I think everyone's safe. But when I turn forty-two, I should probably break off all communication with the world and hibernate until I'm forty-three. Maybe everyone will stay safe then."

"That's right. I remember now." He nodded. "Maybe that's something you could talk to your housekeeper about. Seems to me she's got some connections." He waved to the waiter and ordered us another round.

"On to business," Piper said, which startled me. Suddenly I wasn't so sure if I was on a date. "Does your old boss live here, on island?" In the lamplight, his eyes held a relaxed expression. I thought I saw a hint of joy, too. Clearly, he liked my company, which made me second guess myself, or, probably more accurately, quadruple or even quintuple guess myself as to whether or not we were on some kind of date/non-date combo.

And looking into those eyes almost made it possible to tell him everything about Malcolm. But thinking about Malcolm ruined the whole scene. Thinking about Malcolm made me hate the way Piper looked at me when he'd scanned my body earlier. Thinking about Malcolm made me a little scared of Ginger's suggestion that Piper had the hots for me. Thinking about Malcolm made me realize I was a fool for buying that red dress because I knew the looks I'd get in it. Thinking about Malcolm made me wish we were back at the jail, in the interrogation room, when I had no idea that Piper was good to dogs.

"I'm not sure." The words came out in an almost whisper and seemed to have an effect on him. Without saying anything, he leaned back in his chair and after a few seconds, removed his eyes from mine to look around the crowd.

I did the same, not recognizing a soul until a man brought my food to me.

"Babylon gyul," the Rasta-probably-not-named-Charlie said. He dropped my plate of macadamia mahi-mahi down on the table. "Wha mek you here?"

"Um, Piper!" I said, reaching across to grab his arm. "This is my Rasta friend."

"Hail up," Piper said to him. He stood and pulled his wallet out of his slacks to show the Rasta his badge. "We came for dinner. You work here?"

"Ine no confusion." The Rasta held up his hands and slowly shook his head.

"We're not looking for trouble," Piper said, sitting back down. "But we would like to ask you a couple questions."

"Meeno—"

"No!" I slammed my palm on the table. "You made sure I knew what you were saying when you were staring at my boobs. Do it now. My friend, Chance, was killed. You're one of the last people to have spoken to him. And you told me he had someone angry at him. Who? And talk so I can understand."

His eyes darted between Piper and me.

"Look," he finally said. "All's I know is Chancey loaned me some cash once and needed a favor de udda day. Said he promised a friend he'd pick her up at de airport but couldn't do it. I said I would. After I took you to his place, I tought maybe he didn't want to get you 'cause you parah in de car."

"Para?"

"Crazy, paranoid," Piper interpreted.

"You drove like a lunatic!" I glared at the Rasta. "But that doesn't matter now. When I saw you at the Fruit Bowl, you mentioned something to me about Chance making someone angry. Remember?"

Again he looked at Piper before answering.

"Who was angry with Chance?" I stood up, putting my face close to his.

"Big person from Sout America. Maybe Brazil? He friend of Chancey," he said, stepping back. "Well, friend no more."

"Because Chance died?"

"Well dere's dat, too. But Chancey had a big qual w' him one night.

"Had a what?" I asked.

"Fought," Piper said.

"What about?"

"Meeno—I don't know. De Sout American," the Rasta spread his hands out wide. "He vexed."

"When was the argument?" Piper asked.

"Maybe T'ursday last? But de man come back Saturday night looking for him. Right after Chancey left. And again Sunday morning, right 'fore Chancey call me 'bout you. De man was asking if anyone knew where Chancey be." Someone pounded the Rasta on the back. He looked behind him then back at Piper. "Yo food be ready. I be back."

He kept his word and retrieved Piper's burger then left us alone at the table.

Piper tapped in a note on his cell phone before eating. We dined in silence. I concentrated on the taste and texture of my meal. The mahi mahi was glazed with some kind of an orangey-teriyaki sauce and encrusted with toasted macadamia nuts and coconut. The mixture of the textures blended as smoothly as the tastes. The shack must have had a castle chef hidden away somewhere.

Near the end of our meal, by the time I'd decided I could probably mimic the sauce in my kitchen at home, the Rasta came by with the check.

"Dere's a jam," he said, pointing toward the bay.

"Good to know," Piper said, slipping him some cash.

"Think there's a language course I could take at the university here?" I asked.

He grinned at me while he chewed a last bite.

"It would help. But I don't think they teach it. It's something that would come with time though." He wiped his mouth. "That sounds like you're planning on being her long term."

"If I succeed at the restaurant, why not?"

"Nothing keeping you on the mainland?"

"I don't have a job there," I sipped the last of my drink. "And I've discovered an income is usually a good thing."

"Right. But no special someone?"

"I've some family," I said slowly, leaning back toward the we're-on-a-date camp. "But they're scattered all over Florida. No one is within an easy drive."

"I get the feeling with you there is no such thing as an easy drive."

I didn't answer. I let my eyes wander the parking lot and the shopping center across the street. I could hear music coming from somewhere behind it.

"Anyway, it would be an easy move. I like it here," I said.

"Not afraid of rock fever?"

"Ha!" I laughed at the thought. Many people from the mainland move to the islands eagerly looking forward to living in paradise without realizing how boring it can be. It's a small island with not much to do besides eat and drink. Most leave within a year, dying to get off the "rock" stuck in the middle of the water. "Piper—"

"My first name is Matt."

I smiled. "Matt, when Chance offered me partnership, I thought it was the greatest idea ever, in part because it is such a tiny island. Small is what I want. I'd planned on getting a place within walking distance to the restaurant. My Uncle John said he'd help me find a house boat if I wanted to live on one docked nearby."

"So you do boats?"

"Sure. Boats and planes I can handle. It's just cars that make me crazy. One of my therapists thought it had something to do with being in close proximity of the hard ground."

He laughed.

"As Butterworth says, everyone has their own brand of weirdness. So, now that you know mine, what's yours?" Although the meal was done and our glasses empty, I leaned back in my chair as if I intended to stay there a while. Which I may have. I mean, it was a rather long way home on dark and twisty roads.

"I am perfectly sane and normal." He, too, reclined in his chair, eyes bright from the reflection of the streetlights.

"Of course you are. Every single dad takes in a pack of dogs, is aloof, arrogant and has a hero complex. And all of them are sane."

"I do not have a hero complex."

"You do to."

"Do not." He laughed and stood up. "So do you want to check out the jam?"

"I don't know. What is it?"

"It's a party."

"Sure." Anything to postpone that long ride and then being alone in the house trying to stay sober until I fell asleep.

We walked through the parking lot to the other side of the shopping center and approached the docks on Vessup Bay. A band was playing, people were dancing. Moko Jumbies stood tall, hovering above the crowd. It looked like there had been a wedding, but a public celebration is a public celebration. No one objected to us being there. The band played Quelbe music, in traditional St. Thomian style and people quadrille danced.

Matt and I danced in place with them, a kind of shuffle step that I was once taught the name of but couldn't remember. The crowd was heavy and thick and kept growing. Eventually, I was pushed from the crowd so that I was dancing directly in front of him, my back barely touching his front. We continued that way, growing closer as our movements slowed to a gentle back-and-forth sway.

The rhythm seemed to lull me to sleep. Though I was standing up, my eyes wanted to close. My head leaned back and found Matt's shoulder. His hand went to my waist. We danced-swayed like that for several beats.

"You keep leaning your head against me, I'm going to respond," he whispered in my ear.

I forced my eyes open wide and turned to face him. Our fronts now touched, sending sparks through me.

"What do you mean?" I asked. It was hard to see him well, as we were not close to any of the larger streetlamps.

"I mean." He paused. Both hands were on my waist now. I could feel the sensation all the way through to my dusty womb. "I like your head. It's pretty. It's funny. It's intelligent. It's also a little nutty, but that only adds to the charm."

I snorted.

"So I'm giving you fair warning. I'll reciprocate if that's what you want, is it?"

We'd stopped dancing/swaying.

"I honestly don't know," I said. The only thing at that moment I was sure I wanted was a good night's sleep *and* I really wanted sex, maybe not in that order. "I'm not really good with relationships."

"Ha!" His head tipped back as he laughed. "And she says that to a divorced man who is ... what did you say? Aloof, arrogant and with a hero complex. As if I'm any good at them."

"Yeah well, there's that and the ten-year thing on my part, too. What if I'm cursed? I mean, you have kids to think of. And dogs."

"I still think you could talk to your housekeeper about that."

"I'm too tired to think, Matt."

"Then I'll take you home. You think on it and when you're ready, you'll let me know." He took me by the arm and led me out of the crowd. It was dark. I stumbled over a curb and bumped the tall legs of a Mocko Jumbie. He grabbed hold of a lamppost to keep balance and leered down at me. The large dark eyes within the bright green mask scared the hell out of me. I couldn't help but wonder if I was an evil spirit.

Matt's hand tugged at my arm. I let him lead me away from the tall guardian.

"One thing though," he said once we were near the Jeep. "You need to keep your head to yourself until you have an answer."

Chapter 23: Jumbies

I made Matt wait while I sat in the passenger's seat and practiced therapeutic deep breathing techniques for several minutes. I envisioned myself lounging on a white sand beach in one of those anti-gravity chairs at sunset. The temperature was the right kind of hot. I could smell gardenia in the air. I could hear the ocean's rhythmic whispers. I transported myself there so thoroughly, I thought I felt the trade winds caressing my skin and heard someone who must have been named Raul calling my name.

Actually, it was the Jeep's air conditioner and Matt.

"Mandy," he tugged on my arm. "I don't mean to rush you, but it's getting late and we're supposed to get a storm soon. You about ready?"

"It's possible." I slowly opened my eyes, blinking them several times. "Let's go."

We made it to my house without me having a panic attack. Granted I was panting and had clutched the assist handle above the passenger door so hard my hands were cramping. But still, no panic attack.

I walked up to the house while he headed toward his SUV.

"Do you want that camera?" He opened his driver side door.

With light only coming from the porch lamp and his car interior, I could see his silhouette backlit and frontlit, detailing an arm extended, a white plastic bag in his hand. The bag with the camera. *That* bag. *That* camera. The camera where the photos of Malcolm were stored.

"We're done with it at the station," Matt said walking toward me, carrying it.

"Right." I cleared my throat and tried to picture myself reaching out to take the bag, the camera. In my head I saw myself do it several times. Each time it only made me nauseous. "I think . . ."

Matt stopped a few inches away from me.

"I can stay a little if you think it would help you look at the photos again," he said. "If you could place a name with the other man, you might open up some new possibilities."

The other man? I was so shocked to see Malcolm's picture I had completely ignored the other man. Without answering, I went to the front door, unlocked it, turned off the alarm and left it open for Matt to follow me.

Inside, at the dining table, I powered on the camera and without letting myself think about what I was doing, I scrolled through the photos until I saw the picture of Malcolm with the mystery man.

I glanced at Matt. He smiled at me. I wanted another drink. But not in front of him.

"I don't know this man," I said. "But I'll try to do some research."

He nodded at me.

"I'm okay now." I stood. "Don't you have dogs to feed or something?

"I do." He stood too. "I don't suppose I need to tell you to lock the doors and set the alarm after I leave, do I?"

I shook my head.

I let him out and shut the door. As soon as I turned the lock, that deep, hollow sense of loneliness descended upon me again. I tried to make it go away thinking about how his hands felt on my waist at the jam. That only made it worse. I opened the door.

"Matt," I called. He was almost at his SUV.

"Yes?" He turned and approached me.

I couldn't think of anything to say.

"You want me to stay awhile?" he asked as he stepped back onto the porch.

Yes. "You can kiss me good night," I said instead. He grinned, touched my cheek and lightly brushed his lips against mine. "Good night, Mandy."

I shut the door and barricaded myself in before returning to the camera. It was heavy in my hands again. As were my eyelids.

"Tonight could be the first night I actually sleep," I said to my reflection in the sliding glass doors. "I should probably take advantage of it."

But if I was going to sleep, I should have had Matt take me to a hotel. By the time I washed up for bed, checked the doors were locked, and set the alarm, then re-checked the doors and alarm, I was wide awake again.

I climbed in bed and stared at the outline of the window. Outside the wind grew from a light rustle to wild blasts and gales as a storm brewed and broke out full force over the house. It seldom storms in April on St. Thomas. That's an August thing. But someone in charge must have forgot just where in the calendar we were because this storm raged hard enough that the Weather Channel should have given it a name. Lightning flashed halos behind the curtains. Thunder made my house rattle. Wind blasted the rain against my window so hard that I wouldn't have been surprised if it broke.

Yet all that was nothing compared to the storm brewing inside of me.

"God damn it, Chance!" I yelled and threw off the sheet. I tore out of the bedroom and stomped into the kitchen. "Why the hell did you do this to me?"

Of course the little shit had no answer.

I ripped open the cabinet door and faced a horror: there was no rum. The wine cabinet held no wine. The only liquid spirit about was cased in a lone, dusty bottle of tequila. I pulled it off the shelf and stared long and hard at the hornet on the label. It was a damn good brand of tequila. But I couldn't do it. Once you've had a bad experience with tequila, you don't want to risk another. And I'd had that bad experience all ready.

I mixed water with orange juice and told myself it would taste just like a V & O. It turned out that I was lying but, ever the champion of denial, I drank it anyway and kept pretending. The real danger was I had very little food to work with.

Anger can be controlled with a series of slicing and dicing, hot oil splatters and salt. Usually. This anger was different. This anger surged with such force it pumped through my veins as if trying to explode out of my body. I wasn't sure how I would contain it. Nor did I know if it would be safe to contain. But I had few resources in the damn kitchen to help me deal with it.

Neither Chance nor I were fans of prepared, convenience foods. We shared the philosophy that that was why restaurants were invented. We preferred to cook with fresh, therefore perishable ingredients, which explained why the pantry held only a box of cereal, old bread crumbs he must have bought for emergency situations, and baking staples. The refrigerator was almost equally bare, aside from an overabundance of condiments.

There was, however, a large plantain in the hanging basket by the sink. I ripped it out, almost throwing it across the room in my desperation to find something, to do something, to get control of something. There was also coconut oil. The plantain was green and firm. I would do up some Cuban chichachirritas.

Peeling the plantain didn't quite quell the rage as well as I expected. I was still making snorting sounds and stomping as I searched the kitchen for a slicer. Where the hell could it be? I blasted around the room, yanking open each cabinet drawer and door one after another to no avail. Not a mandoline anywhere.

"Jesus Christ, Chance!" I hollered and slammed shut the broom closet door. As if to add emphasis, the rain slashed against the windows. I didn't really expect a mandoline to be in there, but I couldn't leave any stone unturned. "You couldn't find a God-damned slicer but you managed to track down Malcolm Wenner. Right? Sure as hell sounds like you finally got your priorities straight."

With a large chef's knife–at least he'd bought decent knives–I concentrated on cutting the thinnest slices of plantain I possibly could. Then while the coconut oil heated, I pealed and pureed a head of garlic. I fried the plantain slices and salted them while they drained on paper towels. Knowing full well how sacrilegious it was, I mixed the garlic with some store-bought mayonnaise. I had no other choice as I didn't have any eggs. If that shit had been alive, I knew there'd be eggs in the refrigerator and I'd able to create a real aioli. Granted I was the one who had polished off the dozen he had, but he ate eggs all freaking time like every proper Englishman does. He never ran out. If he were still alive, we'd have eggs in the fridge. But no. He had to do something stupid like follow Malcolm and get himself killed.

The chopping, frying, mixing and mashing worked. It soothed me enough that by the time I sat at the table to eat, I was able to forgive Chance. He had behaved true to character: on impulse, constantly looking for entertainment. Why not spy on Malcolm and take pictures of him without him knowing?

With the last of my orange juice-water mix, I cheered his eternally-twenty-one-year-old spirit and stood up to wash my dishes. That's when the lights went out.

It might sound crazy, but I find power outages during storms to be rather peaceful and settling. Growing up in Florida, I realized the least likely like time for anyone to do something harmful to you was during a storm. And my tenure covering crime had revealed a similar fact: no one ever had their house broken into during a tropical storm in the middle of the night.

I knew I stood a good chance of being safe from Chance's killer, Malcolm, and any other real-life jumbie until the storm ended. Once that happened, if the lights were still out, the looters would come out with their guns and knives and it would probably be wise to find some place to hide.

In other words, it should have been the perfect time for me to go to bed. My belly was full, my anger had subsided. I was tired and I knew I was safe.

But I took it as a sign from Chance.

My laptop had been plugged in since my arrival and had a full battery of life left and my AirData wireless card was a good, reliable friend who always gave me internet access. I had to look up Malcolm. If I were to be honest with myself, which I hated to be but it was either be honest or risk another bad adventure with tequila, I'd admit I was never angry with Chance at all. I was angry with myself. I was mad at myself for the crazy, lonely, scared little nut-bag I'd become after I'd met Malcolm Wenner.

Google offered more than a quarter of million results when I plugged in his name. I ignored all of them and went directly to the images.

God he was still handsome as ever. Chillingly so. Dark, slicked back hair, a little white at the temples. Tan, but naturally, not from anything sprayed on him. Perfect teeth and piercing Mediterranean eyes. Each photo showed off his chiseled jaw, his natural poise and grace.

In every picture where he was with a woman, she was the hostess of an event or she was on the arm of her date and the three of them were photographed together. Either he hadn't replaced me, or he'd found another one to keep at home, shut in, looking pretty, up on her pedestal until he decided she could go outside.

Malcolm was an admirer, a collector of things that needed to stay perfect, out of sight and out of reach from anyone else who might be interested in seeing or touching them. His prized possessions remained in their proper place, privy only to him, or else steadfastly in his hands when out in public.

I paged down through hundreds of photographs, alternately pissed off at the bastard of a man who had hurt me so badly and equally pissed off at myself for letting it happen. Occasionally, I'd grieve for the person I used to be: the one trusting enough to risk a relationship, to risk loving someone, to risk losing myself.

I'd just about given up on finding a photograph of him and Chance together when I saw one with him and the man in the photograph from the camera. To be sure, I clicked the camera back on and checked. The glow from both pieces of equipment made it clear: it was the same man. I clicked on the image on the monitor and learned the man's name was Carlos Quispe Catunta. Quispe, I knew to be a common Peruvian name.

"Interesting," I said out loud, leaning back in my chair. The name rang a bell. It was a loud bell. I knew I knew it. And after digging around on the internet some more, I knew I was right.

The electric came on before I woke up the next morning. While my cell phone charged, I called the Tutu post office from the house phone to get specific directions. Tired, but not hung over, I drove feeling like my reflexes were on a delay switch. I had trouble making the turns in time.

I still don't understand why none of the countries who had ever laid claim to St. Thomas couldn't have blown a couple of holes in the mountains and made tunnels of straight, wide roadways. There were too many curves and turns climbing and descending the mountains. And I still couldn't figure out exactly where the wheels were on the road, especially when I had to make a right-hand turn and remain in the left lane the entire time.

I neared the juncture where Forty-Two meets up with Donoe Bypass Road. I had to make a right, which isn't a ninety-degree turn there. It's more like a twenty-five degree turn with not a stop sign in sight. I slowed on my approach and the idiot driver behind me decided to pass me on the right, even though my right blinker was on.

I slowed even more to allow him to pass quickly. He thanked me by pulling back into my lane too early, cutting me off, making me swerve and slide against the wall, efficiently smashing the driver's side mirror, until I stopped.

I had to wait for another car to pass before I could backup and get into the road again, where I had to immediately make that stupid, tight, right turn.

I overshot the left lane on Donoe Bypass and went off the road again, into the bushes. Once more I had to backup before I could proceed. Then I drove with a tree branch sticking out of my front grill. I really didn't care. I hoped it scared all the other drivers around me and make them steer clear.

I made it to the post office, went inside and found Chance's box was loaded with mail. Too much to even try to weed through it standing there. I rolled it into a large wad and tucked it under my arm before heading back outside.

My Jeep still glinted in the sun, but along with the back bumper barely intact, the scrape on the passenger side, the broken parking light, driver's side mirror hanging by its wires, and the branch sticking out the front, I noticed all four tires had been slashed and the passenger window was broken.

Matt arrived in about ten minutes.

"Where are you?" he asked when I answered my cell phone.

"In a corner of the post office where I can see everyone come in."

He entered, found me and then walked me back outside.

"You all right?" He put his arm around me.

"Yeah. I'm fine."

"Really?"

"Really. If someone had wanted to hurt me, they would have done so. Taking out my tires was meant to scare or warn me, right?"

"Right." He stopped in front of my Jeep and reeled back on his heels. "Though it frightens me that you think that way."

We watched as a team of police officers worked around the branch to dust for fingerprints.

"So, which part happened when you were inside?"

"Just the tires and window." In vain, I tried to come up with a segue to a different topic.

"And the rest?"

"Do you realize how dangerous it is to drive on this island?"

"Ever since you arrived." He walked over to speak to the tow truck driver. I waited, leaning against his police SUV, wondering why someone had gone to this trouble.

"Where are you heading now?" Matt asked when he returned to me.

"The restaurant."

"I can take you."

"Are we too far to walk?"

"Just keep your eyes closed." He placed both hands on my shoulders and gently shoved me out of the way so he could open the passenger door of his SUV.

"I'll fall asleep."

"So you had a rough night again?"

"Yes, but I stayed sober."

He pulled my hand, inching me closer to the waiting passenger seat.

"And I learned something that I don't want to keep to myself." I kept my feet planted on the cement. There was no reason why we couldn't have a chat in the parking lot.

He grinned and touched my chin. "I'd love to hear it. Why don't you try that self-hypnosis thing you did last night? It almost made you normal on the drive home."

"I am perfectly normal." I shook his hand away. "I just happen to be the only one around who's aware of just how insane this world is."

He stuck his hands in his pockets and raised his eyebrows.

"Fine." I closed my eyes and tried the therapeutic breaths. But there was just too much going on in my head to concentrate. I gave up when I became dizzy instead of relaxed and climbed into his SUV.

"This baby is armored, right?" I asked.

"If you need to think so," he said and slammed the passenger door shut. I clicked on the seatbelt but slid out from under the shoulder harness portion so I could bend over and put my head between my knees.

"What are you doing?"

"Making sure I can't see anything. I'm going to try the breathing exercises again. Please don't talk to me."

I heard him turn the car on and put it into gear. Once I sensed we were on the road, I gave breathing the ole college try. It probably wasn't the wisest thing to do, considering how gravity wanted to pool all my blood in my head. My eyes began to black over.

I shot back up in my seat, shook my head and prepared to die.

"Where the hell are we?" I screamed as he rounded a turn so tight I thought we would end up making a circle.

"We're heading into town," Piper said, not looking at me.

The road straightened and immediately my body pulled up in reflex to an anticipated sideswiping by a car heading toward us. Somehow we missed.

"Eeee!" I thought we were about to slide against a wall. My knees were up to my chest, as if they would be better than an air bag.

"It's all good, Mandy. Close your eyes and breathe."

"Aack!" I swear I felt two wheels leave the pavement as we took a hairpin turn.

"Close your eyes, OK?"

"I love being in cars. I love being in cars. I love being in cars," I chanted with my eyes squeezed shut, knees up, as close as I could get to being in fetal position, all the way to the Revenge Café.

Chapter 24: Potatoes, Asparagus and Dye Jobs

Ginger was already at the restaurant.

"Good morning," I said to her as I strode in. If there's a positive to having a phobia, it's feeling that rush of invincibility that you get sometimes after surviving a near-death situation.

"Mornin' sugar." She handed me several papers. "These are menu ideas. You have a great palate. Let me know what you think."

I had a purpose! Finally there was a line item listed on my job description. Who know I could feel even more empowered?

"Just a warning, there's no mention of a bacon day," she added.

Well that was a letdown. Regardless, she was asking for my input. I could finally offer something to the restaurant. Hallelujah. But first, I needed to talk to Matt.

"So here's the thing," I said after I sat down at my desk. "That other man in the photograph is named Carlos Quispe Catunta."

"You're faster than my people at the precinct." Matt took a seat across from me.

"I needed something to do besides sleep."

He nodded and took out his phone. "Can you spell that name?"

I did as he tapped it in his cell.

"Should I know who he is?" he asked.

"Only if you're into potatoes and asparagus."

"Should we start this conversation over?"

I sat straighter in my chair.

"Senior Catunta is an agricultural specialist from Peru," I said slowly, anticipating his raised eyebrow response.

"That is interesting." He fulfilled my expectations.

"Indeed."

"Peppers?"

"Nope."

"Coca?"

"Nope."

"Do I need to continue guessing?"

"Potatoes. I'm sure that was next on your list, right?"

"Not exactly."

"He was the president of the International Potato Center in Peru and sat on the advisory committee of the World Potato Congress."

"Are you sober?"

"I'm not even drinking Polish vodka, which is made from potatoes."

"Which somehow would make sense right now."

"Yes, well notice I said he *was* not he *is.*"

"I did notice. Why no longer *is*?"

"Asparagus."

"I can get a breathalyzer in here in a matter of minutes."

"I was hoping you'd say *interesting* again."

He laughed. "Go on."

"So, as head of the CIP, which is the Spanish acronym for the International Potato Center, his main goal was supposed to be to further research into growing potatoes in Peru. Peru has the longest potato growing history on the planet, and yet it now imports potatoes and rice as staples. They even import bags of potato chips."

He leaned back in his seat, crossed his arms over his chest and smirked at me. God, he was sexy.

"Well, anyway, the CIP had set up initiatives aimed toward alleviating poverty in Peru by enlarging the potato crop, increasing the number of farmers and farm workers. They also were striving to feed the people with fresher, healthier homegrown products. Sounds good, right?"

"So far."

"OK, so here's the kicker: while Catunta did his part to encourage potato growing, he also got involved with asparagus."

"Those foods go well together?"

"If you use enough butter."

"I'll just stop interrupting with questions. You go on and tell me whatever it is you're trying to tell me." He leaned forward, elbows on knees, fingertips pressed together, shirt falling open so I could see his powerful chest that was such a magnet for my head.

"Yes, well, someone in Peru got the idea that they should grow asparagus, which at first the soil there did well with. So well that the World Bank started investing in the exportation of asparagus from Peru. However, it only did well for a while. Asparagus does not grow naturally in Peru and is quite taxing on the land and water supply. In fact the Ica Valley's ecological system has nearly been destroyed by the demand for asparagus in the States and Britain."

"But they continue to grow it because?"

"Its popularity makes it quite profitable."

"Really? I hate asparagus."

"Me too. Unless it's breaded in Panko crumbs, fried in peanut oil and dipped in a wasabi ranch sauce."

"That might be tolerable. You'll have to make it for me sometime."

"I will."

His grin broadened. My stomach fluttered.

"So..." Piper said.

"So the potato people took notice of the damage asparagus growers were doing and tried to fight it, with Catunta at the helm. However, guess who received millions of dollars from the World Bank to become an agro-exporter of asparagus?"

"Catunta?"

"Right. And when word got out that he was supporting a rival crop, and one that was destroying the Peruvian ecosystem, he had to be let go. Interesting, right?"

"So far."

"Oh, well that's all I got."

He laughed.

"Seriously. I don't know what it all means, but it seems like it should mean something, doesn't it?" The restaurant phone rang. I reached for it but someone answered elsewhere in the restaurant.

"It does." He glanced at his watch and stood. "It's very coincidental that Abbott was recently in Peru and that he'd been taking photographs of the Peruvian man. But how does your old boyfriend fit in?"

"I have no idea."

"Hey sugar," Ginger rapped on the open door. "There's an alarm company on line one saying something about a house alarm going off."

I picked up the phone.

"This is ADT calling for Chancellor Abbott. His home alarm is signaling a glass break and movement in the motion detector."

"Call the police." I slammed down the phone. "Someone broke into my house! We have to go," I said to Matt.

"I have to go," he said. "You'll stay here."

"No way!"

"I'll be going over the speed limit."

"You'll call when you know something, right?"

He left.

I sat at the desk and blew out a long stream of air.

"You all right, honey?" Ginger asked, taking Piper's place in the other chair. "You look like hell."

"I could use a decent night's sleep," I said. "Crazy shit is going on. I'm so confused, I can't sleep."

She stood, shut the door to the office and returned to Piper's seat.

"Tell me all about it, hon."

I gave her a rundown of all the events to date, leaving out the part about looking her up on Intellius.

She puckered her lips and made a kissing sound. "Damn! You sure know how to lead an interesting life."

I laughed. "I guess so. But I'm still tired as hell."

"I know just the thing." She retrieved her purse from a file drawer and handed me a card-key to a hotel room. "My suite at the Wyndham has plenty of room. You go take a nap there. It's room 828."

"Are you sure?"

"Sure I'm sure. You need to be on top of your game tonight."

"Right, but we need to pay everyone today." I picked up the bank statements and glanced through them.

She dragged her chair over next to me.

"All right then, sugar. Let's get it done and over with, then. I hope you know more about this computer than I do. What kind of payroll software do you have?"

I heard the sound but wasn't quite sure what she'd said. Cash register bells rang too loudly in my head. I held in my hands what appeared to be both personal and business bank account statements. Both were well stocked. By the looks of things, Chance, and now I, had more cash than what I thought a bank could insure in an account. I wondered if Butterworth knew a trusty financial planner on island.

I blinked to be sure my eyes still worked after popping out so far in surprise. Oh how I hoped Chance got that cash via legal means. For now, I'd just pretend that it was. At least as far as payroll was concerned.

"Mandy? Honey you OK?" Ginger shook my arm.

I handed her the statements.

"Looks like we're loaded," I said.

She paged through them with a long, low whistle.

"Good Lord," she eventually said and handed the pages back to me. "We can quit that discount for cash customers."

I turned to the Mac and wiggled the mouse to make the screen come to life and found where the program icons hid. Within minutes Ginger said, "I know that one," and pointed. I clicked on it

"That's the most used restaurant payroll program around. Now, if everyone's info is plugged in, this will be a cake walk." She clicked around on the screen. "And it looks like it is. We're sitting pretty, honey. I can do this in my sleep." She gripped my hand. "Which you need. Why don't you go to my room, nap, then get yourself all gussied up. I'll take care of this, print out the checks and then you can sign them when you come back and hand them out to everyone. What do you say?"

"I say it sounds like something I can handle."

I stood and grabbed my purse.

"Don't forget to take your dress."

"My dress?"

"The one hanging on the back of the office door. Remember? Here?" She stood and pulled the dress off the hook. "You hung it here when we got back yesterday and forgot to take it home."

"Oh, that." I hadn't forgotten it. I was seriously considering returning it for something that covered more of my body. And something that wasn't red. A woman has to have the confidence of the winning SuperBowl quarterback to wear a tight fitting red dress in public. I was going to have to do something major with my hair and make-up to pretend I was that strong.

"Yes, that." She shimmied up the plastic." It's just gorgeous. And you'll look just gorgeous in it for our first major soiree."

"Right, our first major soiree. You got any tricks on camouflaging under-eye bags?"

"Sleep! Just get yourself some sleep. Did I tell you?" Ginger continued. "On top of the cruise ship, I called around to the local shops and boutiques to offer discounts to workers there in exchange for putting out our brochures in their shops. Tonight, we have enough reservations from them and that cruise ship that we'll be at full capacity. See? I meant it when I said you need to be at your best." She pulled the dress off the door. "Take it." She forced it into my hands. "And get over to the Wyndham. Take a nap in my suite. I'll be in around five or so to get ready. It'll be like we're young roommates fixin' to go on a double date."

Something I'd never experienced in my life as I'd moved from my grandmother's home to living with Malcolm. I wasn't sure if it would be fun for women our age. But the thought of sleeping anywhere other than Chance's house where the jumbies railed outside so loudly they woke up my own inner demons, was too sweet to resist.

I braved a taxi for the short ride to the Wyndham, made it there alive and found her suite. I also found an old and battered Hawaiian-style shirt I'd seen on Butterworth the day before draped over a desk chair. I tried not to think about its significance. As she had said to me, I might one day sign her paycheck, but that didn't mean I could tell her whose shirts should be in her hotel room. Still, it'd only been a couple of days since she'd met him. Was that really a healthy thing?

The sheets were beautifully white and welcoming. I tried sleeping. But then I thought about the red dress and that I wasn't wearing the right kind of bra and that I needed heels for it.

The Royal Dane shopping district was just a few blocks away. I walked over in search of a lingerie shop and a shoe store. The heels were an easy find. The bra, not so easy. I finally managed to find a sex-toy shop that had an overly ornate thing that was probably never meant for a utilitarian purpose. It held tight, though, and I wouldn't have straps showing.

I was just signing my credit card receipt when I glimpsed a magenta head go by the store window. It was accompanied by a bleached blond one.

I couldn't let go of the theory that the Revenge Café was in a territory rival drug gangs were fighting over, possibly with Reggie Callwood involved in one of them. I headed out the door of the shop and flirted with the idea of calling Ginger to see if she thought the intrigue and suspense from the restaurant being in the center of warring factions would be a good publicity stunt. But then I realized dead tourists were never good for business.

Besides, as I stared in the direction the women were heading, I also realized that I hadn't noticed any other suspicious people in the parking lot. And why would they insist on jobs?

Instead of heading back toward the Wyndham, I followed my vibrant haired acquaintances down the narrow alley lined with shops. At first I was sure to keep a good distance between us and to stay within easy reach of something to hide behind. But after about thirty feet, I realized they were too self-absorbed and stoned to be completely aware of what was going on around them. They stumbled down the street through the light shopping crowd, laughing and pointing at whatever they found amusing. Frequently they had to lean against each other for unstable support.

They tripped passed a store near the end of the alley and realized they'd gone too far. Magenta stopped very quickly and grabbed Blondie's t-shirt, nearly toppling her friend backward. I ducked in a doorway as they turned around and went in the shop. I approached and peaked in the window.

I couldn't see a damn thing. A white, tent-type thing was blocking my view. I had to go inside. Not stopping to think clearly about what I was doing, I went in to get a better look.

The white thing was a screen set up for a photo shoot. I tried to blend in with the few shoppers who had stopped to watch the show. Soon enough, my funky-haired friends came wobbling out of the dressing room wearing bikinis.

"Jesus Christ," I heard the photographer whisper to his assistant. "They're wasted already. You'd think they were supermodels." He sighed. "Okay everybody. Let's get to work."

I left as the assistant tried to direct the girls, calling them Amy and Jessie, into poses fit for an ad campaign.

Matt called just as I returned to suite 828.

"I'm at the restaurant," he said. "Ginger told me you were sleeping. Why are you answering your phone?

"Why did you call if you thought I was asleep?" I set my bags down on a chair and kicked off my sandals.

"I assumed, if you were sleeping, you would have turned the ringer off and I would leave a message."

"Oh, I should do that. But why did you call?"

"To update you. Nothing was stolen from your house that I can tell. Someone came in and was obviously looking for something. But your laptop is still here and the television. Do you have any other valuables tucked away somewhere?"

"No. The only jewelry I brought is the stuff I'm wearing. How could you tell they were looking for something?"

"The place was ransacked."

"Oh hell. Now who's going to clean that up?"

"Call your housekeeper."

"She'll yell at me." I fell on the bed.

"Then you'll have to clean it. Anyway, there weren't any prints inside or out of your Jeep except for your small fingers. But I'm certain whoever slashed your tires is the same person who did this."

"It would make sense. They immobilized me so I couldn't return back home when the alarm went off."

"Right. You're good at this."

"I don't want to be. Any prints at the house?"

"We're still looking. I'm doubting it though. However, the tire slasher also went through your glove box. Unless you had opened it and left it open when you went in the post office. Did you?"

"No."

"Had you looked in there recently? Do you know if there was anything valuable in it?"

"I have looked and all I found was the registration and insurance papers. Did they leave those?"

"Yes, and your unpaid traffic ticket."

"Oops. I forgot about that."

"I didn't hear that. Don't suppose you have any idea what they could be looking for do you?"

"Potatoes? Asparagus? Peppers?"

He laughed. "Get some sleep. What time would you like me to pick you up? You've got quite the job ahead of you if you're not calling your housekeeper."

"I can't go home today. We have our first major soiree tonight."

"What's that?"

"I'm not sure. I'm just repeating what Ginger said. I'm under orders to get some rest and then get all dressed up and be at the restaurant for dinner."

"Will you need a ride home after that?"

"Probably."

"I'll meet you at the restaurant tonight then."

"Thank you."

"You're welcome. Now turn off your ringer."

I ordered pasta from room service then, with a belly full of refined carbohydrates, I snuggled between the super clean, smooth sheets and closed my eyes.

I was able to sleep for almost three hours before Ginger burst in and suggested we go down to the spa and let them do our hair and makeup—her treat. I guessed I paid her well.

Chapter 25: Ex-Beaus and Old Worries

I was a knock out. That's what Ginger and everyone at the spa said anyway. I agreed, with reservations. While I have learned to use my looks to my advantage, it had been a long time since I'd worn something like that dress. And as I stood there, gazing at myself in the mirror, I saw too much cleavage, too narrow of a waist, and too tight of a dress for me to be comfortable let alone confident.

But it wasn't unfamiliar. It was the kind of thing Malcolm used to insist I wear.

I almost hoped Piper wouldn't show up. I didn't want him to see me like that. What if he liked it too much? Would I turn him into a monster, too?

Ginger suggested we have a glass of wine while we waited for the valet to hail us a cab. I sucked down two and was on the verge of ordering a third when she dragged me outside and forced me into the taxi. In hindsight, I was glad she did it. I'm not sure I could have walked in those shoes if I'd kept drinking. It might have been a wiser move to have actually walked around in them a few minutes when I'd bought them instead of just shoving my feet in and deciding they fit fine. Those babies were high. And, not only were there platforms under the toes, the heels were long, thin and pointy. Probably thin enough and pointed enough to blind a man if I needed to.

Not wanting to snap an ankle climbing up the stairs, I took the shoes off when we arrived at the restaurant. I had no idea how far my ankles could bend inward, but when it became painful I figured I was better off looking a little goofy for a few minutes then wearing a cast for several weeks. And besides, who could I trust to take me to the hospital? Those ambulance drivers always took for granted that other drivers would move out of their way. I seriously suspected there were more accidents involving them than were reported.

At the top of the steps, I bent over to put my shoes back on. Standing up required a wiggling and a jiggling motion to re-position the dress over my breasts. Ginger giggled as she watched me.

"Good Lord, honey. You're the funniest person I've ever met. Even when you're not trying." She hooked her arm in mine, giving me ready support, and led me down the walkway.

Moko Jumbies danced to a boom box set in the center of the courtyard, by the fire pit. I stopped to watch. Not wearing masks, their faces shone in the evening light as they jumped and clapped their hands to the rhythm of the music. One turned toward me, met my eyes and smiled. I smiled my gratitude back and let Ginger take me inside the restaurant.

We walked directly toward a group of men setting up musical instruments in the corner near the piano. She introduced them to me as our house band.

"I didn't know we had a band," I said as we watched them tune and arrange.

"We didn't until yesterday." Ginger's eyes surveyed the restaurant, gleaming with satisfaction.

"How much do they cost?"

"They're free tonight. But if they do a good job and our diners like them, they'll be here most nights and we'll work out a price."

"When are you doing all this?" I found myself peaking down at my boobs as best I could without being obvious. The way they strained my dress made me think of a dam at near capacity. "Seriously . . . Finding cruise ships, arranging bands, reserving Moko Jumbies, ghost hunting with Butterworth? It seems like you're always here in the dining room running the place."

"Sugar, I loves running me a restaurant. But I'm good with time management, too. The cruise ship was just a couple of phone calls. Chester got these boys here incorporated as a band and told me about them. And you sent Lydia to me who gave me the contact for the Moko Jumbies. I didn't do much." She took my hand like a school girl and we walked toward the office and kitchen doors. "And that baker you hired has quite the artistic touch."

"He turned out to be good?"

"Better than good, honey. Slim is probably one of the best pastry chefs I've ever known."

"Slim?"

"His real name is James DeGraaf. But everyone calls him Slim."

"Now I get what Matt said."

"What?"

"Nothing. He's good, huh?"

"Just you wait and see what he did for dessert tonight. You did right with him. But uh," she stopped, faced me and pointed her eyes at my boobs. "Why don't you go and properly tuck those babies back in, OK? If I didn't know better, I'd think you were about to offer up a new item for the drink menu." She turned me around and gave me a gentle shove toward the office. "Now that would have been funny if you'd have said it."

I wobbled into the office, feeling a little giddy over what she'd just implied: I did right with that baker I hired. And I'd sent Lydia to her. It almost sounded as if I was acting like a real restaurateur. They were rather inspiring thoughts for me as I rearranged my dress to cover my breasts. So inspiring, I thought I might even attempt to do some paperwork before the evening crowd hit. That's what I told myself anyway, although I suspected I was looking for an excuse to remain in there so I could hide.

In the stack of mail I'd retrieved from the post office I found bank statements that I assumed were identical to the ones I'd been given copies of the day before. I threw them away. There were also a few invoices for restaurant supplies that I put in the in-box on my desk. I threw away some *thank you* cards to Chance from the recently photographed and loads of junk mail that went in the trash, too. There was nothing was from Peru. Nothing was about potatoes, asparagus or peppers. And, to my huge relief, nothing was from Wenner Publications.

With nothing left to do and the scent of garlic luring me out of the office, I stood, tottered around my desk and nearly bumped into Ginger at the office door.

"I was just coming for you." Her face was set in a frown. "Some fool's out there insisting on talking to the owner and drinking flaming drinks."

"Oh God." Malcolm liked flaming drinks. "An Irish Car Bomb?"

"Maybe, it has Baily's and Guinness in it?"

"And Butterscotch Schnapps, Goldschlager, Rum, and

cinnamon."

"That's what he wants."

I sighed. "That's Malcolm's favorite drink."

"Malcolm?" She gripped my arm. "Would that be your ex-beau you told me about this morning?"

I nodded.

"So your old flame still has it burning for you, huh?"

I nodded again. "What the hell is he doing here? What do I do now?"

"Go talk to him." She said it like it was something I could easily do in that dress. "At least make him drink something else. There's not an employee in the building who will go near that bar right now."

I took a deep breath and glanced down. Both boobs were in their rightful place. And there was something about them, their gentle curve held tight, that reminded me of a shield.

I walked as fast as my pointy-heeled shoes would let me until I had to slow down when I saw him at the bar.

Time slowed down with me. My world narrowed. In tunnel vision I watched his eyes take me in and devour me, obviously savoring what he saw.

"Malcolm," I forced my voice to sound like he was a pleasant surprise. "It's been a long time."

He stepped off his bar stool, took my hands and kissed me *hello,* on the lips.

"My God," he said. Keeping hold of me with one hand, he caressed my cheek with his other. "You're still stunning. As you always were."

I smiled and stepped back as far as his grip would allow. "Thank you, but, um, listen. I came over to tell you, you can't order those drinks anymore. This place has a history of fires and it spooks the employees."

He laughed and pulled me to the bar stool next to his. He sat. I remained standing, gripping the bar. He'd let go of my hand, but was still touching it, his fingers resting on the backside. It was something he always did whenever we were in the same room together. He always had to be touching me. At the beginning I was young and stupid enough to think it was an endearing gesture, like he couldn't get enough of me. Later I realized he was letting everyone know he owned me and I was off limits. I pulled my hand away and fingered my hair.

"Francis," I asked the bartender. "Could you pour me a Something Better?"

He laughed. "Is that really what you're naming it Miss Mandy?"

"It fits, doesn't it?"

"Sounds like you still got a way with words," Malcolm said. "You know every time I see a food column written by you, I have to read it."

"I doubt you'll be reading much any more. That was my former career."

"What are you doing now? What are you doing here?" His fingertips grazed my arm. My hand clenched tighter to the bar as if by sheer physical strength, I could will myself to be patient while I waited for the drink.

"I own this restaurant." I made him lose contact with me when I accepted my glass from Francis.

Malcolm stepped off his stool and stood closer to me. I had no where to go but on the next stool.

"So, since I believe you were asking for the owner, what can I do for you?" I tried to twist around to make it awkward for him to reach out and touch me.

"I want to buy this place," he said, sitting again, giving enough distance between us that I could breathe. "Coincidentally, I've decided my next venture would be in my own line of restaurants around the world."

"It's not for sale."

"Everything's for sale, sweetheart. Sometimes it's just a matter of finding the right price." He smiled, deepening the creases at his eyes, which remained fixated on my face. "It's funny. I had someone look at this place for me and he told me a beautiful woman owned it. I had no idea it'd be you. But since it is, maybe we could work on something together?"

I drank instead of answering right away, trying to give myself enough mental space to summon my journalism objectivity and ask the right questions. Could it be a coincidence that he'd want to buy that particular restaurant so soon after Chance had taken his photograph? Perhaps. But, his offer coming on the hills of Callwood's was too much to take lightly, especially since the place wasn't listed for sale anywhere. Why did so many people want my restaurant?

"Why this place?" I asked. "It's not for sale."

"It was up until a couple of months ago. I was on the verge of making an offer when someone bought it out from under me. I didn't realize it was you."

"Actually it was Chance."

He said nothing at first. His eyes were unreadable, black pools.

"What do you mean?" he finally asked.

"Chance was the person who bought this place, back in February."

"With what money?"

"With his."

"Chance." He picked up his drink and downed it. "Never has money."

So there was another use of present tense.

"He doesn't anymore. He gave it all to me," I said.

Malcolm slid off his stool and stood close to me. He had always hated that Chance and I were friends. When he needed me to write with my *amazing ability to describe food*, as he called it, he had accused me more times than I could count of sleeping with Chance when I never had. That was before Malcolm had made enough money to hire more writers. When he eventually had a full stable, he took me off assignments and away from Chance. He kept me holed up in our beautiful penthouse where I cooked and played with food to keep me company when Malcolm wasn't home. I went out only when I was on his arm, like a chain gang of only one prisoner.

I had to admit, I was a complicit inmate. While I hated most of it, I did feel safe with him so I chose to stay, using him as he used me. I knew he'd protect me from anything bad in the world. Granted it was because he wanted to make sure his prized curio piece stayed in mint condition. But it was still protection. So

I let him do it. Despite remembering my grandmother saying he had a bad aura. Despite my Aunt Maggie saying my mother didn't approve of him. Despite something inside me suggesting that maybe, if I looked hard enough I'd find my own inner strength and wouldn't need him. I took the easy way with him and I chose to stay with him for years. The whole thing was partly my fault.

I knew that. And standing there, even after not seeing him for so long, standing there so close to him with both good and bad memories flooding back to me, I knew it would be easy to do it again. Prized curio pieces never felt alone and scared, unlike how I'd spent every night since I'd landed on the island. I couldn't keep going like that. Something had to give. Or I needed to find some strength in something that wasn't liquid.

But his hand was on the small of my back, which seemed to encourage the idea that I was weak and needed his power. If it weren't for the scary undertones of his movement, I would have easily leaned into him.

I slid off the other side of the bar stool, putting it between us, and took a long drink of my Something Better.

"Where is Chance now?" he asked.

"He's dead."

First he frowned. Then he opened his mouth as if to say something. But before any words came out, behind him I saw Matt enter the restaurant talking, as if they were old friends, with Reggie Callwood.

My face must have registered some kind of expression because Malcolm turned to see what was there.

"Malcolm, my man!" Reggie slapped him on the back and then noticed me. "And Mandy Breen. You're looking fine, gyul." Matt stood next to him, grinning at me. Fear tingled down my arms and legs.

"She is," Malcolm said turning to him. "How do you know her?"

"I did some reporting here when Reggie was on the police force," I answered, letting anger come to the forefront, ever grateful for its ability to stem the flow of panic. How could Matt have acted like he didn't know Reggie and now waltz in like they're good buddies? My breath forced through my nose as if I were about to snort fire. "How do you know him?" I asked Malcolm.

"He's my business associate I was just telling you about," Malcolm said.

"Right. I get it now." I glared at Matt. "Apparently Reggie came in the other day on Malcolm Wenner's behalf."

Matt nodded.

"Dat's right," Reggie said. "You tink you might sell now?"

I jutted out my bottom jaw and put my hand on my hip.

"As I said the other day, Reg, this place isn't for sale, at any price."

I stormed away as best I could on my weak ankles, heading back to the office.

Piper caught up with me at the edge of the dance floor, near the office door.

"Are you all right?" he asked, grabbing my elbow.

"What the hell are you doing with Callwood?" I ripped out of his grip, nearly losing balance in those damn shoes and flailed my arms to right myself.

"We met up by chance in the parking lot," Piper said, helping me stabilize. I shimmied away from his touch. "After what you'd told me, that he'd been in to look at the restaurant, I thought it might be prudent to speak with him and see what he's been up to." His hands were spread open wide, as if I were pointing a gun at him. Apparently he'd noticed how pointy my heels were.

"And I'm to believe that?"

"You can believe whatever you want. It's the truth." He took a step back.

"Right. So you're telling me you never had contact with the man prior to Chance's death?"

"With Callwood? Yes, of course I had some contact. He was leaving the office when I was coming in." Piper shook his head. "What are you getting at?"

"I don't know. But . . ." I pressed my fingertips against my brow. I wanted to rub my face and try to erase the whole evening, but I didn't want Ginger's good money going to waste by ruining the makeup. "It's Reggie Fucking Callwood. He's corrupt. You know that right?"

"His record has some curious incidents." He lowered his hands and tucked them into the pockets of his slacks.

"Curious? Is that what you call it?" With a clenched jaw I let out a long sigh that more resembled a hiss.

"Your old boyfriend is staring at us," Piper said. "Is there something else you need to tell me?"

"I need to process some things. Just go away, will you?" I stormed into the office.

Chapter 26: For Dessert, a Lobster Tail

I sat at my desk, not knowing, yet again, what to do with myself and I was getting tired of feeling that way.

I called my Aunt Maggie and got her voice mail. I called my cousin Bob, who assured me he found nothing else on Piper. Then I called Babs, who I probably should have been calling on a daily basis since I landed anyway.

"I can't do a reading for you, hon," she said.

"Why not?"

"I never do readings for people I love, you know that."

I wished I had thought to get another drink before coming into the office. I hadn't even finished my Something Better that I'd left out on the bar. "Well can I just get advice, girl-to-girl?"

"Of course."

Tears surprised me by filling up my eyes. I dabbed as gently as I could, though the thought occurred to me that if I went back out there with mascara smeared all over my face, Malcolm would look at me differently. But then the diners would look at me with horror and the employees might even think the ghost lady got to me and I'd have to find a new job.

"How do you know if you can trust a man, Babs?" I sniffed.

"I can feel it in my gut."

"What if I have no idea what my gut is feeling? Right now all I'm feeling is hunger."

"And before that?"

"Anger and fear."

"Because of what?"

I sighed. "Babs, I called for answers, not for more questions."

"Mandy, I know it's tough. Particularly with men, I mean, look at me." She paused, giving me a chance to remember what it was like for her. Her husband had cheated on her and got another woman pregnant shortly after she had miscarried their only child.

"I'm sorry," I said. "God, I'm so self-absorbed. I keep forgetting everyone else has their own issues."

"You're not any more self-absorbed than the rest of us. But listen, all I can tell you is you can't trust someone unless you want to trust them. And you can't trust them until you're ready to stop mistrusting them. That's the bottom line."

"Thanks."

"You're welcome. Now, go eat something and then check in with your gut."

"Right. Well, um, also, thanks for the birthday wishes. I got your voicemail."

I hung up and went into the kitchen where I devoured a plateful of the pastries my new baker had created. For dessert, I had a lobster tail. I stayed in there observing the orderly chaos of cooks and wait staff, relishing the noise and smells. I couldn't help but notice how every single person there was clearly comfortable, clearly confident the rug would not be pulled out from underneath them as they went about doing what they loved to do. Ginger popped in walking steady on the earth because it never occurred to her it might open up and swallow her whole.

"Mandy! This place is happening, honey! If we keep this up, we'll have nothing to worry about." Her face shone with joy. She was smiling, beaming with genuine happiness because she had the freedom not to frown. She was free to not be afraid of living out her dream. It was all I could do not to cry. I needed Francis and another Something Better.

Matt met up with me at the bar before Francis even had a chance to notice I was standing there.

"I promised you a ride home," he said. "You look ready?"

"Why are you still here?" I asked. I didn't see Callwood or Malcolm around. "Didn't I scare you off?"

"I'm a man of my word," he said. "I made you a promise and I'll keep it regardless of what you decide to do. And I promised I'd take you home."

"You're unbelievable." I glared at him, kicked off my shoes and tore back into the office to get my purse. "Let's go," I said to him when I returned to the bar and picked up my shoes. "Why didn't you leave?"

"Is that what you wanted?" He walked beside me out of the restaurant as if it didn't matter to him I was shoeless and scowling.

I didn't answer. I was too busy touching my brow to feel how deep the impression from the scowl was.

Outside, the Moko Jumbies were still dancing.

"Hey!" I yelled at them. They spun around toward me. "You let one of them in. Were you on break or something?"

"Mandy," Piper dragged me down the walkway before they retaliated.

"Don't you dare touch me!" I jerked out of his grip and ran down the stairs.

"Why are you mad at me?" he asked at the bottom. "I've done nothing wrong." We headed toward his SUV.

"That's just it!" I yelled, standing beside his car. "God! Do you have any idea how frustrating it is to deal with you? You're calm. You're rational. You keep your promises and you're good to dogs!" He opened the passenger door and I threw myself into the seat.

He went round to his side, opened the door and climbed in.

"What did that man do to you?" he asked as he turned the car on.

"What do you mean?" I bent down to wipe the sand and pebbles from the bottom of my feet.

"Callwood's new business partner. Your old boyfriend."

I let my head rest on the dashboard and closed my eyes.

"Are you asleep?" Piper whispered after several minutes passed.

"No, I'm still trying to figure out how to answer your question." I'd been so caught up in my head that I just realized he'd been driving. I sat up straight and partially opened one eye to look at him. He was calm and relaxed at the wheel, confident as ever.

"How about you try using words?" He risked a grin when he glanced at me.

"OK." I inhaled. "He ... no, I..." I snorted. "I am a product of Malcolm Wenner. But it's my own fault."

"I still don't understand."

Headlights went by outside our window, startling me. My breath came in shots through my nose.

"How's your night vision?" I almost shrieked as another car passed. "You know it goes bad as you age, RIGHT?" I gripped the assist bar and nearly pulled myself out of the seat as he rounded a corner the same time yet another freaking car was coming toward us.

"Close your eyes," He suggested.

Instead, I covered my face with my hands and tried to do the deep breathing techniques again. The image of my grandmother came to me. She was cooking pancakes for dinner. My sister, Maddie, and I were setting the table. We were laughing about eating breakfast for dinner. I could smell bacon.

"Did I tell you my father left us soon after my sister was born?" I asked with Grandmom's laughter ringing in my ears. She laughed like a woman with no worries.

"You mentioned something. You were young."

"I was two."

Piper said nothing.

"After my mom died, my sister and I had to live with my grandmother in a mobile home outside Orlando. Grandmom waitressed in a little diner and was an astrologer on the side. My grandfather had been a shrimper. Apparently he smoked a lot when he was on land and died of lung cancer before I was even born. So it was just us three girls. Money was always tight. As soon as I was old enough, I got a job waiting tables at a tourist restaurant. I was good. Customers liked me. I was great at upselling. The owners had several other places and wanted me to work at one of their more high-end establishments. It meant more money for me and my family, so it was a no-brainer."

I felt the car take a turn and slow to a near crawl. I leaned back again and rubbed my face with my hands, forgetting about my mascara. I pulled down the visor and opened the lighted mirror to prevent me from seeing anything outside my window. The pale blond reflected back at me looked nothing like the hot number she was when she showed up at the restaurant earlier. The bags were coming through the concealer, the eyes were blood shot. I looked about as strung out as the models I kept seeing.

"And Malcolm Wenner comes in . . ." Piper encouraged me. He stopped the car.

I shut the visor. At first, the darkness seemed more dark after the light from the mirror, but then I noticed we were in my driveway. The headlights shone on the upside-down broom on the porch.

"Malcolm comes in the restaurant several times, eventually insisting I wait on him. I was only in high school. The restaurant fudged my age a little so that I could serve drinks. He thought I was older than I was at first. He'd flirt with me and tease me, telling me he loved the way I described the food. That I have a good palate."

"Everyone agrees with that."

"I told him how old I was because he wanted to see me, outside the restaurant. He didn't care. So, I know it was stupid, but we dated. When I started college at a community school to be a journalist, we . . . we became more serious." I swallowed hard, thinking how stupid it was of me. "Soon after, when Maddie and my grandmother died, it seemed only right that I move in with him. I . . . I was young. You know? And it finally seemed like I had a dream come true. I know it sounds bad."

"Actually," Piper said. "It sounds like you found something close to a father figure."

I didn't answer right away. He was right, although I'd never seen it that way before, despite all the time spent in therapy.

"Yeah, well, he had just started his food magazine and suggested I combine my new journalism skills with my palate and see how it worked. It worked well."

"And you became a food writer."

"Soon after that he hired Chance as a photographer. Chance and I hit it off perfectly. He was like a long-lost brother to me. We bounced jokes off each other, simultaneously got the same ideas about articles. Malcolm both hated it and loved it. He resented Chance and me building a friendship, but our work earned his magazine awards and helped gain a wider audience. As he became more successful, he started other publications and eventually didn't need me to write. By that time, I had been living with him long enough that I'd become accustomed to his over-protectiveness. Again, it seemed only natural that he wanted me to stay home, unless he was with me. I could cook and play with food to my heart's content. I was well-fed. I was safe. I didn't have to drive anywhere."

"So he had you in a cage of sorts, but it was a comfortable one and you trusted him."

"Yeah. So what could be bad about that? Right?" I stared at the yellow and purple house with the broom still on guard.

"And then?" he prodded.

"And then, as he grew more powerful in the publishing world, he grew more possessive. He branched out to do travel magazines and others on art and collectibles. I started feeling like a collectible. He'd have me dress up, all the time, in heals and slinky dresses for breakfast even. And whenever we went out, he constantly was on the prowl for men looking at me, and for me to be looking at men. He became jealous at the slightest communication. He ..." I couldn't go there. "It got to the point where I never left the penthouse. Not even to go somewhere with him. It was just easier that way."

Matt turned the car off.

"Then one morning," I broke the silence. "Chance bursts in. We were eating breakfast. He insisted on showing me all these photographs of Malcolm in bed with models. Malcolm attacked him, they fought. I thought Malcolm was going to kill Chance. I threw my coffee at him, in his face. He–I don't know. He crouched down, like he was wiping his eyes or something, but then suddenly he was on Chance, choking him. Without thinking I grabbed this stupid ancient vase that he admired almost as much as me, and slammed it into the back of Malcolm's head. Knocked him out."

"Remind me never to get you mad."

I gave a small laugh.

"After that, I hid at Chance's for a while in Miami, waiting for Malcolm to press charges, waiting for the police to come."

"He couldn't, though. Once you told your tale—"

"I know that now, at the time I was too paranoid to think straight." I got out of the car and walked to the door, carrying my shoes, stepping gingerly on the gravel driveway in my bare feet. Piper followed me.

"Listen," he said. "I need to get home and let a puppy out before he messes on the rug again. I'll come back if you want. Do you want me to?"

Yes, I wanted him to come back. The last thing I wanted was to be alone. But, as I reached out to touch the end of the broom handle, I realized maybe I needed to be alone.

"No," I said, turning to him. "I think I'll be OK."

He touched my cheek. "Any chance you'll sleep? Would you prefer I take you somewhere else?"

"Go home to your dogs. I faced my jumbies last night. I think

I'll sleep."

"I wasn't worried about jumbies."

"I know. But I think after them, I can handle anything."

He looked like he wanted to say something and was unsure. I took his hand off my face and held it.

"There's nothing for you to worry about, I'll stay sober," I promised.

"You out of rum?" he asked.

"Yep."

He squeezed my hand. "I'll be by to get you in the morning. Your Jeep should have new wheels by then." He kissed me good night, again, very lightly.

Ensconced with triple-checked locked doors and a set alarm, I peeled off the dress and removed my makeup. Standing naked before the bathroom mirror I tried to make myself conjure up what Malcolm's eyes had looked like when he saw me. Glutinous came to mind. Possessive. Was it really there, though, or had I seen it because I'd expected it? I squeezed my own eyes shut and focused on the memory of seeing him at the Revenge Cafe. Covetous. That was the word.

How had Piper look at me? He'd grinned his fun-loving, kind grin. It was Chance-like only with an added level of maturity and sensitivity.

He answered his cell phone on the first ring.

"Are you all right?" he asked.

"Yes. I was wondering, do you know why you are here?"

"Is this a philosophical or religious question?" A dog yapped in the background.

"It's an employment question. Do you know what happened to your predecessor?"

He laughed. "Yes. I know why the vacancy occurred. Why?"

"I think I need to tell you a story." Wrapped in a thin, white terry cloth robe, I sipped my orange juice and water and told him all about the last story I covered on St. Thomas and why Reggie Callwood might not like me or Chance.

"Interesting," he said when I was done. "Very, very interesting. I knew there was something else you weren't telling me."

"That's it." I admitted.
"Good. Now let *me* tell *you* all about Reggie Callwood."

Chapter 27: About to Anyway

The jumbies stayed away. But I still didn't sleep.

The ransacker had ransacked well. The place was a disaster. I stayed up nearly all night cleaning and setting the house right again. After all, I had no idea when Lydia would pop by for a visit.

I'd slept only a few hours by the time Matt called and woke me, saying he was on his way. Soon after I showered, he was at the door with a puppy in his arms.

The only pet I'd ever owned was a goldfish that had died on me, not surprisingly, when I was twelve. I'd won it at a carnival after aiming and hoping for stuffed teddy bear. I liked it alright, but I never understood why people would want a pet. Why sacrifice so much time, money and energy on something that invariably eats your shoes and doesn't use a toilet? Or in my case, didn't notice you were around unless food was for offer?

But this puppy noticed me. His sweet, dark brown eyes met mine with such a ferocity of happy eagerness, I had to touch him. I rubbed his head. He leaned into my fingers, as if wanting more.

Matt put him in my hands. At first I held him under the front legs, his round belly swinging gently, his uncomplaining face looking at me to see what would happen next.

"Try sitting down on the floor and petting him," Matt said.

I did as told, sitting cross legged on the sisal rug, not sure what to do with the thing. But the puppy knew what to do. He tackled one knee with abandon, tumbled over and spun around to face me in bowing posture, his rear sticking up in the air and his skinny tail wagging back and forth.

"He's trying to get you to play with him," Matt explained.

"How do I do that?"

"Just respond. Scratch his head, pretend you're grabbing his paws."

I played with the puppy for a few minutes, enjoying his keen willingness to have fun until he curled up in my lap.

"My God! He's the cutest thing ever!" I picked him up to rub noses. He looked at me with nothing but pure, eager curiosity, as if asking: *would you love me? I love you already. Please?* "Where are you taking him?"

"Here." Matt sat on the floor in front of me and scratched behind the puppy's ears.

"Here where? Do I have a neighbor?"

"No. Here to you. I thought he might be good for you."

I looked into the puppy's shining, happy eyes. They were so full of hope and enthusiastic anticipation for whatever wonderful thing was coming to him next that I wanted to watch him experience it.

"What's his life expectancy?" I asked.

"About twelve years."

"Do you have one who's at least two already? It would just be wrong to chop that down." I laid the puppy down on his back. He willingly let me rub his belly.

Matt touched my cheek. "You haven't spoken to your housekeeper about that yet?"

"No," I said thinking his eyes were just as nice as the puppy's. "I was serious when I said I'm a little afraid of her."

"Everyone is. But she's got connections." He stood.

"What does that mean anyway?" I stood too, and picked up the puppy.

"It means she might be able to help you."

I cradled the dog to my chest. I'd never heard my biological clock tick but I was beginning to suspect I had a canine one.

"Thank you," I said to him. "For everything. I appreciate how you're going out of your way for me. Really."

"My pleasure," he grinned at me.

"You're having fun?"

"You could say that." His eyebrows lifted into their trademarked position. "You're never boring."

I put the puppy down and went into the bedroom to get my purse. The puppy followed me. Matt was clearly thinking I'd given him a signal last night. And maybe I did. But what did that say about him? What kind of sane man would be a witness to my insanity and still want to be with me? There must be something wrong with him.

I checked my hair in the mirror.

Or maybe I did have trust issues. I looked down into the puppy's innocent eyes. Clearly, he didn't have any trust issues.

Chance's cell rang.

I ran to the kitchen where it was still plugged in.

"Hello?" I looked into Matt's face and mouthed *Chance's* while pointing to the phone pressed against my ear.

"Is this Chancellor's friend who rang his family up on Sunday?" I recognized the voice immediately.

"Yes, it's Mandy Breen. We met before Mr. Abbott. At your other son's wedding."

Matt reared his head back and raised his eyebrows in anticipation.

"I remember you. I assumed you were the one who phoned. Do you have a few minutes this morning?"

"I guess so. Is there something you need to talk about?"

"There is something I need to give you."

"Where are you?"

Bertrand Abbott IV was staying at the Ritz Carlton, all the way down on the southeast part of the island, past Duffy's Love Shack. He refused to meet me at the house or the Revenge Café, instead, he insisted on me meeting him at the Ritz. Matt refused to let me drive.

"You're going to hurt the dog," he said as he removed my feet from the dashboard.

"I'm protecting it." The puppy squirmed against my stomach, probably uncomfortable. I may have squished it a little as I cringed.

"You don't like my driving?" He swerved into the opposite lane to avoid a pot hole.

"I like it as much as I like anybody's." I righted myself and looked behind to see if we'd hit anything. I thought I'd heard a loud bang.

"That dog is going to feed off your tension. You're going to make him scared to be in cars, too, if you're not careful."

I held the puppy's face to mine and chanted: "The car is a safe place. The car is a safe place. The car is a safe place."

"Good start." He slammed on the breaks when a man sauntered across the street, on a diagonal. I don't know where he came from as both sides of the road at that point were flush against white walls. The puppy's body swayed back and forth in my hands.

"I can't believe the car is a safe place if you're going to insist on driving so fast," I shrieked and hugged the puppy tight.

"I haven't gone over thirty-five miles an hour."

"Really? Have you had your speedometer checked recently?"

"Why don't you try those breaths again? Or try petting the dog. Petting animals is supposed to be calming."

I breathed and breathed and breathed. And I pet that dog so much and so hard, I was surprised to find it still had hair when we arrived.

Abbott was in the general lobby at the Ritz, as he said he would be. Matt stayed outside with the puppy, positioned by the front door.

"Mr. and Mrs. Abbott," I said upon approaching them.

He stood. She remained sitting, eyes focused on the floor.

"It's Breen, correct?" he asked, waving his hand toward an empty chair across from the rattan sofa where they were sitting.

"Yes." I sat, catching a glimpse of Piper talking to a bellhop. "I am so sorry about your loss." It was all I could think to say.

"Yours too," Mrs. Abbott said, still not making eye contact with me. She held a wooden box in her lap.

"Yes, well, I guess we'll see you at the memorial?" I braved. I was aggravated by what I could only recognize was their lack of grief. Granted he was estranged from them, but he was their freaking son.

"I hope so," Mrs. Abbott said, raising her eyes to glare at her husband. "But we are here now."

"Right." I cleared my throat. "Did you want something from me?"

"No, as I said I want to give something to you," Mr. Abbott said. He reached out to his wife, who ignored him and handed me the box. I took it and almost dropped it. The heftiness was surprising.

"Please wait until you are in a private place to view the contents," Mr. Abbott said.

I let the box sit in my lap unopened. It was a plain, brown wooden cigar box with a hinged lid. It couldn't have housed cigars though; the contents rattled and it had to weigh a couple pounds.

"Chance gave that to his mother recently when he was in

London. I'm not sure why. I can't believe he legally owned it. I am hoping you could get it back to its rightful owner without implicating us somehow?"

"What is it?" I asked his mother.

"You will see for yourself when you have privacy." Mr. Abbott stood up and held his hand out to his wife. "Good day, Ms. Breen."

"Chance had asked me if I could possibly convert it all into money for him," Mrs. Abbott said upon rising, ignoring her husband's hand. "Of course I'd do anything to help my son."

"Of course," I said as he pulled her away. They left together, yet obviously apart.

As soon as the Abbott's had rounded a corner and were out of my sight, I met up with Matt at the entrance and we returned to his unmarked SUV. With me bent over so I could play with the puppy on the floor instead of seeing where we were going, we headed westward, toward Charlotte Amalie. I recounted the strange conversation I'd just had with Chance's parents and sat up to open the box.

That's right about the time he turned onto a one-lane, walled road that did not have a *one-way* sign informing us we were going the right direction. The road was so narrow, I expected both mirrors to be crushed off the car.

"Holy shit!" I yelled, feet on the windshield.

"Calm down," Matt swiped at my feet. "We're about to head up Donkey Hill."

"What's that?" I clutched his arm.

"It's the most dangerous road on the island, so stay off it, got it?"

"I'll never go near it." I think I lost sensation in my face at that point. I actually understood the phrase *frozen with fear* as I could do nothing but stare out the front window as he took what's called a switch-back turn, something tighter than a hairpin turn, at the same time a bus took it coming toward us.

"It's a good thing that rain stopped," he said, as if it were a normal day and we were the only people out and about. "Can't always climb this hill when it's wet." He took another tight turn.

"Isn't there another way?" I squeaked.

"Not if we want to get there within the hour."

"I'm in no hurry."

"I'm technically on the clock and I still need to get this dog back home. Just shut your eyes."

I put the puppy on my lap and curled over it as best I could. My ears tingled and my breath came in short and fast.

"You know if we were in an accident and the air bag deployed—" Matt started.

"Shhh. I know. I didn't say it was a sane position. But death would be quick and painless."

After an eternity of my body swaying back and forth with the turns, Matt stopped.

"We're on Thirty now. You might considerate it safe to sit up."

I did as suggested, but when the light changed and he accelerated, I couldn't handle it so I bent down to occupy myself with opening the box.

"Oh my God!" I yelled, making the puppy cower at my feet. "I'm so sorry sweetheart." I rubbed its head. "Good thing you're driving, Matt!"

"Sure it is." He patted my back. "What's in there?"

"Looks like gold. Gold coins, and gold . . . gold things." I held one of the larger figurines up in the air above my back. No longer than my thumb, it resembled a dog with a long neck. "What do you think it is?"

"Your friend have any theft on his record that was preventing him from becoming a citizen?"

"No! Well, not that I know of." I returned the figurine to the box. "No. No. Chance wasn't like that. He had a code of ethics that would have prevented him from stealing. Unless ..."

"Unless?"

"Well, you know, in a Robin Hood sort of way."

"Which is still illegal. Didn't his mother say—"

"Right. He wanted his mom to pawn them or something. That kind of makes it look like he didn't want to risk anyone who knew him finding out." I felt the car stop again and sat up. We were at the citrus colored government building. Fort Christian was on our right and I knew Blackbeard's Castle was nearby.

"Were there any burglaries at the Inn at Blackbeard's Castle recently?" I asked.

"No. Why?"

"I don't know. Just grabbing at straws I guess."

Matt dropped me at the restaurant, promising he'd let me know about my Jeep as soon as he heard anything.

I called my aunt from the office phone instead of my cell, thinking she'd feel the Revenge Café's vibes, or whatever she felt, stronger from the landline.

"So I'm at the restaurant and it's Saturday," I said. "Nothing bad happened last night." I paused wondering if Malcolm counted as bad. "I mean, the ghost didn't do anything. Is it waiting to do something tonight? None of my workers are willing to work past sundown and, again, it's Saturday. We need to be open."

"I can't predict the future, dear. You should call Babs for that." I heard her sip a drink.

"Maybe I will, but really, I was hoping you could help me get rid of them."

"Who?"

"The ghosts!"

"Why not learn to live harmoniously?"

"How do we do that? What are they saying? Are you getting anything specific from them?"

"Now?"

"Yes!"

Aunt Maggie was quiet.

"Still picking up on the revenge concept, my dear. But really it's faint."

"Would it help if you were here in person? I could fly you out here on the restaurant's dime."

"I'd love to dear, but I am booked solid. My business always picks up when the economy goes down. Your Uncle John was just joking about how it was too bad he couldn't have bought stock in me. Right now I'm more valuable than gold." Her voice cackled with laughter. "Gold!" she repeated. The word could have been coincidental, but Aunt Maggie doesn't believe in coincidences.

"I don't want to keep you for too long, but just one more question," I said. "Can you ask Chance how or why he got the gold?"

"Just a minute, hon." I waited, hearing nothing on the other end.

"You know, I'm still picking up revenge or maybe making amends. And . . . wait . . . an apology."

"To who?"

"You! Who else?"

I hung up and called Butterworth's number. His voice mail picked up after several rings.

"Come on, Breen," I said aloud to myself. "You've been sober for a couple of days now. Why aren't you thinking clearly?" I left the office and found him at the bar of my restaurant, where I should have gone to begin with.

"Do you know what this is?" I asked him, plunking down the golden dog-like thing.

"Why yes," he said, grabbing and immediately dropping it. He popped off the barstool to retrieve it from the floor before continuing. "It's a llama. Judging from the size, I think it would be called a fertility charm." He turned it over on his palm. His body completely still as he studied it. I didn't think he even breathed.

"Llama? As in from South America?"

"Yes. Peru, to narrow it down more. The Inca's would bury them with their crops in an attempt to increase the yield." He held it up, pinching it between his forefinger and thumb. "This is quite the collector's piece!" His body started showing signs of excitement, he was on the balls of his feet.

"How do you know?" I took it from him, lest he inadvertently send it flying through the restaurant.

"It's gold. Usually they are made of stone." He squeezed his hands together, as if restraining them from reaching out to touch the llama again. "The gold alone would fetch it a pretty penny on the market, but the artifact itself would be worth tens of thousands. Where did you get it?"

"Chance's mother." I didn't think Butterworth needed to know she got it from Chance. "She gave me a whole box of stuff. It's in my office. Want to take a look?"

"Yes!" He literally jumped up in the air.

"It's worth how much?" Matt asked.

"According to Chester Butterworth, who studies art and whatever in his spare time, over three-quarters of a million dollars." I handed him the box. He let out a whistle as he glanced inside.

"And you can trust him on this?" he asked.

"He wasn't standing by the off switch to my life support system when he told me."

He grinned at me.

I sat back at my desk and put my feet up. The sounds from the restaurant had ratcheted up as everyone sped through their efforts to clean for the day. It was close to four o'clock and the workers were getting restless to leave. I had expected, since nothing had happened on Friday, they'd be OK working Saturday. But no. They were doubly worried something horrible was in store for that night. Ginger wasn't pleased, but she promised me she and Butterworth had a plan to fix it all before the following weekend.

"I hate to say this, I really really do," I said.

"But you're about to anyway." Matt sat across from me.

"Right. Do you think you can find out if there were any reports of artifacts gone missing from Peru?"

"I was thinking along those lines myself."

"Good. I can't believe Chance would, you know."

"I know. But he'd been keeping plenty of secrets from you, right?"

"Right."

"How long do you need to be here?"

"Until everyone leaves. I told Ginger to go already. She and Butterworth have big plans for the night."

"And you?"

"I had planned on getting a decent night's sleep."

He stood and put the box of Incan relics on my desk.

"You need it, but, I don't think you should get one at your house tonight." He came over to my side of the desk and squatted down to be eye level with me. "I don't mean to scare you, Mandy, but I'm worried that whoever attacked your car and hit your house will now want to talk to you to see what you know. And then, if you don't know enough, I don't want to think about what they might do, especially if they learn you have this gold and it's connected somehow."

He touched my face with the back of his hand.

"Are you inviting me over so I can make dinner for you?" I teased with faked bravado.

“I wouldn’t be opposed to it. As long as you keep the vegetables to a minimum.” He kissed my cheek. “I can take you to a hotel afterward if you want. Call when you’re ready for me.”

Chapter 28: It Seemed to Make Sense

The restaurant employees all bid me goodnight. I made a lap through the building, to make sure I was alone and then I went into the office to play with the safe. I wanted to put the artifacts in it, but I couldn't figure out the combination. Eventually, I left the box on my desk and headed out to the kitchen, thinking I'd scare up some food for Matt and me before I called him.

I stopped as I passed through the rear of the dining room. There was a shadow of someone standing on the other side of the frosted glass doors. I assumed it was Matt. I was wrong.

Malcolm was there when I opened the door.

I couldn't speak.

"Are you all right?" he asked.

"Um," I shook my head. "Yeah. But, um, we're . . . we're closed." My lungs must have thought I was in a car because they shrunk and became unable to take full breaths. "There's a . . ." I forced a long inhale through my nose. "It's a long story," I said and exhaled. "You'll have to go elsewhere to eat."

"Maybe this is best. I came here to speak to you. Hoping to have a moment in private. Can we?" He tilted his head to one side. I noticed his hands had remained at his sides; he hadn't tried to touch me, to stake a claim. Maybe I could just talk with him. Maybe I could ask how he knew the Peruvian, Catunta. Maybe he could help me make the connection between the photos on Chance's camera with the Peruvian artifacts and possibly even Chance's death.

"Sure." I stepped back to let him in.

Malcolm led the way to the bar. He sat on a stool. I went behind, glad for the fortress the bar provided me.

"No flaming drinks." I handed him a shot of Johnny Walker Black scotch. I almost drank water in an attempt to stay sober for the conversation, but the way my hand shook the scotch bottle told me it might be a good thing if I dabbled, just a little, in the rum. I poured it over a pineapple juice and coconut milk mixture.

"Cheers." Malcolm lifted his glass. I lifted mine, but didn't clink his. We drank.

"You look cute." He reached out to run his hand along the halter strap of my sundress.

I stepped back, took a breath and reminded myself I was a reporter. If I was covering a story and he was just another man I was interviewing, I'd be the one in power. I should try acting like one again.

"So," I said and swallowed. "Before we have a nice chat to get caught up with each other, I need to know, are you the person who slashed my tires yesterday?"

"What are you talking about?"

"I was driving Chance's Jeep. Someone slashed the tires on the same day that I see you for the first time in years. It seemed a little coincidental."

"I didn't slash any tires." He leaned his elbows on the bar. "I honestly didn't know you would be on the island."

"Why are you here then?" I sipped, suddenly not feeling the need for alcohol. I was handling Malcolm Wenner, on my own, unfortified.

"I told you last night. I want to buy this restaurant."

"And Reggie Callwood and you are suddenly business partners?"

"Reggie and I met some time ago. He was trying to help an exporter from South America find a buyer for some art."

The weight of his words made me put my glass down.

"Callwood's in the art business? Really? What kind of art?"

"Artifacts, Incan. It's not important now. I didn't want them. It was actually a funny thing. I had met the man before. He'd already tried to get me to buy them. But he couldn't ensure me they weren't smuggled illegally. I don't need that kind of bad press."

Matt had explained to me that Reggie Callwood was able to stay out of jail because he had admitted to making the connections between buyers and sellers, but had not actually facilitated the deals. He named names and provided bank drop details in exchange for his freedom. He had a different sort of connections than Lydia did. And now it sounded like he'd moved from illegal drugs to artifacts.

"Anyway, Callwood and I hit it off. I mentioned I had a fondness for the area, he knows it well. We agreed to try and work together." Malcolm finished his scotch and let his eyes travel from my face, down my body. "My God, Mandy. You are so beautiful. I have missed you so badly. I was such an ass to you. I have so much I want to atone for."

"That's nice." I scratched my head. "But really. I'd like to leave the past in the past." My voice was impersonal, objective, reporter-like. "Right now, though, I'm hungry. Why don't I find something for us to munch on as we talk?"

He smiled at me and slid off the stool.

"Go have a seat at a table." I left the bar and headed into the kitchen.

I hadn't cooked in there before so I wasn't sure where things were or even how to turn anything on. I didn't need much. There was no need to have a whole meal with the man. I just wanted to spend enough time to try to make a connection between Catunta and Chance.

I fumbled around the various storage cabinets and opened and shut several drawers, making quite a bit of racket while I searched for food and proper utensils to cook it with.

I knocked over a tall stack of stainless-steel bowls, making even more noise that didn't quell much as I re-stacked them. Frustrated, I gave up on making any warm food and opened the freezer to get ice cream.

That's when everything went black.

It seemed to make sense that death would be quiet. The coldness I hadn't expected. It was better than the fires from hell, though. And I was finally sleeping. Yes, I was going to sleep. I could feel it coming. A long, deep sleep.

But then a bright light came on and someone screamed.

By the time Matt arrived at the restaurant, Ginger and Chester had me seated in a booth, swathed with table cloths. There was a large puddle of dark, brown-red liquid on the floor.

I listened, not sure if I understood, as Ginger filled Piper in on what had happened.

"Chester and I came in to finish setting up the cameras for the night. We didn't see that mess on the floor at first as we went directly to the office to start setting up the rest of the gear."

"What gear?" Matt asked.

"We were planning on getting footage of the ghosts." Her hands moved in an agitated blur as she spoke. "I'd bought all sorts of cameras and had them shipped overnight, but we just didn't have time to set them up before. We had to work when the Islander employees couldn't see us, as Chester assured me they wouldn't take too kindly to us filming the ghosts."

"Yes. Some might think the ghosts would be unhappy if they knew we were trying to catch them in action," Chester added.

"So we had to work top-secret like."

"You're putting up cameras?" I asked. I felt an arm around my shoulders. It was Matt's. I leaned into him as I tried to make sense of what was going on around me.

"Yes, sugar. Good to hear you talk, finally." She sat across from me in the booth. "I guess it was a good thing we were setting up tonight, huh?"

"Were you putting cameras in the freezer?" Piper asked.

"Good Lord, no," she waved her hand. "I was getting Chester and me some pastries. I went into the freezer and found Mandy, tied up with napkins and left there to die." Her voice shook. Chester pulled her to him. "It was awful!"

"So, you came in and went to the office to set down your gear," Matt said. "At that point, Ginger, you went to the freezer?"

"Correct and..."

"And what did you do?" Piper asked Chester.

"Oh, I headed out here to make us drinks. I turned on the light and saw that blood there just as I heard Ginger scream." I looked where he was pointing. So that's what the puddle was.

An officer approached the table. Matt slid out of the booth. I fell over. He helped me right myself again and walked to the kitchen area with the officer. Ginger excused herself and left. My head hurt like hell but the room had quit spinning.

"Here." Ginger returned and handed me a cup of hot water with lemon. "You could probably use some cocoa, but this was faster, honey." She set a plate of pastries on the table.

"Thank you. It's fine." I sipped.

Ginger stood with Chester's arm around her shoulder. She

looked frightened and unsure.

"Don't you dare frown over this," I said to her.

She laughed. "I won't now that I hear you making a joke again. Oh Mandy, don't you ever do that to me again, you hear?"

"I'll do my best."

"So are you all right?" Matt approached the table.

"I think so. My head hurts. The blood's not mine is it?" I put my hand on the back of my head and felt a lump, but no wetness.

"No." He tilted my chin up toward him. "I should take you to the hospital and get you checked out."

"No. I'm okay."

"Let me see your pupils." I stared in his eyes. "Do you remember anything?"

"I was locking up." That was all I could remember.

"Were you getting ready for me to pick you up?"

"Maybe." I shook my head. "No. Someone was here. Malcolm! Malcolm was here."

"What did he want?"

I took a longer drink of the hot water. My head blank.

"Sir, you might want to take a look at this." A uniformed officer called to Matt from the office door.

"I'll be right back," he said to me. "Try to remember as much as you can."

I ate a few pastries, sure that a combination of wheat and sugar would be good for the brain cells.

"You need a real drink, love?" Chester asked.

I nodded. Rum would also be good for brain cells.

He turned on his heels and headed toward the bar, tripping a little when he almost stepped into the blood puddle.

Matt returned.

"Your safe was shot open," he said.

"Good. I didn't have the combination." I accepted my glass from Chester, knowing it was clean.

"So you don't know if anything was in it?" Piper asked.

I slowly shook my head.

More officers came in the room and approached our table.

"You sure Wenner was here?" Piper asked.

"Yes. He came to the door. I thought it was you. I'd just left the office ... wait." I sat up straight. "The safe was open?"

"Yes."

"Did you notice the wooden box on my desk?" Yes, nothing like sugar and alcohol to get one's memory back.

Piper stood. I followed him to the office. The box of gold artifacts was gone.

"I want you to check the hospital for Malcolm Wenner," Piper said to an officer as we headed back to the main room. "Call customs, too. I don't want him leaving this island." He turned his focus to Ginger and Chester. "I'm afraid you will have to set up the ghost cameras tomorrow night. My crew will need to search for evidence tonight. We can't have you in here setting up while we do it. But I got your statements, you can go."

"All right," Ginger said. "But Lydia is coming here tomorrow to do her thing. Should we cancel that?"

"Lydia Abiff?" an officer said.

"Yes. She was going to talk to our ghost," Ginger explained as if that were a normal thing to do.

"She can do whatever she wants when she wants," the officer said. "Right sir?" he asked Matt.

He grinned and nodded.

"Very good. Let's go Chester." Ginger slung her purse over her arm and tugged on Chester's hand. Like a love-sick puppy, he trailed alongside of her.

"Will you take me home?" I asked Matt. "I'm so damned tired."

"Just a minute." He went to speak to his men again while I slumped back in the booth. It was comfortable enough. I could probably just sleep there. I wadded up the table linens into a makeshift pillow and settled in. But Matt came back before I dozed off.

"I'll take you home. But to my place. I don't think you should be by yourself right now and certainly not at that lonely part of the island."

"You're probably right. But it's too late for me to make dinner."

"There's always breakfast." He pulled me up.

Too tired to worry about crashing, I slept all the way to his house.

"It's small, only two bedrooms," he said turning on the main room light. The little white puppy came running over to us, his tail wagging so hard his entire rear end moved with it. It was actually a tail wagging a dog. “You have your choice, you can sleep in one of my sons’ beds, but they are single beds and since they have to do their own laundry, I can’t guarantee how clean the sheets are. Or you can risk sleeping with me.”

“I’ll go with you.” Because really, I just didn’t want to be alone.

“So you finally trust me then?”

“I’m so damn tired I wouldn’t even notice if you tried something.”

He grinned. "You’d notice and you’d be pleased”

I rolled my tired, burning eyes as much as I could. “Which one’s yours?”

“In there. I’ll be in as soon as I let this dog out to do his business.”

“Can I borrow a T-shirt?” I called from the bedroom.

He came in, pulled a VIPD T-shirt out of a drawer and left the room.

I stripped to underwear, grateful I wasn’t in a thong, put on his shirt and slipped under his covers.

I knew I was either asleep or unconscious when I felt something, someone touching me. A hand came around my stomach and an arm under my neck. Someone was trying to strangle me!

“Aa!” I came too in the darkness. Matt shushed me.

“It’s just me. You’re OK. Go back to sleep.”

I lay back down, spooned into his arms, where I felt safe, but I could hear pounding somewhere.

“What’s that noise?” Someone was frantically pounding.

“The rain.”

Rain, I inhaled and let myself drift back to sleep, almost.

“Is the door locked?”

“Yes.”

“Is the alarm set?”

“Uh huh.”

“Good.”

“Mmm.”

Once again I felt the lull of sleep.

“Good night,” I said.

“Mmm.”

My eyes almost opened. "Did you call your boys to say good night?"

"Of course, much earlier. Go to sleep."

I settled back into his arms again, I was so damned tired, but no! Where was the dog?

"The puppy!" I shrieked and sat up. "Where is it?"

"On its bed, sleeping. Like we should be doing."

"Oh." Once again I lay back down, but awake now. I stared at the outline of the window and listened to the rain, hoping sleep would come back. After a few minutes, Piper's hand left my stomach and touched my face.

"Your eyes still open?" he whispered.

"Yes."

"Close them. You're safe. Everyone is safe."

"Impossible." I closed my eyes. "But I'll try to sleep anyway."

"Thank you."

Chapter 29: It Was Nothing

"I thought I was supposed to make breakfast," I said. I padded barefoot into Matt's kitchen and got a great view of him from the rear. He was shirtless, shoeless and in snug fitting khaki pants.

"You that good with cereal?" he asked, looking over his bare shoulder.

"I'm even better with a coffeepot." I bent down and picked up the puppy who'd run over to say hello. "Good morning, sweetheart!" I rubbed my nose against his. "Did you sleep good?"

Matt came over to us and scratched the puppy's head. "If you name him, you have to take him."

"Sweetheart is not a name," I said and silently added, "yet."

"It can be. Coffee's already brewing. Get yourself a cup when it's done. I'm going to shave now."

I sat on the floor and played with the puppy like all was right in my world. Like no one had attacked me or my car, or had ransacked my house and robbed my business. Like there wasn't a puddle of blood in my dream restaurant. And like my breath didn't stink from not having a toothbrush with me. The puppy didn't care about any of it either. He was content with playing a simple game of put-me-on-my-back-and-rub-my-belly-while-I-nibble-at-your-hand. I was sure in puppy speak, there was a shorter name.

Matt returned fully clothed and poured us both coffee.

He handed me a cup. I drank it from the floor where I continued to sit with the puppy.

"No one bothered your house or restaurant last night," he said. And we found Malcolm Wenner at the hospital. He had a gunshot wound to the thigh and was out cold when we got there. He's awake now. I'm going to drop you to get your Jeep and go question him."

The warm fuzzies from playing with the puppy left me. I sighed.

“I guess that means Malcolm isn’t a suspect with anything regarding me?”

“Doesn’t look like it, but you never know.” Matt sipped his coffee. His eyes watched me over the cup. “You’re good with the dog. You going to take him?” He sat on the floor next to me and reached out to rub the dog’s ears.

I wanted him to touch me, too.

I put my cup down and leaned into him. “I’m intentionally putting my head against you. You can respond if you want.”

He didn’t verbally answer. But his body suddenly became as stiff and as responsive as a concrete slab.

“Aw, Mandy. I wish you hadn’t chosen now to do that.”

“What?” I leaned back to look at him.

“I can’t take you seriously if you do that now. It’d be wrong for both of us.”

“How . . . What the hell?”

He stood. “I need to know you mean what you’re doing. After last night–”

“Didn’t I just say I was *intentionally* putting my head on your shoulder? I think that means I meant what I was doing.”

“I’m just saying, I think it might be best if we waited until this mess you’re in is over. That way I can be sure your head is clear when you make those decisions. That’s all.”

I struggled to stand without exposing my underwear beneath his T-shirt.

“When my head is clear? So I’m an hysterical female, is that it? All panic stricken and–”

“I didn’t mean that.” He spun around and walked over to the sink. “I just need to know you’re reaching out because you want to, not because you’re scared.”

“Go to hell.” I stormed into the bedroom and slammed the door behind me. When I re-emerged, he had cleaned both coffee cups and appeared to be calmly waiting for me, petting the puppy on his lap.

“You should be proud,” I glared at him. “You’ve perfected that aloof and indifferent attitude.” I flung my hair behind me.

“Mandy, that’s not at all–” His pants vibrated. He pulled out his phone from his pocket and read a text. “Wenner has called an attorney. I need to go and talk to him as soon as I can. Come on. I’ll drop you at the garage for your jeep on the way."

I gave Piper the silent treatment all the way to the garage. He probably figured I was cowering in fear, which I might have also been doing. I grunted at him and waved him off while I spoke to the mechanic to make arrangements to pay for the damage. I'd left my purse at the restaurant.

The ride home wasn't as filled with danger as it usually was. My GPS god took me past a golf course where the road was slightly wider and more hilly than mountainous. Best of all, there was little traffic that Sunday morning. I almost drove as fast as the speed limit the entire way.

I entered Chance's house, my house, using the spare key I'd put back in the conch shell. It was silent, but not eerily. It was nothing. Just a quiet house.

I brushed my teeth, took a fast shower and thought about making a decent breakfast. But there were still no eggs and I was out of bacon. I called Ginger and explained my purse-less situation. She welcomed to treat me to breakfast at the Wyndham.

"We'll have ourselves a bite to eat before we meet up with Lydia at the restaurant," she said.

"Why, exactly, are we doing that?" I asked into the phone. Not that I would cancel out on the woman, but I thought I deserved to know why she was getting preferential treatment in my restaurant.

"She's got some kind of process to talk to the ghost and find out what we need to do to make it happy."

"It wasn't a ghost who shot Malcolm or knocked me out."

"Maybe not. But the ghost might have encouraged it. Anyway, this will be good for marketing."

Ginger and Chester were already seated at a table, but had waited for me to get there before attacking the buffet.

"Sugar, you look the best since I've met you," she gave me a hug and led me to the buffet. "I guess you got some good sleep."

"I did."

"Do they know who bopped you on the bean?" Chester asked, handing me a plate.

"They don't."

"That man of yours investigating?" Ginger wanted to know as

Chester handed me another plate.

"The police are." I set the extra plate aside.

We loaded up on traditional hotel breakfast buffet foods and returned to our table. A bus boy, reeking of marijuana, bumped into me, almost making me spill my eggs. I watched him trip out of the room. He reminded me of the models.

"Chester," I started, then waited for him to spot clean coffee droplets off his shirtfront. "A couple young women came in to apply for a job earlier this week. I think—"

"Mandy! You're not thinking of hiring them, are you?" Ginger asked.

"No. I just keep seeing them around."

"Who?" Chester asked.

"I think they might be models. One has blond hair, the other magenta or purple. Very skinny. I think the blond is named Amy or some kind of name that begins with an A. Oh!" I set my coffee cup down. "I spoke to them at the steps of the Revenge Café the day you helped me pick out an urn."

"Oh them. Yes. They came here to work over a college summer break a couple years ago. One is Jessie. Jessie Alvarez and the other is Amy, Amy . . . something. They got into some trouble and couldn't go back home."

"Where are they from?"

"I don't know that. It's odd though that they were looking for a job. They do a lot of modeling for local agencies, but they don't actually work."

"Modeling is work," I said. "But what kind of trouble did they get into?"

"Not sure about that either." He paused with his fork full of scrambled eggs and sausage poised in the air. "Milton! That's her name. Amy Milton. And, yes, from what I understand, it wasn't legal trouble. More like family trouble. They just couldn't stay home."

I wasn't sure what that meant, but he continued to chew his food as if he made perfect sense so I let it go. It didn't really matter anyway. There was just something about those girls that bothered me. I suspected it was because it looked like they were wasting their youth, like I did, and I hated looking at reminders of my own bad choices.

We finished eating. Chester drove Ginger over to the restaurant.

I drove myself. He left the Wyndham after I did and yet somehow arrived several minutes before me.

There was a policeman on duty, telling us Piper had told him to stay until one of us showed up. He left and we went inside. We stood before the round, dried puddle of blood.

"Where was he shot?" Chester asked.

"Um, right there," I answered, pointing to the floor.

"What?" he asked. Ginger laughed.

"I'm sorry. He was shot in the thigh." I cleared my throat. "You think the blood will stain the floor, Ginger?"

"I don't know, sugar." Ginger bent closer, as if to get a better look. "But if we can't bleach it out, maybe we can use it as a tourist attraction."

"Ew. Really?" I asked.

"No! See? If you had said that, everyone would have known it was a joke." She put her hands on her hips. "I don't know what we're going to do with it."

"Maybe Mrs. Abiff will know. When is she getting here?"

"In ten or fifteen minutes," Ginger said and then turned to Chester. "I know we have to be outside, but do you think she'll let us have the cameras run?"

"What cameras?" I asked.

"The cameras I bought, sugar. We have some on time-lapse and some on motion sensors. Wouldn't it be great to have the photos from this de-ghosting or whatever you call it?"

"I guess so."

"I was thinking," Ginger continued, "that we could put them on our website. Did I tell you Chester can build us a website Mandy?"

"Um, no. Can you really do that?" I asked him.

"Oh sure, love! I've already got lots of information on the area and pictures stored in my cloud that I can use. I just need images specific to this restaurant now. And something talking about the food. You could write that, right?"

"Right." But I was still back on that word *cloud.* "What do you mean, *cloud*?"

"You know." He walked over to his usual stool at the bar and sat down. "Where I store all my data and information."

"If Chance had a cloud, could I find it?"

"You'd have to check his computer and know what his log in info would be." I grabbed his arm and dragged him off the stool to the office.

"Show me."

Within seconds, I logged into the iCloud website with the *ChanceEnconters* ID, using *Never2L8* as the password. Soon I was looking at all the information stored in Chance's cloud. There were thousands of labeled photographs, because Chance acted like a big boy when he needed to. They were well organized. I easily found Evie Schwartz's photos from the destination Bar Mitzvah.

But what took my attention the most were his emails. They were all in his cloud, including the ones between him and Catunta.

"Oh my," I said aloud as I read through them. Chance had been a very bad boy. I found my purse, shuffled through for my phone, and dialed Penelope Abbott.

"What can you tell me about Serge Beauchance? Who exactly is he?" I asked Chance's mother.

"Oh," I heard her sigh and expected her to hang up on me. "I was going to talk to you about him when I came to the memorial this afternoon."

"I understand now may not be the best time. I'm sure your husband would rather—"

"I just informed my husband I'm leaving him. I don't care what he would rather."

"Oh, um, well." I cleared my throat and hoped it took a long enough time to allow me to respectfully change the subject. "So, about Serge Beauchance?"

"He's Chance's real father. That's where his name came from."

"I see." I leaned back in my desk chair and stared at the open, empty safe.

"I was so very young. Too young. My parents were insisting I marry Bertrand. I didn't want to. I wanted to be an artist. I wanted to live a little before I settled down. They let me have a summer in Paris, thinking a few months of freedom would be enough. I met Serge there and fell in love. It sounds foolish and stereotypical, doesn't it?"

"It sounds like something many women can relate to, Mrs. Abbott. I call it the YNS syndrome. It stands for Young N Stupid. I could chair the committee for it."

She laughed. "Please don't call me Mrs. Abbott. Call me Penny. I'm going to change my name as soon as the divorce is final."

"Very good, Penny. So you fell in love with Serge," I encouraged her.

"Yes. I had a beautiful summer with him. When I returned home in the fall, I told my parents I wanted to go to school in France to study art. They wouldn't allow it. Back in those days, I don't know, parents had more sway over their children I guess. I did what they wanted. I agreed to marry Bertrand. A few months before the wedding, Serge came to London. I told myself it was just one last lovely memory with him. That was all it was to be. But then Chance..."

"I see. Now I understand why Chance's younger brother is—"

"Bertrand Abbot the Fifth? Yes, I guess you could say I was rather passive aggressive with their names. When I realized I was pregnant and that the baby had to have been Serge's, I begged, pleaded with Bertrand for a divorce. But he wouldn't let me go. Between him and my parents, I felt I was stuck. I had no job skills, I couldn't support myself. I—"

"I understand, Mrs.-Penny. I do. And I don't mean to sound insensitive, but I need to know for sure what happened. Chance asked you to ask his real father, who happens to be an art dealer, to sell some Peruvian artifacts for him. And his father did, right?"

"Yes. Somewhat."

"What does that mean?"

"Serge gave Chance the money for the artifacts, but he worried that perhaps the artifacts were, well, possibly illegally gained by Chance, so he secretively returned them to Peruvian authorities."

"Ah ha! That was my missing piece."

"I don't understand."

"I know. But right now, I need to go and take care of something. You said you're coming to the memorial?"

"Yes."

"Then I'll see you this afternoon and will explain everything. Thank you so much."

I hung up and blew out a long, slow breath. Yes. She gave me the missing piece. I returned my attention to the emails and re-read through them, letting all the new information solidify in my head before I called Matt to fill him in.

"No, I need to call Piper," I said out loud. "He's not Matt to me anymore." I went out of the office to get a cup of coffee to give me the stamina to do it. When I returned I couldn't find my cell.

I sat at my desk shuffling through my bag, swearing at myself.

"If I'd just get a smaller purse I wouldn't be able to carry so much stuff." I dug deeper in my bag, ripping the opening as wide as it would go. "If I had less stuff, there would be less mess." I shook the insides around. Still no phone.

"I just had the damned thing!" I dumped it onto my desk and rifled through the pile.

Lydia Abiff came into my office.

"What de matter wi' you? Why you always making a mess?" she asked.

"Huh?" I looked at her. She had her hands on her hips, scowling at me. Smoke from a lit brown cigarette curled up from her hand. The no-smoking sign at the entrance obviously didn't apply to her. "I can't find my phone."

"Course not. Look at dat mess!" She ran her hands through the purse trash and came up with my phone and the pack of matches.

"H'ya. Take dis." She gave me the phone and pocketed the matches. "Now go. I need to do dis alone."

I started putting everything back in my purse.

"No. You do dat later and do it right. Go now." She picked up the Jeep fob. "Take dis, too. Go somewhere." She waved the cigarette in the air.

I followed orders.

Ginger and the others were seated in the patio area, chatting like it was another typical day in paradise, which it was. I almost joined them, but Jessie and her blond friend, Amy, had arrived at the top of the stairs.

"Can I help you?" I asked Amy because Jessie was giggling too hard to speak.

"Yeah. Like, we really need that job."

Ginger came over to us. "Sorry, darling, but all positions are filled. Again, you can complete an application and we'll keep it on file in case we have an opening."

"No, seriously, you have to hire us," Amy, though unsteady, narrowed her gaze as if to bore into Ginger. "You have to."

"We need the job. Like a real job. And Chancey promised us," interjected Jessie. "He did."

"Well Chancey isn't the one who's calling the shots now," Ginger said. "So you will just have to–"

"But we need work!" Jessie shoved Ginger's arm. "He promised us!"

"What did Chance promise, exactly?" I asked, stepping between her and Ginger. No one was going to shove my general manager around.

"We could be waitresses. He said it was the least he could do for us," Jessie said. Her eyes rimmed with moisture. "He owed it to us."

Owed not owes.

"Why?" I leaned closer, "did he owe you a job?"

"He ruined our fucking careers," Jessie said. Tears were, indeed, flowing down her cheeks. "And when he finally admitted it, he said he'd make sure we had jobs."

"Shut up, Jess," Amy warned her and tugged at Jessie's arm. Jessie nearly lost balance, she was sobbing.

I grabbed her other arm. "When did he say that to you?"

"Sunday! He said–"

"SHUT UP!" Amy screamed and jerked her friend down the stairs.

I ran down the steps after them and jumped in front of Jessie.

"Why did you kill Chance?" I demanded.

Chapter 30: Stopped Myself

"What?" Jessie blinked her wet eyes in slow motion. Realization crawled across her face.

"Why did you kill Chance?" I grabbed her shoulders and shook her. Her body wobbled like a jellyfish right out of my grip. She and Amy ran to their car, hopped in and took off.

I flew over to the Jeep, jumped in and pressed the ignition button. I punched the Jeep in reverse and slammed into the guard rail. Back in drive, I pressed harder on the gas pedal than I think I've ever pressed before and totally ignored the sound of what was probably the back bumper falling off.

We headed north then went east on Veterans Drive, one of the few, or maybe the only, four lane highway on the island. I drove without care for my safety. I just wanted to get caught up with those girls.

I swerved off the road to pass a tour bus. In fact, I went sufficiently far off the road that a lamp post completely scraped off the driver's side mirror. Back on the highway, I heard my cell ring.

I was doing fifty on the highway, not sure what the speed limit was but because I was weaving in and out of cars going in both directions, I had a feeling I was going way over it. I knew it had to be Piper calling and had to answer it. Besides, I was already living dangerously, why not add one more flaming knife to the juggling act?

I hit the speaker button.

"What?" I yelled.

"Listen, Mandy," Matt started. "I–"

"I'm chasing Chances' killers!" I yelled.

"What? Who? Where?"

"Two girls. Jessie–Aaaack!" I careened off the highway onto a stretch of grass by a parking lot.

"Where the hell are you? Are you driving?"

"I'm on Veteran's Highway. Heading east. I think I just cut through the Riise Shopping Center parking lot."

"What do you mean cut through?"

"Drove over the grass."

"Jesus Christ! I'm on my way. Don't hang up."

"OK. But try not to talk to me. I'm going like," I glanced down at the speedometer, "seventy miles an hour."

"Stop now!"

"NO! They killed Chance!" I caught site of their car again and may have sped up even more. We continued east along the harbor. I could hear Piper shouting to someone other than me.

"Keep me up to date if you're going to insist on driving," he said to me.

"We're passing Bluebeard's Castle." I yelled. "Is he different from Blackbeard?"

"You'll have to ask my sons. But what the hell? Stay focused." He said something, I guessed into his police radio, about Bluebeard to someone else. "What kind of car are they driving?" he asked me.

"A red one."

"That's all you can tell me?"

The road took a sharp turn to the right. I bumped my head on the window. "Ow!"

"You OK?"

"Yeah." Next was a hard hook to the left. Two of my wheels came off the ground. I knew for sure because when they landed, I bounced in the seat. "Holy shit! I'm gaining on them. Just passed the Marriott."

"No you didn't. Not that fast."

"Don't make me take my eyes off the road to look, Matt!" I slammed on my breaks to keep from hitting a bus in front of me, screeching to the right, briefly closing my eyes while the car heading toward me barely scathed by. I pulled in front of the bus. "The road is branching. I'm on the right branch."

"NO!"

"It's a Nissan, I think!"

"Stop!

"NO! They're not getting away from me!

"You're heading to Donkey Hill!"

Now that would have been the perfect time to do something smart. To think clearly. To act rationally.

I could have slowed down and let the police do their thing. They knew to look for a red Nissan speeding down Donkey Hill. I could have easily pulled over and given Piper a complete description of what the girls looked like. It's not like they could drive for infinity. We were on a small island, after all. And even if they did get away, Chester knew who they were. I had both their names. I knew which shop they had been recently photographed in. They could easily be found now. Yes, the sane and smart thing to do would be to stop testing my non-existent driving skills and let justice be served.

However, that bitch killed my one and only true friend and she had the balls to stumble onto his property, laughing.

I was right behind them at the top of a hill. And right behind me was a VIPD car with lights flashing and siren blaring.

Sparks flew from somewhere. It was from my front left fender scraping a guard rail. I jerked back into the lane and bumped Jessie's car. She fishtailed and floored it. We took a switchback turn to the right. I lost control and went through the scrub on the side of the road, somehow winding up in front of her.

I needed to pin her between me and the policeman behind us to keep her from turning off.

We went through a series of S-shaped curves with me slamming on the breaks every time she started to get distance between us. Just after a few times, I mastered staying in my lane when she bumped into me. There was a positive: I was improving my skills.

I could see the exit for the Bolongo Bay Resort and Iggies restaurant ahead. I knew a little further down would be the entrance and came up with a plan.

I forced Jessie to slow down to a respectable speed and then at the last minute, I floored it into the exit did a one-eighty turn out the entrance and rammed down on the gas pedal again, intentionally slamming head on into Jessie's car.

Stopped that bitch cold, I did.

Stopped myself, too.

Air bags are amazing inventions. I was able to unhook my seat belt and plunge out of the Jeep, a little shaken, but not hurt. Before the police cars even stopped, I ran over to Jessie's car and yanked her door open.

"Why did you kill Chance?" I yelled. Jessie struggled to get out from behind her air bag. Whatever was in her system making her laugh so easily also seemed to be interfering with her motor skills. "Why?"

"We didn't mean to," she yelled.

"Shut up!" screamed Amy. She struggled out the passenger door, ran around the back of the car and shoved me out of the way.

I stumbled and caught myself, then just stood there almost amused by watching the women. We were surrounded by police officers who'd arrived at the scene from a variety of direction. Piper was among them. They all seemed equally enchanted by the scene: A skinny blond, with one foot against the back door and one on the ground, trying to pull her magenta-haired friend out of the car by her head.

But I wasn't amused enough to forget why I was there. "Why did you do it?" I yelled.

"It was an accident," Jessie yelled back, her voice muffled by the air bag.

"Shut up, you stupid bitch!" wailed Amy. She jerked on Jessie's head, hard enough to hurt her, I thought.

"We didn't know he would die," Jessie shrieked.

"Shut up! Shut up!" Amy pummeled Jessie's head. "You bitch, shut up!"

There weren't any expensive vases lying around so I didn't try to break up the fight. Instead, a uniformed officer pulled Amy away and another helped Jessie get out of the car. She fell to the ground, crying. She looked up and made eye contact with me.

"It was his fault," she said.

"Who, Chance?" I knelt down in front of her, feeling a hand on my back. I knew it was Piper.

"Yes," she sobbed.

"How? Why?" I grabbed Jessie by the hair exercising my multiplication skills to see if there were too many witnesses for me to pay off in order to strangle her without going to jail. I was now a wealthy woman. But there were a lot of cops around. I didn't think I had that much money. Besides, I still didn't know if it was legally mine. And I had a feeling, Piper couldn't be bought.

"Easy," Piper said. "Come on, I can't let you touch them."

I couldn't release my hold.

"Why?" I screamed at her.

"He–"

"He ruined our fucking careers!" yelled Amy, a uniformed man holding tight to her arm. "It was his fucking fault. We didn't mean to kill him but he deserved to die."

Piper tugged on my arm. I let go of the hair and stood up.

"What the hell are you talking about?" I asked.

"Mandy," Piper interrupted. "I know you deserve to hear this, but I have to go by the book." He turned to a uniformed officer. "DeYoung, you take over and read them their rights. They're under arrest for the murder of Chancellor Abbot."

Piper led me to the Grand Cherokee while the officer started the familiar chant.

"Congratulations." He squatted to look at the Jeep from the side. "I think you finally killed it."

"That's too bad. I really liked that car."

"You have a strange way of showing affection." He put his arm around my shoulder.

"Don't touch me." I shrugged him off.

He sighed. "I know. We need to talk. But –"

"I've nothing to say to you." I turned my back to him.

"But I have a few things to say to you."

"Sir?" A uniformed officer interrupted. "We read them their rights but they are more interested in incriminating each other. Can't get them to stop yelling. We're ready to take them to the station now."

"Do you think someone could take me, too?" I asked the uniformed officer.

He looked at Piper.

"I'll take you, Mandy." His hand was on my back again. I stepped away.

"I'd rather go with someone else."

I heard him sigh. "Brandford has enough on his hands. Let me take you. I need to talk to you about your ex-boyfrind and Catunta, anyway."

I snapped my head over to look directly at him. "What?"

"We need to talk about who attacked you last night."

"It wasn't these women?"

"No. It was a Peruvian agriculturist."

"Catunta?"

"When he was exporting asparagus—"

"It was a front for exporting Incan artifacts."

"How did you know?"

I wanted to sit down, but my Jeep was crumpled. I walked over to Piper's SUV and climbed into the passenger seat.

He followed me over. "So will you at least talk to me about what you suddenly know? Or is there something else you were holding out on?"

"I wasn't holding anything out on you. I was completely open about everything. Everything. Unlike you. But you know something? I totally understand your ex-wife. I can clarify exactly what she was talking about when she gave you that ultimatum, *if* you'd care to hear it."

He got in the driver's side. "My ex-wife has something to do with Catunta?"

I looked at him, feeling my jaw hang slack. "Are you really that obtuse?"

"Let's start over. How do you know about Catunta's export business?"

"I finally found Chance's emails on his computer and read through them. Now, ask me what your wife meant."

"I'm more interested in the case." He put his key in the ignition of his SUV.

"Of course you are."

"Are you ready?" he asked.

"Ugh!" I threw a hand in the air. "That's exactly my point. You avoid intimacy. You can't handle truly getting close to people. You really are aloof and possibly indifferent." I crossed my arms over my chest and stared out the front window. "*And* you have a hero's complex. So there!"

"I do not have a hero's complex."

"Really?" I turned to look at him. "Trust me. I've spent enough time on a shrink's couch to be able to see underlying motives of behavior and analyze unconscious decisions, at least in other people. I may not be able to fix any of them, but I can analyze like the best of them. *You* have a hero's complex. And now that I'm not in any kind of danger, you have no need for me. So the aloof and indifferent part of you took over to prevent you from getting close to me." I faced forward again and glared out the front windshield, arms still crossed over my chest. "Go ahead. Drive."

Chapter 31: Way to Freedom

He started the car. I could feel his eyes on me, but I held tight to my resolve not to look at him. After a few minutes, he put the SUV into gear and headed out of the parking lot.

We drove in silence for a few minutes.

"Are you all right?" he eventually asked.

"Why wouldn't I be?"

After another couple minutes in silence. "You seem OK with being in a car," he said.

"Yeah, you know. I am. Good observation skills, detective." Though inside, I was elated. Ecstatic. I wasn't freaking out. I was relaxed and at ease. I was pissed off at him and a little bit confused about what had happened the previous night, but I was calm while riding in a car.

"You're not panicking?" he asked. "Not even a little bit? Are you medicated?"

"Maybe it's a natural high. Adrenaline. I just intentionally wrecked my car. I could have killed myself or them. Actually, I think I might have been trying to kill them."

"Shh. Don't say that in front of me."

I slid my eyes over to him, he was smiling. I couldn't help but grin, too.

"What I mean is: I faced my worst nightmare and survived. The girls even survived. It's all good."

"Yes it is." He reached over and tugged at my arm. "Please."

"Why?" I squeezed my crossed arms tighter.

"Because maybe you are right. About me. About the intimacy thing. But maybe I'd like to conquer my fear. You can understand that, right?"

I relented.

"Just because I let you hold my hand doesn't mean you're forgiven and all is good between us, Superman."

"What would it mean, then?"

"That maybe I'm willing to think about things."

"I promise to keep my cape locked in a trunk."

I held onto his hand and enjoyed the view outside my window, relaxing further and further into the seat.

"I don't mean to ruin our moment or anything," Matt said. "But it sounds like you were awfully busy this morning cracking the murder case and learning about Catunta. Care to enlighten me on what was going on?"

"First, where did you find Catunta?" I asked.

"He was staying at the Inn at Blackbeard's Castle."

"Of course."

"What?"

"I'll tell you later. When I tell you all about my Aunt Maggie."

"What are you going to tell me about now?"

"I found Chance's cloud."

"The hospital is on the way. But they'll probably do a blood alcohol test and then I might have to file charges against you for driving under the influence."

"They'll find I'm clear headed for the first time in my adult life." I explained about Chance's cloud and the login information from his letter.

"I get it now." Matt nodded his head. "And in his cloud you found proof connecting him with Catunta?"

"Plenty of emails between them."

We'd made it all the way up Donkey Hill and were now heading down toward the harbor. I had yet to have a panic attack. Instead, my breath was taken away by the gorgeous view: the islands off the shore, the ships sparkling white in the blue sea.

"Chance stumbled upon Malcolm and Catunta meeting and got curious as to why," I said. "When he learned that Catunta needed a contact who would want to purchase the artifacts, he volunteered himself."

"Had he ever done anything like that before?"

"No, but his real father is an art dealer in London."

"The man you met at the Ritz?"

"No. That was something Chance had never told me. After

reading the emails where Chance asked his mom for help, I called her cell and got the whole story. The man I always thought was his father was horrible to him. As it turns out it was because his wife had had an affair, producing Chance, while still being married. And in those circles, in those days, divorce wasn't tolerated."

"But Chance knew?"

"Yes. And he contacted his mother to get his real father to help him sell the artifacts. She did. He made boatloads of money."

"I see." I saw him work his jaw as he thought it all through. "And then what happened?"

"When Chance's dad gave him the money, Chance split it with Catunta and then Chance's father sent the artifacts back to Peru."

"What?"

"His father knew they were illegally taken from the country and felt they belonged back in Peru and didn't want Chance to get in trouble for it."

He frowned out the front window as we passed Bluebeard's Castle. Blackbeard's should be coming up soon. I looked for it thinking I should ask Chester if they were two different hairy, pubescent, pirates.

"Catunta caught wind and was pissed off at Chance," I continued. "He felt Chance was intentionally endangering Catunta, setting him up somehow by returning the artifacts. Chance assured him he had nothing to do with the art's homecoming. Catunta demanded he get back the last batch of artifacts to sell them to someone else, someone who wouldn't return them to Peru. But Chance had already sent them to his mother."

"Which she subsequently gave to you."

"Yes. Apparently she had yet to get them to her old lover and when Chance was killed, maybe she thought it was over the artifacts and for some reason she told her husband."

"That would make sense." He pulled into a parking spot at the police department and turned off his SUV. "Maybe she feared she'd be connected to the sales somehow, too, and was now at risk."

"I didn't think of that. So, uh," I squeezed his hand to make him look at me. "I'm not sure. Did he legally buy the house and restaurant?"

"I don't think there's any proof that he didn't."

"Good. Because I can't move here if I don't have a home and a job."

"Right." He grinned. "Now let's go see what we can find out about those girls."

So intent they were to make sure the other one looked like the worst offender, Jessie and Amy began telling all back at Bolongo Bay, continued while en route to the police station and still had more to add once they arrived there. All despite the fact they didn't have a lawyer present. At the station, Matt let me listen to them yell over each other, alternating between coming to each other's defense and yet trying to make each other look the guiltiest.

"Look," said Amy to me. Handcuffed to a desk, suddenly she appeared to be sober, as if whatever had made her loopy had worn off. "It was an accident, really."

"You accidentally killed a man with hot peppers?" I took a chair from another desk and sat near her. The arresting officers had already taken their possessions and fingerprints. We were waiting for the official complaint to be filed and for them to have their mug shots taken.

"We didn't know he'd die. We just wanted to hurt him a little. Just 'til he agreed to give us a cut," said Jessie from another desk. She somehow had rubbed her nose when the ink was still fresh on her fingertips and looked like she'd been punched.

"A cut of what?" I noticed Matt standing on the perimeter of the room. I was sure he was there just in case I did something to cross the line. But I only wanted information. And I knew their rights had been read.

"He fucking owed us!" Amy wailed, a little spit came out. She started crying. "He ruined our careers. You think I wanted to be a stripper?"

"What does that mean? Did Chance make you strip?"

"NO!" She shot her head up and glared at me. "I had no other way of making money."

"Ever think of college?" I asked.

Jessie laughed. "College is what got us here." She laughed harder until she, too, cried. "We were here on spring break and Chancey asked us if we'd be in a video he was shooting for a friend."

"Oh, that," I found myself raising my eyebrows and looking at

Matt. One of the things Chance did on the side was videography for a guy who made cheap movies he then sold by 1-800 commercials and on the fraternity circuit. They were very risqué; filled with bikini or topless college girls drinking, dancing and slurping Jello shots off each other. He'd told me all about the easy money he'd get from them.

"We were stars!" shouted Amy. "We rocked those videos."

"Yeah!" Jessie cheered like they'd aced their SATs. "But then ..." she leaned her head on the desk. "I think I might throw up," she said. An older officer used his foot to scoot a trash can in front of her.

"So I don't understand," I said. "You were in a video and?"

"And my brother saw it at school," Amy said. "And he showed it to my parents."

"Who showed it to my parents," Jessie added. "My daddy's the fucking attorney general of the state."

"They wanted us to move home, go to a local college or something." Amy was crying again. "We came back here thinking we could do more modeling work but, but. . ."

"There isn't much of that here," Jessie finished.

"Yeah, most girls go to New York." I said and sighed. "So you thought you'd tie Chance up because?"

"We did some gigs for him, modeling stuff," said Amy. "And he'd hired us to jump out of cakes and stuff, you know."

"I know." Though really I didn't.

"Last week, we were supposed to do this gig for a bachelor's party, but the bride saw us and ruined the party. She threw a shoe at Chancey and hit him in the eye."

"Yes, I know about that."

"Yeah, well, when he got hurt, I drove him in his Jeep back to that restaurant. He told me he'd just bought it and wasn't going to do any more photo gigs or arrange for strippers or anything. He told me he'd help hook us up with other photographers though. But, like, he owned that fucking restaurant! And when I realized he owned it, it was, like, obviously with the money he made from our video!" Amy shrieked.

"That's not how–" I started.

"So I left and told Jessie. We went back the next day, just to talk to him. You know, remind him he wouldn't have had that money if we hadn't been in the video."

"Yeah!" Amy interjected. "But he kept lying to us. He kept saying that he didn't make much from that video. It just pissed us off, you know? He was like making this salad in this gorgeous restaurant–"

"That we bought him!" yelled Jessie. "But he wouldn't give us a cut. So, we drank a bottle of wine with him and when he got relaxed, she tackled him." She pointed to Amy.

"No I didn't!" Amy tried to lunge at Jessie, the cuffs pulled her back. "You said to get him!"

"I said to keep him still!"

"That's what I was doing!"

"No! She got a table cloth or something and threw it on him and shoved him down."

"Well she took an apron and tied his hands behind his back with the strings!"

"But she was the one who found the peppers."

It was a like watching a screeching table tennis tournament. My head bounced back and forth between the seething girls, listening to their inane rant.

"We didn't mean for him to die!" Jessie hollered, tears running down her face. "We just wanted to hurt him, you know, the way he'd hurt us."

"I believe you." I nodded.

"That's why we put him in the freezer. When we started thinking we'd gone too far we tried to take his clothes off. Get him cooled down. You know?"

"I know." So Chester had that part right.

"And then it seemed like he'd be OK. He said he'd make it up to us."

"He'd give you a job," I finished and stood up.

"Yeah. So we left."

"I've heard enough," I said.

I went out into the information area, near the front doors thinking I was plenty brave enough to take a taxi anywhere I needed to go. But Matt followed me out and offered to take me back to the restaurant instead.

Chapter 32: All Is Well

At the Revenge Café, I found Ginger inside. Other workers were there, too. Everyone was cleaning in a somewhat déjà vu sort of circumstance. The stain was gone.

"And?" I asked.

"Oh honey, it was wonderful!" Ginger said. "And after a while, Lydia did let us in so we could see the end. Chester got some photos. Can't wait to show them to you. He's with her now. She had to return the frogs."

"What frogs?"

"The ones she needed for her ritual or whatever."

"What does this all mean?"

"It means all is well, honey. And we'll be able to open on the weekends! We're staying open extra late tonight!"

I turned to Matt.

"Good thing I got a decent night's sleep. Looks like I'm working tonight."

He grinned. "Think you can at least take a break sometime to have dinner with me?"

"I don't know. I mean, did we finish the conversation? Do I know why, exactly would I do that?"

Before Matt could answer, Chester came stumbling into the restaurant and dropped his camera. Lydia stepped over it shaking her head.

"Is everything all right?" I asked her. "Is the ghost gone?"

"Nah," Lydia smiled at me, or maybe she snarled. "She ain't going no where."

"But–"

"We need to talk." She pointed to Ginger and me and strutted over to the bar. We followed.

"It's all good, Mandy," Ginger said.

"What's all good?"

Lydia asked Francis for a whiskey and pulled a cigarette pack out of the bag she was carrying. "You ain't got nothing to worry about," she said. "De ghost is happy now dat women are in charge. She'll protect this place. You just got to take care of it de way only good women can."

"Am I a good woman?" I asked, realizing I'd been referring to myself as a girl for at least a decade too long.

Lydia pounded a cigarette out and squinted at me. "You might do," she said, nodding. "Dat ghost was mad at all de men who'd done her and de others wrong. Don't let one do dat to you now." She tossed back her whiskey in one drink. "We'll talk more another time. Just know she expects you to behave yourself."

I watched her leave and surveyed the restaurant. It was back to normal. I took in the perfectly decorated room, the uniformed staff bustling about, Chester on a barstool gazing over at Ginger, Penny was there, too, looking at a menu. All of them, even Chance's mom, looked like they belonged there. I felt like I belonged there, too. And, despite the yellow caution tape and the smell of bleach, I liked feeling like I belonged there.

I found Matt.

"Can I still get that dog?" I asked.

"Sounds like a good idea."

"Good. I'll talk to Lydia about ten year curses."

"And when do you think you'll talk to me?"

"Haven't I been doing that all morning?"

"About us."

I sighed and turned to him.

"You go first," I said.

"I want your head on my shoulder. Whether or not you need my help." He looked at me from under his brow and put his hands in his pockets. "Your turn."

The sound of a glass breaking took our attention. Chester had dropped his drink. Ginger grinned at him as she cleaned it up. He beamed back at her.

"I think," I said slowly as I returned my eyes back to him. "Maybe we've been doing it all wrong."

"What do you mean?"

"Maybe the first move should be you putting your head on my shoulder."

ABOUT THE AUTHOR

Lisa Shiroff writes because she's not sure what else she can do with herself. Oh sure, she's a wife, mom of two kids, and manages to walk her dog every day, but as far as careers go, the only thing she knows how to do is write, cook and mix a drink. Chefs and bartenders have to work weekends, though, so she's sticking to the writing gig. She currently resides in south Jersey and gets to the Caribbean as much as possible.

You can learn more about her books, check out photos from St. Thomas and find the recipes to Mandy's go-to foods from this book on Lisa's website at (where else?): www.lisashiroff.com.

31134712R00156

Made in the USA
Charleston, SC
06 July 2014